NOT
FOR
NOTHING

stephen graham jones

DZANC
BOOKS

1334 Woodbourne Street
Westland, MI 48186
www.dzancbooks.org

The characters and events in this book are fictitious. Any similarity to real persons, living or dead, is coincidental and not intended by the author.

NOT FOR NOTHING

Published 2014 by Dzanc Books
Design by Steven Seighman

ISBN: 978-1938604539
First edition: March 2014

This project is supported in part by awards from the National Endowment for the Arts and Michigan Council for Arts and Cultural Affairs.

Printed in the United States of America

10   9   8   7   6   5   4   3   2

for Bruce and Randall, my uncles

and for Benny P.

Now and then,
I save a child from drowning
—Bob Hicok

1.

SHE'LL BE WAITING for you when you walk back from the water station next door. And of course you'll have the tip of your thumb in your mouth, will only realize it after you've stopped walking, when you're standing there like some animated character trying to blow his flattened hand back up. All that's left to do then is waggle your fingers before your face in "Hello," your eyes kind of squinted. Not so much against the glare coming off the storage units, but in apology. For being who you are.

It's an apology you make more often than you'd care to admit.

Instead of smiling with you, making this easy, she'll just stare at you through her alligator print sunglasses. Trying to classify you, place you in her country club world. When you obviously don't fit, she'll shrug, re-cross her legs, one slingback heel riding down the sole of her foot an inch. She'll lower her hand, guide that shoe back up. It pulls her eyes away from you just long enough for you to drop your hand from your face, hide it behind your neck. Or what you think's long enough.

But be honest with yourself here, if you can. Your mouth's still half-open, you're wearing the same clothes you have been for a few days now—easy to lose track—and, really, there's no delicate way to explain what you were doing when you rounded the corner: using the ridge of your lower teeth to dislodge the barbecue sauce packed under your thumbnail. You're not even sure if it's from just now—chopped beef at the water station— or from your lunch there yesterday.

In your other hand is a gimme calendar from the John Deere house. You raise it against the sun to see this woman better, tease her apart from the shadows, and for a moment your throat catches with recognition, some rush of nostalgia you can't quite follow all the way back to a memory. It has to do with the way she's sitting, her hands at her bare knees. Or, no: it's the knees themselves.

You know her, don't you? Probably should already have said her name.

Think, think.

She sits on the edge of the bench you've liberated from one of the storage units it's your job to guard. The bench you've liberated from 4B, to be specific. Your vague plan is to use it as a couch. It's from an International truck, you're pretty sure, like the one up on blocks at the closed-down Exxon up the street.

"Your secretary let me in," she says.

It's hard not to smile, here.

Not only do you not have a girl working the desk, but, unless you count the wooden spool you've been swatting flies into for six weeks now, you don't even have a desk. Your "office"—that's how she would say it, if it were important enough to say—is just an empty storage unit, a one-car garage, pretty much. There's a single bare light bulb at exactly forehead level, unpainted cinderblock on three sides and a door you left rolled up all morning because the bench seat hasn't been smelling too good. You're thinking about giving it back to 4B, really.

And you have to say something to her now.

Luckily you've been drinking all morning.

"Surprised she found the time," you tell her about the secretary. "All I can do to get her to answer the phone, most days."

The woman who should really have a name by now doesn't laugh. This makes you feel better about not remembering her.

"Ringing off the hook, is it?" she says.

You give her your best pleasant smile then shrug your way in out of the sun, looking both ways first.

"I know you, don't I?"

This is funny to her.

In the stillness of the storage unit, her lipstick bending up into a smile is still wet enough to make a sound. Meaning she just put it on. For you. Before you're even all the way aware of it, you're wiping your mouth on the back of your forearm for any pecan pie crumbs you might have missed. This is the first time in weeks your appearance has come close to mattering. Now, though. That she's even sitting on that bench seat has you interested in her. And the amount of leg she's showing. The amount of leg that she knows she's showing, that she catches you climbing.

Instead of admitting she's caught you, you stumble ahead, say the obvious: "So that'd be your Town Car out there, yeah?"

She shrugs, her shoulders bored, as if to suggest that this is common knowledge. And maybe it is; you've only been back in town for a couple of months. Less if you don't count all the nights you already don't remember.

"Don't worry," she adds, tilting her head at the idea of the water station. "I didn't park on Sherilita's precious parking lot, *officer.*"

The cool thing to do now would be to recite her license plate back to her. Say something about the air pressure in that back tire. How you already have the maroon-black paint, chrome spokes, and tinted back glass of her Lincoln filed away. Just like the homicide detective you used to be.

Except of course you don't even know enough about the plates to be sure the car's local.

"Mind?" she says, threading a Winston 100 up from her purse.

"Careful," you tell her. It's the opening of a line you heard a lawyer use once.

"Careful?" she says back.

You stall a bit to be sure you have it right then deliver it at just the right speed: "You can get addicted to that, I mean. To asking permission."

She shakes her head, rolls the wheel back on her lighter, and you pretend not to watch her lips take the cigarette. There's a place on the cinderblock wall you were going to put a nail. To hang your calendar on. So you can keep up with the days.

Look there instead of at her mouth.

The idea she's supposed to get from this is that you have other things to do here. But you are who you are, too. When you come back to her face with what you were gambling was going to be an innocent, accidental snapshot of a glance, she's already watching you, has been holding her smoke in just so you can get caught up in her exhale.

You swallow, the saliva loud in your ears.

How long has it been since you've been this close to a woman? One who was even remotely interested in you?

The answer comes before you want it to: two months. Except that woman was a judge.

She was very interested.

The exhaled smoke rises to the top of the storage unit, goes all paisley around the yellow bulb, and it's then that the woman you know you should know says your name. The one nobody's called you since grammar school.

You track back down to her, suddenly unsure if you've had four beers or fourteen. Hours before you're ready, minutes too late, she pulls her sunglasses off eye by eye, lowering her face to do it, and looks up at you all at once, from twenty years ago.

Gwen Tracy.

You rub the loud skin around your mouth, try not to let her see all the muscles in your face wanting to smile.

As apology, maybe, or in sympathy, she offers you the 100, and you take it as casually as you can, breathe the cherry deep red. When the nicotine hits the capillaries of your brain, you almost laugh in your throat but catch it just in time.

Instead of taking the 100 back like you offer, she slaps you hard across the face.

It's Gwen all right.

"That why you came by?" you ask, rubbing the heat of her hand deeper into your cheek.

Her answer is to pinch the 100 away from you, flick it out the wide door. The orange sparks go spastic in the caliche dust, looking for a new home.

"Can't believe you're back," she says.

You shrug, are kind of surprised at how it's all turned out as well.

"Instead of jail," she tacks on.

"Guess they thought this was bad enough," you say, meaning Stanton, Texas, in July.

She just stares at you about this.

What she gave you once, what for a long time you said had ruined you, was the picture in your mind of the delicate print her hair left against the passenger side window of her father's single-cab Ford. Because there hadn't been enough room on the driver's, with the steering wheel. It had been January. The windows had been fogged with urgency.

That's twenty years gone, though. You should have forgotten about her already, Gwen Tracy. Erased her, replaced her.

But you're kind of sentimental, too.

And she's not here for what you're thinking she's here for anyway. What you're wanting her to be here for. It's probably just the bench seat she's still sitting on that's making you think that. You rub a spot on your forehead so she won't be able to see your face, say in your best fake voice, "Five dollars off a month on the large units. If you pay a year in advance."

It's like you're sixteen again—awkward, embarrassed, a little bit guilty. Still hiding behind lame jokes. Or trying to, anyway.

She stands, the bench seat rocking behind her.

"You used to be a cop," she says. It's not quite a question, but it's close enough to one that you feel you have to answer.

"You could say that," you tell her, your voice not so fake anymore.

Again she's just staring at you, like she's trying to say things with her eyes. When you don't get it, she finally just comes out with it: "I'm not here for a storage unit, *Nicholas*."

You tell her that's not your name anymore and set the calendar down on the wooden spool, careful not to let it slap.

"St. Nick?" she corrects.

It's because, in elementary, you were fat.

"Gwen Tracy," you say back. It's all you can come up with.

She cocks her head, turns half away from you, amused. "You have been gone a long time, haven't you?"

She stares at you for longer than you want her to, and just when you're about to touch a spot on your cheek—anything to look away—she says it again, that she's not here for a storage unit.

"Then what?" you say, lifting a beer from the cooler, offering it to her and taking it yourself when she won't. The plan all along, really.

"This was a mistake," she says. "I mean, if you're what I want, then you should know why I'm here."

"You mean if I'm a—" you say, meaning to end with *psychic*, but cut it off before you can get there. Just to double back, make sure you're hearing what she's saying. As expert cover for this stall, you drink a third of your beer in one long mouthful, and take time to wipe your lips after that.

She doesn't want a psychic. She wants the next best thing.

"My detective days are over," you tell her.

What she says back is "Good," then turns all at once to the open garage door, as if she half-expects somebody to be standing there. Nobody is. Nobody ever is. She watches it for a breath longer anyway, then turns back to you, pinning you with her eyes the same way she used to during pep rallies, when she was leading all the cheers. That way she had of making it feel like she was looking just at you. She still has it. And more, the whole package, and—

That's it.

She's got the whole package, the whole *cheerleader* package. What you recognized right off from twenty feet away, through the glare of the sun and the aftertaste of water-station barbecue, were her knees. How, a crowd of people stacked up before her, she used to sit with her knees tight together like that, her pom-poms framing them.

You never watched the game. Just those knees.

"What?" she says.

"Why 'good?'" you say, a lucky save. "Tell me why it's good for you that I'm not a cop anymore."

"Because the cops can't do anything," she says, shrugging, saying the next part quieter, like a suggestion. "But a private investigator...*could*."

You laugh through your nose. "You think that's how it works? That when you stop being a detective they just issue you a PI license, like a consolation prize?"

"Isn't that what you were doing already, though?"

You keep smiling like this doesn't hurt you. It's why you've been keeping a low profile, though: when your career in Homicide had gone into a public tailspin—no murders cleared off your part of the board for twenty months, a Midland PD record—you'd started moonlighting. It had made sense at the time, odd-jobbing in your off-hours, taking pictures, finding dogs, knocking on doors, whatever. Always the shield to hide behind. It had felt like something, anyway. Maybe not like solving a real, official homicide, but close enough for you and the girls you went with.

Until the judge.

But don't think about her.

"Let me explain something to you," you say, picking the calendar up just to keep your hands busy, your eyes safe. "What I do here is provide live-in security for Aardvark Custom Economy Storage. Free room, free board, so long as nobody complains about me taking liberties with their stuff. And, know what?" To show her who you're about to talk about, you tilt your head next door, to the water station. "I let Sherilita's kid's band practice in one of the empty units after dark, and she gives me four chopped beef sandwiches a day. *With* Fritos. And sweet tea. Pie, if they've got any left over."

When you're done, she's just staring at you.

"Sherilita goes to my church," she says. "Real devout. So what do you do on Sundays?"

"Liquid diet," you tell her, your face so straight it's slack.

"Guess you've really got it made then," she says after a few beats, shaking her head with disgust, digging in her purse for her keys. "Don't need to hear about anybody else's—listen, don't worry about it, *Nick*. Nice seeing you again. You're a great guy. Real gem. Look you up in twenty more years."

Like every other woman you've ever known, she turns, starts to leave. You nod about it, already telling yourself that it's for the best. That she was trouble, not worth it. Probably would have wanted you to clean your act up anyway.

On the way out, she says, "Get your mail here too?"

You ask it before you can stop yourself, even though you know it's a set-up: "Why?"

"I'll have my mother drop you the program from my funeral. She still remembers you."

Instead of leaving, she just stands there, her eyes welling up.

None of this is anything like what you wanted. If she wasn't in the only exit, you might already be gone, even. Mentally if not physically.

Except that she came to you for help.

After all these years.

She came to you for help when, to everyone who reads the papers, you're a leper, a criminal, an embarrassment.

"Open or closed casket?" you say.

"Closed," she says, and you nod, say it, that one word like a gate opening up onto another world: "What?"

Gwen steps through it with you, her arms crossed high on her chest.

"You don't—" she says, her voice soft, as if reconsidering. "I'm a teacher, Nick. English."

"What grade?" you ask, ready to file her answer away with the Town Car. You might even need a little flip-notebook soon, like a real detective. But then, instead of giving you a classification to write down, she says, "Remember how you had that crush on Miss White, in geometry?"

You still think about her every time you see a protractor in the right light.

Gwen closes her eyes, as if making herself say the next part. "Well, I'm Miss White now, I guess. Except the—the student. He's a lot more…it's not as innocent, I mean."

"You have that effect," you tell her.

"Nick," she says back in her teacher voice.

Not bad.

"Then tell the principal," you say. "Call his parents in for a conference. *Fail* his narrow ass, Miss Gwen."

She just looks at you.

You breathe out through your nose, chew the inside of your cheek. "You want me to talk to him, right?"

She shakes her head "no" too fast, like she doesn't even have to think about it.

"He's our age," she says, in explanation.

You look to the concrete floor for a way to make this fit, but it doesn't. "What grade do you teach?" you finally ask.

"Tenth," she says. "But this was a special class. In Big Spring."

"Howard College?" It's the only one there, last you checked.

She flashes her eyes up to you. "The prison," she says.

Now you look to the open door. How wide it is. "And you told the cops?"

"They say he hasn't done anything," she says. "Untouchable, as long as he doesn't break his parole, or probation, whatever it is."

You nod, already knew all of that.

"Just to be clear," you say, in case she's wired or has a stenographer around the corner or something, "part of not being a private eye is not being a hit man either. Cool?"

"That's not what I want," she says, touching your arm now, the underside of her long nails cool, a place to hide. "You said you—that you provide security for this place."

You nod once.

She picks it up, keeps nodding, adds, "That's what I want too, Nick. Security."

You exhale like it's your lungs that are smoky, not your head. "If you're interested," you say, quieter now, "I can turn you on to some gentlemen I still know over towards Odessa, who can, y'know, help your secret admirer break the terms of his parole—"

She stops you with a finger across your lips, the nail just brushing the underside of your nose. It's intimate, almost. "*You*," she says, standing on her toes, so her mouth can brush against yours, her lipstick dry now, a red taste you want to catalogue too, particle by particle.

"Gwen," you either say or think, it's hard to tell, your hand groping out for the wall behind her so the two of you don't fall over. But then, at the last possible moment, the bench seat already an important part of what you're fast-forwarding to, wondering if you're still athletic enough for, she pushes away, forces the sunglasses back over her eyes.

"What?" you say.

"I—" she starts, then opens her purse instead, pulling out an alligator wallet that matches her sunglasses. It makes you linger over what she might be wearing under her dress. But then there's the wallet, the sheaf of bills pressing up from it that, for the first time in your life, make you think *bank notes*. Two separate, distinct words.

"Ten dollars off if paid in full, right?" she says, laying three hundred dollar bills down on your wooden spool that still isn't a desk.

In a trance of some kind, like you've just been paid for something you would have done for free, you nod, remember an interview you saw on late-night once. It was some past-his-considerable-prime porn king, and he's talking about how, just after *Deep Throat* came out, all the up-and-comers—the girls not so fresh off the bus—would walk up to him and say they could do it, deep throat. Did he want to see? No names or hellos or anything, even.

In the interview, this is where the guy just kind of shrugs, helpless, and says it perfectly, the way you're feeling now: I'm a pig, what can I say?

"So?" Gwen says, still holding the money across.

You're not a good person.

The bills are folded into your wallet before she even makes it back to her Town Car.

Two beers later—bent nails scattered on the concrete floor of the storage unit, your thumb pounding, the air thick with profanity—another vehicle noses up to the chain link fence that's either supposed to keep other people out, or you in.

Without looking away from the open door, you set the hammer down onto the calendar, crack open a sixth beer—could be eight, depending on how you count—think to yourself that you should call Guinness, maybe. Two customers in as many hours has to be a record for Aardvark Custom Economy Storage.

"How am I supposed to get anything done around here?" you say out loud, trailing off some at the end because you hear it for what it is: the exact thing your father used to say every afternoon of every weekend of your childhood. The childhood that happened exactly three blocks east of where you are right now, one street up. Your dad's probably still there in his faded green recliner, his right hand dropped down to the wooden lever like he's about to eject from this life he never really planned.

For a flash you have to look away from, you think it's him at the fence, that he wants a reconciliation, an explanation, an apology. But then, too, you know he's you, more or less, just older. Even at thirty-six, you wouldn't ever drive three blocks for any kind of gratification that wasn't immediate, and you can't imagine you'd be any different at seventy-three.

It's funny enough that you smile a bit, then feel bad about smiling, then suspect maybe you're just faking your way into a laugh because the silence has become uncomfortable. When that happens in a movie, it's because the person on-screen's being watched, isn't alone. This is real life, though. The wide door's still just an empty block of light, a diesel engine clattering in the heat out there. Under that, footsteps crunching through the caliche.

You hook one side of your mouth up, know without having to think about it that the missing sound here is a truck door closing. That the person walking up didn't want to announce himself like that, give you time to prepare. That it's a man is just a feeling. *Gut* feeling, you correct, in your head. That little voice every detective worth his salt has learned to listen to over the years. That little voice you never could hear in Midland, on the bunny slopes of the homicide beat. It's loud and clear in your hometown, though: those crunching footsteps are male. You nod, smile. It's already starting then, the case. In the only way it can. Because you don't have any wheels, any way to get around, all the players are going to have to start delivering themselves to your storage unit: Gwen's tattooed, lovesick ex-con; her mother, with a plateful of cookies; your dad, even though that's not what you want; some local badge to cramp your style, put a damper on your big homecoming. Most of all, Gwen, her skirt getting shorter with each visit.

It's your case, after all.

Part of her's still with you—in the muscles under your lips, on the pads of your fingertips. On the circle of red on the half-smoked cigarette drifting up onto the slick concrete of your storage unit, like the caliche out there's lapping, a sea of chalk.

It's then that you realize the footsteps have stopped, become a pair of work boots.

"St. Nicholas," a man says, and this one you know without even having to look up: Rory Gates. It's from the way he has of making the *St. Nick* longer, dragging it into something more painful than it already is. Like he's letting it out some, just to get it all the way around you. In elementary school, his way of saying it made you fail a spelling test once, because you got *St. Nicholas* and *Santa Claus* mixed up, spelled your own name *Nicklaus*. It wasn't part of the test, but you spent so long erasing it that you didn't have time for any i-before-e games.

It was Rory Gates's fault. Along with a lot of other stuff.

"Rory," you say.

He laughs a breath out, and you know there's not a single thing you could have said that could have kept him from it, because he's not laughing at what you *said*. He's laughing at you.

"Been a while, yeah?" he offers.

It's another set-up.

"You must be lost, I mean," he finishes. "Motel's a bit north, I believe."

What he's talking about is the peeling green Bellevue practically next door, on the other side from the water station. Even when the two of you were kids it had been closed down. Not haunted like the convent, but that's just because it's only one story tall. For a moment, walking up from the south two months ago, past the IGA, you'd even thought what he's saying, that Aardvark Custom Economy Storage was the old motel in a second life. But then the storage units turned out to be a pair of buildings running alongside each other for seven units, not a pair of buildings connected into a horseshoe at the bottom.

"Thanks," you say. "Was starting to wonder where the ice machine was."

Rory laughs, extends a hand, and you take it, hope you're not sucking your gut in. What you're wishing is that you hadn't had to turn your service revolver in, and then the next moment you're glad that you did. Better to just let him say what he needs to say, see him off.

"So you gonna let me see it?" he says, catching your eye just before he leans over to the caliche to spit, holding his hand to the brim of his straw hat so it doesn't blow away.

"Been talking to the girls in Midland?" you say back, a thin smile curling your lips just the right amount.

Rory hisses another laugh. Fingers a grain of dip off the end of his tongue, studies it before flicking it down to the concrete.

"Your war wound, man…" he says.

You rub your shoulder.

"Never known anybody who got shot in the line of duty," he says. "What was it? Thirty-eight, right?"

You look away, lower your forehead to your hand in what he can take as a yes, if he wants. Just because *.38* sounds so much better than *.22*, almost justifies your four months in Midland General, then the two more on disability, when everybody knew you were milking it but couldn't say anything, because you were the hero the department needed. At the end of the six months there'd even been a detective shield waiting, a scrapbook of all your newspaper clippings, four chances to take the Homicide test—the one that had no room at the bottom to pen in the main thing you'd learned: that, when a bunch of punk kids start shooting at you, the worst place you can hide is behind a fiberglass boat. And that, if you have to get shot in the back, a .22's not that bad. Not as good as a BB gun, maybe, but far enough from a .38, anyway.

But *.38* does sound better. Especially for Rory. You would have even smiled yes about *.44*, given the chance, raised your shirt the same as you are now, to show him the puckered scar below your right nipple that looks like an exit wound but is really just where the hot .22 slug stopped, unable to push through after riding one of your ribs around under your arm.

Rory smiles, steps closer, and then you realize what you should have already seen: that there are set-ups within set-ups. Instead of touching his index finger to the scar, which would have been weird enough, he cups your belly in his warm hand, gives it a shake.

"Haven't changed at all, have you?" he says, winking.

You let your shirt fall back down, lift your chin to him.

Inspecting the storage unit, he says, "So Stace's parents let you just stay here?"

"Up front," you say. "The office."

"That couch folds out, right?"

Yes.

He shrugs, pushes his lower lip out in appreciation. "Not bad. I mean, after…"

After Midland.

If he wasn't in faded jeans and work boots in the middle of the week, you'd think he was a lawyer, never asking a question he didn't already know the answer to.

"So you needing to store something?" you say.

He laughs again, looks around again. Says, as if in wonder, "People just leave shit here they don't really want, but feel bad about throwing away—" He fake-cuts himself off, eyes wide, fingertips over his lips like this is a tea party.

In your mind, you've got him in various headlocks, are casting around for a video camera to get him on tape like that: beaten, begging, trying to tap out. In the real world of the storage unit, though, the two of you are still four feet apart. Far enough for Rory to squat down, finger one of the bent nails up from the concrete. Rotate it, study it, follow it to the chips and gouges in the cinderblock wall over the wooden spool.

He stands, says as if it's the natural next thing, "Correct me if I'm wrong here, Nicky boy. But when you got busted, it was for taking pictures, yeah?"

Another already-answered question. Like Gwen, like everybody, he read it in the papers months ago: *Midland Homicide Detective Nicholas Bruiseman Questioned for Distributing Explicit Photographs.*

"He told me she was his wife," you say.

Rory smiles, shrugs. "You shot four rolls, right?"

You shrug with him, like you're proud, like it was worth it, like you can't still hear an 8-ball rolling over the warped slate of the quarter tables at Riley's, the corner pocket yawning open to take it, Jimmy Bones looking at you after the break, his chin resting on his cue. In trade for the eight hundred dollars the shot cost you, he'd said you could use your detective skills, figure out who was banging his friend's wife.

It was supposed to be cake.

"Good to see you again," you say to Rory, lifting your beer to him, toasting him away, then turn to the wooden spool. Like you have something to do here. For once, too, it works. Rory Gates becomes what he was before: Vibram-soled boots crunching through the caliche.

Forty seconds later, he's back, silhouetted in the door like a gunslinger, his fingers waggling over his work belt. It's bulging with torpedo levels and stubby T-squares and tape measures. He jacks the hammer up to his palm by touch, digs with his other hand in the bag just in front of his balls, even angles his hips back like he's playing with himself. You look away, grin displeasure, and the next thing you know he has a medieval looking black nail lined up in the middle of all the gouges you've already made.

"No—" you say, reaching, sure this is going to come out of some deposit you never laid down, sure that the cinderblock he's about to shatter is a load-bearing one, but then he hits the nail once with authority and it just slides right on in.

"Masonry nails," he explains, tapping it deeper, the perfect depth. He picks up your calendar, hooks it onto the nail.

"It's not January," you say.

"Never January here," he says back, running the handle of his hammer back into its loop. Then, before you can get anything out, "This is what I *do*, Nicky. I hammer, I saw, work with my hands, and shit gets built. My specialty, you could say. Get it?"

You realize this is another set-up.

He leads off "And what *you* do—"

"...is work security at a storage facility in a town of three thousand people," you say.

"And a few old soreheads," he adds.

It's what the billboard out on the interstate says.

"You think I'm in business," you say.

"Yeah," he says. "I mean, you're famous for it and all. Might as well use it, right?"

To be sure you know what he's talking about, he lifts an invisible camera to his face, takes your picture.

"I should have never come here," you say, quiet enough that he angles his head over. "I'm not a private investigator, Rory. Sorry."

"Well you're sure not a public one anymore," he says back. "What kind would you say you are, then?"

"Listen," you tell him. "Even if I were licensed, and... interested. Even if I were all that, *any* of that, what can I do from here, unless your wife conducts her affair in one of my storage units?"

Rory stares at you about this.

"So that's all you got, George Jones?" he says, hooking his head down the front of the storage units, to the riding lawnmower chained to the steel post by the office door, its battery charging.

Yes.

"Guess you need me same as I need you then," he says, stepping out, waiting just long enough for you to follow him. The only reason you do is so he won't have to lean back in like a dad, ask if you're coming or what.

He doesn't stop at his supercab like you expect, but steps out to the gravel edge of 137 and looks both ways, down to the Dairy Queen and Town & Country first, then south, to all the shiny new Chevrolets at Wheeler's, and you let yourself think for a moment that that's what he's talking about: he has some kind of in there, redid one of the salesmen's offices maybe, so he can get you something fresh off the assembly line, its tires still nubbly. But then he's looking just straight across the road, pretty much. Not at the high school or Graves Plumbing or the church or Franklins'— still Blocker Oil, to you—but at the two-stall carwash.

Under the suds, overspray arcing rainbows across all of Stanton, is an old blue-on-silver Ford.

You try not to smile, would know that truck anywhere— know that no matter how hard the kid washing it scrubs, there'll still be the print on the inside glass on the passenger side, where a girl once laid her head back, ruined you.

"Got it at a farm sale last week," Rory says, then waves his hat at the kid washing it. A boy, maybe fifteen, obviously a Rory-clone—stamped from that same football star material—just the fact of him, that he exists, it cuts right to your heart, doesn't it? It's like—it has a lot to do with that particular truck, really. Had things gone different with Gwen, then that kid might not be a quarterback. He might be drinking under the bleachers instead.

Probably better this way.

On the fourth try he gets the truck started, coasts across the street with the door open, the sole of his boot skating over the hot asphalt.

"Remember being that cool?" Rory says to you.

For once Rory doesn't make you answer, just collects the keys, fake-boxes the boy a couple of times then clamps his hat down, nods to you for his son.

"Watch yourself," he says to the boy, about you. "This guy'll lock you up."

You smile, a cop again, and nod to the boy.

The two of you leave him there, ease back to the storage unit.

"She runs," Rory says. "All I can say for sure. But go gentle. He hasn't even paid for her yet."

The keys to a truck you've maybe been in love with for half your life are already in your hand somehow.

"Just until you get the—" Rory says, filling in the blank with a new-in-the-bag disposable camera he ghosts up from his tool belt.

"And you're sure she's your wife, right?"

Rory laughs, claps you on the shoulder, and takes out his checkbook. "Name's right there with mine," he says, writing. "For better or worse. Fifty keep you in beer and Slim-fast long enough?"

You take the camera, don't even feel his words anymore. "Seventy five," you say, already calculating what you can make from this job if you offer to sell the wife the pictures first.

Rory raises his shoulders like seventy-five hurts, but writes it anyway. He passes the check to you, touches the brim of his hat in farewell. "Be seeing you," he says.

You nod, can feel the Eiffel shadow of the tall motel sign next door falling across the roof of the storage unit you're in, the gravel and tar up there making it blurry, indistinct. Past the Dairy Queen and the bridge there are parachuters floating down from the sky.

Three-hundred and seventy-five dollars in one day, you tell yourself. Three hundred of it cash money, even.

The other seventy-five you unfold, study.

In the top left corner of the check is Rory and Gwen Gates.

You close your eyes, press the check to your forehead.

2.

THOUGH YOU DON'T CONSIDER yourself hardboiled, you spend the next twenty-four hours in a bottle. Standing in the sun between the A and B storage units, staring down the Ford still nosed up to the fence. It stares back, daring you.

Towards the end of it—back to two o'clock in the afternoon again—you play a little telephone roulette, call the number printed on Rory Gates's check.

Gwen answers.

"Hey," you say.

You had an answer ready for Rory, too. The trick is, whoever answers, don't ask for the other. Just pretend that's the one you were calling.

"Nick?" she says, changing ears it sounds like, maybe pulling the phone into a utility.

You place one hand on the edge of the phone booth cemented into the side of Aardvark Custom Economy Storage, have to hold on tight to stand.

"You didn't tell me about Rory," you say.

At first she doesn't say anything, and it lasts long enough that you think maybe she's hung up. But then she's back, closer to the receiver. "You mean you've already started?"

"What?" You close your eyes to hear better, to think.

"The case," she says back, urgent almost. "You already started the *case*, right? That's how you know?"

This makes you laugh a bit, smile longer than that.

"You're married to Rory," you say.

"You've been gone a long time," she says back. "I don't have to defend myself."

"That's my job, right?"

Because you're not coming up with anything that clever for a few years now, you hang up.

Behind you—you don't look, can just feel it—the Ford's still watching you, the disposable camera on its dash now so you won't forget it.

Soon, you say in your head, then crank the a/c in the office all the way up, press your face deep into the crack between the seat cushion and the backrest, your hands balled together under your chin.

What you fall asleep thinking about is what you've been catching yourself dwelling on more and more these last few weeks: Jimmy Bones's eight ball rolling, rolling, the sound filling your chest, tightening the skin over your ribs until you have to look down. It's a doctor. He's cutting a short black line over the hot, live slug under your right nipple. He massages it out into his palm, holds it squirming up to the light, inspecting it through the jeweler's lens he's been wearing all along, but you're not really looking at him anymore, are guiding him out of the way, even—out of harm's way. The punk kids are walking out of the 7-11 again, their eyes flicking as one to your black and white cruiser, an unspoken agreement passing amongst them.

You shake your head no to them, that you're just there for coffee, but it doesn't matter. By the time they're to the ice machine, they're running, slipping around the corner in three easy steps, moving in their fluid, smiling way up Florida street, each of them balancing Big Gulps ahead of them, not spilling even a single drop.

You wake thirsty, to a voice. The payment slot in the door is talking to you. You stare at it until it makes sense: Thomas, Sherilita's kid. He's hunched over, holding the brass flap open with the backs of his fingers, a guitar slung around behind him, the most casual thing in the world.

It's dark, you don't know what time.

Thomas steps away from the door when you open it, stands there with his hands in his pockets.

"Thomas," you say. It's all you can manage.

"Like you're not a walking commercial for the straight and narrow," he says back, smiling his thin smile.

You don't disagree, have to look down to be sure you're even wearing pants. At the fence, brown bottles held close to their sternums, is the rest of the band, and their girlfriends, and their girlfriends' little brothers and sisters, who know too much to be left behind.

You shake your head, study your feet.

"That time already?" you say.

"Always that time, my man," Thomas says and the band pours through the chain link. You lead them to the middle of the B units, roll the door up, then go back for the extension cord.

"What day is it?" you say, handing Thomas the socket-end.

He plugs their amps into it, lifts his chin to you. "Good one, Mr. Bruiseman."

"Nick," you correct, but the bass player is already reaching down deep for a series of notes, the light of the yellow bulb bleeding down over him, his eyes closed against it. You're not sure you were ever this young, really. This perfect.

You sit on a lawn chair one unit away from them, let your head move with the beat of their strange music until the lead guitarist starts looking down the line of storage units.

"Go," you say.

They all do. To take a piss, supposedly. The kind you come back stoned from. The silence they leave is like being at the bottom of a dry well. In it you can hear a cricket picking its delicate way through the caliche, a moth brushing its wings on the single light bulb, the dust glittering down like dry fiberglass.

"That's Dan Gates's truck," Thomas, suddenly standing beside you, says about the Ford.

It's a question, an accusation.

"You know him?" you say back.

"His dad bought it for him, I mean"—he looks down to you—"I thought."

"I'm borrowing it," you tell him. "Moving some stuff. This is that kind of place, right? Where stuff needs moving?"

Thomas flashes his eyes from it to you, his lips pursed in what you know is doubt, but he doesn't press it.

"It true?" he says instead. "That you can't go back?"

"To Midland?"

He nods.

You shrug like the judge is explaining it to you all over again, the deal she's making you thank her for: in trade for your shield and what you promise, swear, and guarantee are all the negatives, the city won't prosecute, won't put you away for six to nine months, will instead just let the statute quietly run out in five years. So long as you never show your face in Midland County again. Not even once. Not even *half* of once.

"Know what they say now, right?" Thomas says, watching the darkness for his bass player.

"About what?"

"You sleeping again, man?"

"Thought you were saying something, I guess."

He smiles. "What they say since Big Springs got the big house."

"You're not old enough to say it like that."

"Pokey, slam, joint, pen, cooler, can, klink, what? Gray-bar hotel? Stony lonesome? Federal *Correctional* Institute? How old do I need to be?"

"What do they say now, Thomas?" you ask, covering your eyes with your right hand.

"That, from Midland, y'know, we're already like half the way *to* prison." He laughs without smiling. "That being in Stanton, you're half in jail already"

"We talking about you or me, here?" you say.

He stares out at the darkness, shakes his head no, not him, then lets his thumb idle down over the strings of his guitar.

You nod like he's as right as he thinks he is, and would like to freeze him right there if you could, so he'll never have to know anything else.

Soon enough he's back in the storage unit, concentrating on a progression the other guitarist keeps missing, can't begin to find, his fingers moving through syrup now, after break. No, not syrup: resin. You watch for as long as you can then grind your empty bottle into the caliche, stand. Study the plastic chrome wells of the Ford's headlights some more.

"Okay then," you say, and walk out to it, running your hand over its passenger side flank in appreciation, cupping your palm over the rounded end of the bedrail just to see if you can.

Slowly, by degrees and by eighths of degrees, you register that you're not alone.

Standing on the dark side of the truck is a woman, her hair down, her hands lost in the pockets of a crinkly skirt.

She's looking at the square of light angling out of the storage unit.

Sherilita.

"He's good," she says, turning to you all at once so you can't lie, her voice desperate, insistent. "Right?"

You nod, let go of the bed rail. "What are you doing?"

"You got your truck back," she says.

You smile, had forgotten she knew.

"Yours and *Gwen's*," she adds, like she maybe wants to spit after the name, and it cues up Gwen, saying how she *didn't* park at the water station, thank you very much.

Bad history, evidently. From after your time.

"So this place like you remember it?" Sherilita asks.

"What else could it be?"

In the same way she knows the truck is yours, she knows who holds the title to it now. She knows the Town Car that was here yesterday, too, and exactly where it did and didn't park. She probably even knows this situation you're in, being paid to stalk a woman who's paying you to protect her from a stalker.

You nod to her, look down at your foot on the rear tire for a moment. "It's the same," you say. "We're all just older."

The silhouette of her head rocks back a bit, with what you don't exactly know, then, her son falling into the melody of a song she probably taught him, she says, "It's all *exactly* the same, Nick. Don't you see?"

"If I'm the same, how could I?"

She stares at you across the bed of the truck. "How long are you staying?"

"Running out of sandwiches?"

She laughs through her teeth some, and it's better that way, to never say anything real.

Ten minutes later, you're walking up to the Town & Country, three hundred dollars cash in your pocket, a set of Ford keys spinning around and around on your index finger.

Because this is Martin County, not Midland, you don't even look twice at the black and white in the parking lot. But then its lights flash right beside you, the switch turned off again before it's even all the way on.

You look behind, for somebody else the cop could want, but there's just you.

The passenger side door swings open.

You swallow, lean down.

The cop behind the wheel is younger than you—one of those ones in training for the DPS, it looks like—his haircut military, stomach hard. A pair of binoculars in his hand, each lens as big around as a coaster.

"You used to be on the force, right?" he says.

"I wearing a sign or something?" you say, touching your chest to see.

"Look." He offers you the binoculars, pointing with his chin out his window.

You take the binoculars, stand with them.

"Past the second pylon," he says.

Until you figure out what *pylon* means, this doesn't help any. It's the concrete columns holding the interstate up, though. You track over to the second, then past it to the military surplus fenced in by the service road.

"What?" You press the binoculars harder to your face.

"Don't see him?" the cop says.

Right up at the tip of one of the rockets or missiles angled up over the fence is a boy. He's sitting on the nose of the thing, his legs trailing down into the night.

You lower the binoculars, look again. He's still there. "Who is he?"

The cop shakes his head. "I get any closer, poof, he's gone."

"Sorry," you say.

The cop—officer—nods.

"You remember the Lawler kid, right?" he says.

The Lawler kid was Dane Wilson's little brother, dead in a stock tank thirty years ago. He was called Lawler because he had a different dad than Dane.

"You're not old enough to," you tell the officer.

"Toby told me about him all the time," he says, and like that he falls into place: Toby Garrett's baby brother, his mouth brown from pudding, socks on his feet all the time because he was scared of grass.

"Where is he now?" you say.

"Toby?"

The officer shrugs, half of his face pulled up like saying where Toby is would take a while, if he could even explain it. That maybe it's more a state of mind than any kind of real place.

You understand, wave his efforts away.

"They still down there?" he says, tilting his head south to Aardvark Custom Economy Storage.

"Them?" you say, trying to make it sound innocent.

He rolls the dial back on his personal binoculars. "They're pretty good, from what I can hear."

You tap his roof twice in farewell.

Before you're even to the door, he's watching the military surplus again.

What you buy inside is a tall coffee and two burritos, their foil baked into a shell by the hot lights.

"One of the new ones, in back," you tell the girl real casual, about the burritos. Like you're a regular.

She gives you the two front burritos, doesn't bat an eye. "Anything else?" she asks, then sags at the hundred you slide over. She has to get manager approval to open the other register for change. Mostly fives and ones.

Fine by you. Better not to be flashing a roll of hundreds all over town. If three bills can count as a roll.

You eat at one of the tables by the plate glass, angled in your seat to watch the boarded-up Dairy Queen—the new Sonic right beside it, smooth and plastic. Nobody's at either of them. It's midnight, Thursday. Your second burrito tastes one day older than the first, and the first was probably there a week ago, in the freezer a month before that. You close your eyes to swallow. When you open them back, the black and white—David Garrett, Toby's baby brother—is gone. The girl behind the counter, she's just watching you, waiting for you to do something. Her and everybody else.

It's late, though.

You toast her farewell with your styrofoam cup—thanks, whatever—and she lowers her eyes, says it on the way out: "That your real name?"

You stop, look back.

"Bruiseman," she says.

"You're only eighteen," you tell her. It's supposed to mean that no matter how hard you try, there's no way you're remembering her too. Not after the yearbook parade you're already been staggering through this week.

You let the door close again, stand by the rack of Auto Traders. "It's real," you say, "yeah. Why?"

"Because it sounds made up."

"I mean, why—how do you know my name?"

She shrugs again. "Fin was asking about you."

"Fin?" you say. "And *that's* a real name?"

"I know." She rolls her eyes. "But he's cool."

"What do you mean?"

"Just—he understands stuff different."

"No," you say, closing your eyes to slow down to her speed. "He was asking about me?"

"Listen, he probably—I don't know. It doesn't matter."

"Does he have another name?"

She doesn't say anything.

"But he knew mine," you say.

"I think you stole his job."

"At the storage unit?"

She adds, "He wanted to be more central, I think."

You just stare at her now.

"He's an *artist*," she says in explanation, lifting the bottom of her shirt an inch or two, pulling the waist of her jeans down with the other hand.

On the ridge of her pelvis, the skin pale and tight, is a butterfly tattoo.

"Fin," you say.

"He's good. You should see his legs. That's where he started out."

You track down the rows of candy, try to figure out who could be even less desirable for a live-in security job than a cop already fired once for corruption.

You look back up to the clerk when you get it. "He's... from Big Springs." It's the polite way to say Big Springs Federal Correction.

The poke, the clink, the big house.

She says, "Like you're mister perfect?"

You lift your cup to her again in thanks, bow out of the Town & Country, walk back to Aardvark Custom Economy Storage, the job you were barely more qualified for than an ex-con. You probably should have saved your burrito receipt. It's an expense, part of the case.

"Fin," you say to yourself, just to hear it out loud. By default, he has to be the one Gwen's scared of.

Except it's more complicated than that. You're not a licensed PI—aren't even sure how to apply for a license—but still, you know enough to know that the woman in the dark sunglasses never tells you the whole story.

For that you have to go to the husband nervous that his schoolteacher wife is messing around on him.

Add *that* to her fear, and bam, it all lays itself out: Gwen, bored with Rory, with Stanton, with all of it, hooked up with one of her convict students. It was only supposed to be for a week, maybe. When she could be the first woman he'd had in ten years. But then he got attached, made parole and moved to town, set up shop. Now she just wants him out of her life. Since he can ruin hers, though, maybe has some see-me-after-class notes in the margins of his English papers, it's proving harder to do than she would have expected.

Enter Nicholas Bruiseman, St. Nick, private eye.

You unlock the chain-link gate, stand still for a moment to be sure Thomas and his band are gone. They are. The orange extension cord's even coiled on the seat of the riding lawnmower, the empty unit on the B-side closed up, your lawn chair folded against the office door.

You shake your head, say to yourself that you should leave more often, then turn to bid the Ford goodnight, don't actually see it until you're in the office: the headlights that had been watching you all day, they're not watching you anymore.

You step back outside, pull the door shut behind you.

The truck's facing the other way now.

You touch the keys in your pocket, pull them up to be sure, then approach the truck, watching behind you more than you mean to.

It's definitely been re-parked. How long were you at the Town & Country? Forty-five minutes?

The easy thing to think—what you want to have happened— is that Thomas and his band dropped the truck into neutral and pushed it around the parking lot some to screw with you.

Except, down along the bottom of the right tailpipe, there's a line of water. From a blown head gasket.

Somebody with a key was here.

But why?

You stand, tracking up the silhouette of the old Motel sign, like somebody could be hiding up there, and then, across the street, the hose at the carwash starts hissing, the sudden pressure jerking the wand from its rack. It spasms from wall to wall.

Because the truck's pointed right at it, you pull the headlights on, walk through them across 137. Catching the hose is a shower, but you do it, unwind the duct tape wrapped around the trigger, hold it until the twenty-five cents that started it is used up. Say it out loud: "Hello?"

Nothing.

Back at Aardvark Custom Economy Storage, distant, the pay phone starts rumbling.

You dive across 137 for it, fumble it up to the side of your head.

"Nicky, Nicky, Nicky," a voice says.

You switch ears, close your eyes.

"Jimmy Bones," you say back.

He laughs. "I'm nationwide, right?"

"What do you want?"

"What do you think I want?" he says back in a way that you can see him leaning forward, giving you all his attention

"She took them all back."

"Nick," Jimmy Bones says. Then, lower, "*Nick*."

"Jimmy," you say back, and feel an 8-ball rising black and smooth in your throat, have to close your eyes, hang the phone up. Swallow.

3.

BECAUSE YOU WORSHIP at the temple of bad ideas, you take your disposable camera down to what Sherilita says is Fin's trailer, in the parts yard behind the body shop on the other side of 80. She packs you a chopped beef sandwich, rolls the bag shut at the top like you're a kid going on adventures in the backyard.

You wait till you're down the road to eat the sandwich. Stop at the IGA for a coke—another expense—then buy a family size bag of chips, too.

"Carryout?" the checker asks. He's an old man.

You keep walking south.

Fin's trailer is supposed to be an old AirStream up on blocks, PERMANENT, INC painted over the door in sharp letters. The last place before it, before you're trespassing, is Caprock Electric, right across from Wheeler's. You stand in its parking lot for two minutes maybe, winding your disposable camera, letting the flash charge up, and nod to yourself about the parking lot: it's working hours. You could have pulled the Ford down here if you'd wanted, parked like you were paying your utilities then just stepped across the street, saved yourself some shoe leather.

Next time.

Holding the bag of chips in your mouth, you cross 80, feel for a moment that you're on a high wire, balancing.

There are no cars for miles in either direction.

From the hump of the turn lane, you can see most of the body shop, some of the tall fence. From the hump of the railroad tracks, you can see it all, even the AirStream tucked into its corner, the fence to one side of it fairy-tale green with weeds, from somebody peeing there day after day. Fin. Already you're knowing him, piecing him together. Later, if you can catch Melinda on shift at the Midland switchboard, you might even get his full name, what he was sent up for. Or—you smile to yourself—you might be able to tell just from looking at him. From studying the picture you're about to take, that he's never going to know about. You are a detective, after all.

Cue the music.

Ace detective Nick Bruiseman swaggers in from the 108 degree heat, checks behind him to be sure he hasn't been tailed. Zeroes in on a senior citizen with an aluminum walker trying to get across the Caprock parking lot.

You lift your chips to him so that anybody from the body shop—the *roof* of the body shop—will think you know him, that maybe he just dropped you off.

It's a good enough ruse, except the old dude falls for it too, leans forward to see you better, his walker tilting over to a hinge point you have to look away from, pretend isn't happening.

You scrabble down the opposite side of the railroad hump, a hundred years of scorched rocks sliding into the ditch with you, and when you finally stand again, trying to salvage your open bag of chips, a punk without a shirt is watching you from his side of the fence. He claps, smiles one side of his face, the hose tucked under his arm dribbling water down onto the knees of his baggy jeans. Behind him is the Caprice he's wet-sanding, the primer dusty red, like he's shaped the whole car from clay.

"Liquor store up here?" you say, looking south, and he smiles all the way now, isn't quite looking up 137 in the hopeful way you are.

"Get to Big Lake, you've gone too far," he says.

You smile like you don't know he's making fun of you, keep walking, the disposable camera hidden in the bag of chips. It was the only place you'd been able to think of.

"Fin still live here?" you say on the way past, and the punk just stares at you.

The front of the body shop is opened wide, a radio on a shelf blaring call letters, particles of bondo hanging in the air.

Bent over a car in some stage of eventual repair is an old Mexican man, years of sun folded into his face. You know without having to ask that, when a car needs pin-striping, he's the one they call. He lifts his chin to you, exhales around the cigarette he knows just to touch with his lips, not with his fingers.

You raise your face back to him, scan across the shop for Fin and find something better: in the corner, its driver's side rearview mirror dangling, is Gwen's Town Car.

As naturally as you can, like it's the prize in the cereal box, you pull the camera up from your chips, snap a picture of the inside of the body shop.

The old man stops smoothing down the roof of the car he's on, narrows his eyes at you.

"No necesitas el flash," he says, opening his hand to the sky. "Es día."

You tell him in Spanish that you can't turn the flash off.

He doesn't believe you, waves you in.

You look both ways—the liquor store, Stanton—and duck into the coolness of the shop, leading with the disposable camera.

The old man takes it, flips it over and back, then nods, pulls a circuit tester from the front pocket of his shirt. Before you can stop him, he's threaded the point of the probe into the back of the camera, given it a lobotomy.

"Ahora," he says, holding it to his face, taking another picture of Gwen's Lincoln. No flash.

"Thanks," you tell him, this time in English, and take the camera back, tilt your head to the car. "¿Qué paso?"

He shows you with his hands: one car sliding up against the other.

You push your lower lip out in satisfaction, like that explains it, and start shrugging your way back out into the heat, stop at the last moment.

The old man lifts his face, waiting for your question.

"It's in here a lot?" you say—the Town Car.

The old man smiles about this, his eyes wet, and nods once, and that's all you need: in a town of only three thousand people, where the Sherilitas can get a pretty good read on your social life just by who's parked out front, you need an *excuse* to park there. So, if your boyfriend lives behind a body shop, you become a sloppy driver.

If your boyfriend works at a storage unit, however, then there's just a flat, monthly fee, one he could probably find a way to comp, since the husband'll already be paying him to find out who his wife's backdoor man is.

Insert self-portrait here.

You crush a handful of chips into your mouth. Up 137 to the north, you can feel the punk kid at the fence, waiting to see which way you're going to go. You look back to him and he doesn't look away, just smiles. You wink to him, funnel the dregs of the chips into your mouth, and set off south, your rear pocket full of undeveloped film.

Twenty minutes later you're trying to drink from a circle system. It's not worth the effort, and the water tastes galvanized anyway, but you're in too far to quit. Soon enough an old gold wrecker slows to a stop, the driver crossing his arms over the wheel to watch you. He's trying not to smile.

You walk over.

He scratches the new buzzcut he's got under his cap. It's probably supposed to make him look less bald. He opens his mouth to say something, to tell you something, then loses it, pushes his shades tighter onto his face instead. He finally gets it out with as much tact as he can muster through the passenger side window: "You know what's in those, don't you?"

You look back to the circle system.

"Rabbits," the driver says, biting the end of the word off, smoothing his beard down along his mouth. "Rabbits and rats and possums and skunks. And all their little babies."

"It's too high," you say, not having to look back to be sure.

The driver points with his chin deeper into the field, says, "Not at the pivot it's not," and you follow the circle system back to there. Picture the single joint of hand line feeding all this water. What a good den it must look like in the winter.

You throw up all at once, wave the guy in the truck on.

He pulls halfway into the ditch instead, waits for you to finish.

"Liquor store, right?" he says, his passenger door open.

You finger a string of vomit away, look up to him. "It's that obvious?"

"Ruby told me. 'Crazy gringo thinks he can walk five miles.'"

You get in, checking yourself for chunks and strings like's polite. "You know Fin, then."

"Big bad Fin..." the driver says, checking his rearview, accelerating.

"I know you?"

He looks over fast, says, "Where you from?"

"Here."

"Maybe, then," he says. "I moved here senior year."

You think about it, tell him he's no older than thirty-six, then.

He spits into the cup between his legs. Says, "My shop back there."

You shake your head no, aren't even sure what question he thinks he's answering. "I mean, *I'm* thirty-six," you say. "I moved away with my mother my senior year. That's why we don't know each other."

The driver extends a hand. "Jim Martindale."

"Nick Bruiseman."

He doesn't question it out loud, but, by the way he's focusing on the dashboard instead of the road, you can tell he's thinking about it, saying it in his head: *Bruiseman, Bruised Man, Bruise Man. Bruise, Man.*

It's nothing new to you.

You sit back and wait for the liquor store you've only seen once. It's five miles out, wasn't there twenty years ago. Just a little modular tan shack—a lean-to, practically. Barely big enough for the one cooler it has. The kid behind the counter isn't old enough to drive, much less drink. You give him another one of your hundreds, pick up a case of longnecks, a six-pack for the road.

"Thanks," you say back in the wrecker, your door closing at the same time as Jim Martindale's. He angles the two of you back to Stanton, puts his foot in it, racking the pipes.

"You're going this way too?" you say.

"Every day's a yo-yo."

You don't really have an answer for that.

"That Lincoln," you say on the way past the body shop. "What happened to it?"

"Today, you mean?" Jim Martindale says, not having to look over to know which car you're talking about. "She says she left it on the curb last night, and bam, some kid sideswiped it."

"Insurance?"

"What?"

The wrecker rattles over the tracks, stops at 80. Jim Martindale's studying you again.

"Does insurance cover that kind of stuff?" you say.

"You a cop or something?"

You shake your head no, no. "Just seems Rory would—I don't know."

"You know them?" he asks, his voice going that kind of nasal usually reserved for out-of-staters.

"Still only one school here, right?"

Jim Martindale eases past the IGA, lets the wrecker coast the rest of the way to Aardvark Custom Economy Storage. Finally says what he's been working over under his beard: "Rory wouldn't be—it's not *him* junking her car up, I mean. He'd be suspect numero uno, wouldn't he? It'd be too obvious."

"How?"

"Since she kicked him out. I thought you knew them."

"Oh. Yeah."

You stare straight ahead, aren't sure how this changes things.

"Where's he been living, then?" you say.

"You tell me."

"His truck?"

"His mom's old house still out there by the dump?" he says, directing his face east, to the idea of the landfill.

You remember the place. But it was boarded up as early as your junior year. You only remember because, for a while, it was the place to drink.

You're about to ask Jim Martindale if he's sure about this, but then, pulling up to Aardvark Custom Economy Storage, he laughs through his nose a bit, lets it wind down to a hiss.

He's looking out his window, at the front of the Ford.

"What?" you say.

"I never saw anything, man," he says back, shaking his head to cover his smile, no eye contact.

After he's gone you walk to the front of the Ford, see what he was smiling about: a streak of maroon-black paint on the outer edge of the aluminum grill. Just at the height of a Town Car's side mirror.

You touch the paint away, use your shirt tail to get what your fingers can't. Stand all at once when you realize that you never told Jim Martindale where you lived.

By the time you get to the turn lane of 137, his wrecker's groaning up over the tracks, disappearing down the other side.

4.

You BELLY UP to the bar of the drugstore. It's been four days, maybe five. Because you don't work on the weekends. Like everything else since Midland, this is a joke: after going to all the trouble of not working on the weekends, which involves some recovery time, you don't work much during the week either. Nothing to tell the IRS about, anyway. Or your so-called clients.

The Ford is parked out front, where you can watch it through the plate glass. All you had to do to gain its trust was rub the water spots off that Rory's son had left, adjust the rearview mirror some. After that, the truck started for you on the first try. The only thing broke on it besides the right blinker, both exhaust donuts, the dome light, the air conditioner, the carrier bearing, and the passenger side window crank is the odometer. But you've only driven it five blocks, too. Maybe the odometer only kicks in at highway speeds.

You study the handwritten menu set under the smoky plastic surface of the drugstore's bar, try to read through all the additional letters scratched there with keys, realize all at once that you can hardly even remember your other life anymore, in Homicide.

Going by the calendar on the wall of the storage unit you're claiming as your own, it's January. Just, one that's 107 degrees in the shade. And there's not any shade.

You order a vanilla coke from the fountain, and a cheeseburger with a green chili on it, no onions, then slide your disposable camera to the kid not needing to write all this down, really.

He looks to the empty stools beside you, comes back even less sure what you mean.

"Want me to take your picture?" he says, drying his hands on his apron. "This your first hamburger or something?"

"Develop it," you say.

He narrows his eyes as if to suggest you're in the wrong town, maybe. Or—you get it, now—the wrong *decade*: what he's looking at for you is a Kodak kiosk by the door.

You put the camera in its envelope, push it through the slot.

The last eleven shots on it, just to use the roll up, get your money's worth, are of the tall Motel sign that's already going invisible, you're so used to it.

The first ten or eleven shots, you can't account for.

Thomas, probably. Whenever he joyrode the truck that first night.

It doesn't matter. All you need are the ones sandwiched between, the two with Gwen's car where it shouldn't be. To her, those two pictures might be worth a hundred each. More, even: the eight that will get Jimmy Bones off your payphone. The eight that's probably already sixteen, the way he counts.

You wonder if she has a tattoo now, Gwen. And where.

If she'd come to her screen door if you pulled up in the Ford, just like old times.

When she was still with Rory, it had been complicated. Now that he's gone, it's not: just get Fin out of the way, and she's available. You take for granted that she's willing. Why else would she have been all over you that first day?

But then there's the boy, Dan.

Maybe he's the one who would come to the screen door, stare at you parked in front of his house. In his truck.

You eat your cheeseburger and drink your coke and study the poster boards of pictures from Old Settlers, two weeks ago. For you it wasn't trying to find shade by the bank but standing in the door of the storage unit you want to be a living room someday, standing there with a beer, listening to the sirens of the parade downtown. The better part of you was still peddling your bike in it, streamers streaming from your handlebars, your mom and dad watching you from the thrift store's overhang, your mother with a scarf pulled down over her hair, your father lifting his hand once to you, as if to say there you are, yes.

But that was eight thousand years ago, Nick.

A lifetime.

"So what's the turnaround?" you ask the kid in the apron.

He squinches his whole face up, says, like he knows he's going to be wrong again, "For another burger?"

"For the film."

"Depends on what you checked," he tells you.

You look at one of the blank envelopes on the way out. See that you could have requested one-day. The default's two to three.

You step back out into heat, slope over to the bank.

Because the seventy-five dollar check is made out to *St. Nick*, they can't cash it. The teller, Janet, just shrugs when you ask her what you're supposed to do, then.

"Have you already rendered the services this is in payment for?" she says.

You study the bullet pen chained to the counter. Open your mouth to tell her kind of, yeah—you took some pictures like he wanted, anyway—but then say instead, "It's Rory Gates's."

Janet nods that, yes, she knows whose check it is.

"Would it even clear?" you say, folding it back it into your chest pocket the way old men do with their pouches of chewing tobacco.

She lifts her chin to the woman behind you, holding onto the velvet rope with both hands.

You smile your way out, know better than to make a scene under a security camera.

On the sidewalk again, you count what's left of Gwen's retainer: one hundred and ten. Minus five for the film developing, one for the gas it's going to take to get back to the drugstore to pick the film up. Six for the cheeseburger you'll buy again. Twenty for beer, three for gas to get the beer.

You're going to need that seventy-five.

Just shy of sixty miles per hour, the Ford has a definite shimmy. It could be a hundred things. You slow back down to fifty, keep on east, not sure where the turn-off for the dump is anymore until the hand-drawn arrow of a landfill sign tells you.

Coming down from highway to caliche speeds, the truck shudders, and you know it's the front rotors, wafer-thin and warped, but at least the brakes work, right? And anyway, this truck was never meant to pull cotton trailers or deliver round bales of hay or be left in a turnrow all day. It's a lover, not a fighter.

You hand-over-hand the wheel, hope there's going to be more landfill signs ahead. The only other way you can stumble onto Rory's mom's old house is if you find some twenty-year-old cans of beer behind the seat, drink exactly the amount you used to after the Friday night football games.

It takes about fifteen minutes to get lost. Not the "not finding Rory's mom's house yet" kind of lost, but the "is this even Martin County anymore" kind.

You're not sure. Your only point of reference is a yellow cropduster plane, swooping down back and forth, dropping rolls of toilet paper each time it starts to lift back up into the sky. To mark its place. Meaning the pilot doesn't have a spotter on the ground, is working alone today. Whatever he's spraying, you can taste it on the air. For a while you try holding your breath, but that falls apart pretty fast, just makes you pull more air in. The only solution is to punch through it all at the best clip you can manage. Several foggy years later, you step off the caliche onto packed dirt, and the surface matches up perfectly with everything broken on the Ford, and suddenly you're driving on glass. You even let go of the wheel for seconds at a time.

Soon enough the road ends, turns into another, even narrower, and then you're not sure if you're on a road anymore at all. Just a glorified turnrow, maybe. But then you start picking up signs—beer bottles, faded silver cans. They're all along the fence on your side, some of them turned upside down onto the thin locust stakes that keep the barbed wire spread.

This you remember: dropping bottles out the driver's side window, tail lights glowing red ahead of you in the dust like a promise.

The *kids* still know where the old house is.

Two minutes later, it's there, just like you remember it except even more trashed. Rory's supercab is angled up to it from some other, probably more direct road.

You nod about this, about what you're going to say to him: that seventy-five's not enough, and that cash works fine, thanks. That it looks like his wife's boyfriend's real trouble. That, what does he want the pictures for anyway? From your limited experience, usually the pictures are just to bring into focus what the husband's already been playing in his head.

But—he's not even *living* with Gwen anymore, right?

What does he care?

You step out, the Ford off because you know more about the starter and the battery than you do about the radiator. The only sound is the plane buzzing behind you, like something you could slap to your neck if you wanted, rub onto your jeans.

Between you and the house is the old concrete tank. At one time there'd been goldfish in it, you remember—this was just after Rory's family moved to town—but for the part of your junior year you were still a Stanton Buffalo, the tank was an ashtray, a trashcan. Down deep in it, caked in the dirt now, there's probably some antique beer bottles, even. Some real live pull tabs. A broken rubber or two, the kid born from that already out of high school himself, making his own contraceptive mistakes.

What you're going to tell Rory is no more *St. Nick*.

And that you know all he's wanting the pictures for is to have the upper hand in the divorce proceedings.

And—how much is there to be had, anyway?

Seventy-five dollars seems a small cut.

That you know the pictures are about divorce will be a lie, of course, but the way he responds will be real.

You step onto the porch, rap on the door, have to back away from the dust packed into the grain of the wood by a thousand sandstorms. Why anybody would want to spend the heat of the day inside a broken-down old house…well, you want to say it's beyond you. It does beat working, though.

Rory's not you, though.

Probably he saw your dust cloud coming and's inside now, getting some new humiliation ready for you.

Not this time.

You back off, call his name through one of the broken windows in front, get no reply. You honk the horn of his truck and come away trailing webs. They're strung from the top of the steering wheel to the headliner, then back to the gun rack, the carpenter's level Rory keeps on the lower hooks.

You turn back to the house, less sure.

You say his name again, louder. Then, backing away, you say it weaker. And you know already that the Ford isn't going to start. That you never should have come out here.

You breathe in, out, go back to the Ford anyway.

It doesn't start.

You stare at the house, shake your head. Don't even have any beer with you. Weren't planning on making a day of the drugstore.

You honk again, only it's not so loud anymore.

Maybe this is something that happens to all PIs. Part of the job.

And then you decide that Rory's upstairs, watching you. Smiling.

You step out, leave the door of the Ford open, pick up the first brown bottle you find and flip it around so that you have it by the neck. You shouldn't, but you do it anyway: sling the bottle end over end at the house.

It doesn't shatter against the wood. Doesn't even dent it, near as you can tell.

You pick up another, throw it harder, and it does break. And the next. The dirt clod you dig up out of a tractor track, though, it just goes right through the wall.

After that, standing there, breathing hard, you decide that Rory probably isn't just a carpenter, that he's probably a pilot by now too. It's the natural next thing to be, after quarterbacking varsity to regionals two years in a row. Being homecoming king. Getting Gwen.

You look back to the plane.

It just keeps swooping up, back down.

"Fine," you say, and go back to the house, push through the front door, check the first floor. It's just like the outside: already broken. Covered in dust. You call upstairs but it's empty too, and the stairs are rickety and wrong anyway, probably only good enough for mice and snakes.

This isn't a joke anymore. Or, if it is, you're not waiting for the punch line, for Rory to pull the yellow plane up to the side of the house, push his goggles up onto his forehead and ask, "What're you doing here, Nicky?"

There'll be no witnesses for whatever he does next.

But his keys are still in his truck. You saw them when you were honking.

It starts on the second try, glowplugs be damned, and for a long, long moment, you know you're just going to take it instead, park out front of Aardvark Custom Economy Storage. Make *him* catch a ride to town.

But then, when neither of you have any jumper cables, you have to take it whether you want to or not. Out the back way, following the dirt road that's obvious now, that swings up around the landfill. The opposite way from the yellow plane.

After a couple of miles, the dirt road becomes caliche, then the caliche asphalt, and you're on the service road of 20, miles east of town. A lot closer to Big Springs than you meant.

The clock on Rory's aftermarket stereo says three o'clock.

You look right towards Stanton, then the other way, to Big Springs.

The judge didn't say anything about not going there.

At the prison you push the visitor's log back to the desk sergeant, give him your old badge number.

He hands you a different log.

You sign your name, try not to smile.

The desk sergeant studies it for half a second then re-shelves it, creaks his chair back to get a better angle on you. "Who you need to see then?"

You rub your chin like a homicide detective might. "It's not like that. He's already out, this guy."

The desk sergeant positions his fingers over his keyboard.

"Fin," you say. "That's all we've got."

"He's wanted for something?"

"Just questioning."

"Fin..." the desk sergeant says, and can't find it, has to call a guard over. He looks you up and down. "That big-ass tattoo guy from D—what'd he do, finally twist some jerk's head off?"

"Not yet."

"ID?" he says then.

You do your best disgusted/impatient act, flash the shield you reported lost six months ago.

"Sorry," the guard says, no sincerity in his voice at all.

"I just need his full name," you tell him. "I can call dispatch for the rest."

"Payne," the guard says, like it's supposed to be funny. "Full name, Anthony Robert Payne."

You repeat it back to him, suddenly aware of the prop you don't have: a flip notebook. "He tight with anybody here?"

The guard rubs his nose. "It'll all be in his file, I'd figure. Right, detective?"

He stares at you after saying it.

Anthony Robert Payne. Fin. Big-ass tattoo guy from D-block. Permanent, Inc.

You nod to yourself about all of it.

"He's in Stanton now, if you're wondering," you say, tapping the counter twice before pushing off, what you've always thought of as a parting rimshot.

The guard nods, still watching you. Says at last, his cheeks drawn up, "I know you from somewhere, right?"

You leave before he can connect you to Big 2 News.

From the phone on Rory's dashboard, you call Melinda at dispatch. She picks up on the first ring.

"Nick," she says, barely a whisper.

"One and only."

"I can't talk to you."

"Just listen, then. I need the sheet on a—"

"Do you know what happens if they find out this is you?"

"I guess we should make this fast, then," you tell her. "Don't want to…get you in any trouble. Like last time."

Last time was in the backseat of your patrol car, your second year out. Because it felt dirtier back there, criminal. Except, afterwards, the doors wouldn't open up, and you finally had to call for help on your shoulder rig. Everybody coming out to clap, somebody throwing leftover carryout rice onto the two of you when you helped her up from the patrol car.

Melinda breathes in, out—is married now, with real rice—and you have her.

Anthony Robert Payne did eight years of a ten-year aggravated assault bid. It was on his ex's new guy, it sounds like. Like the girl he'd divorced was supposed to stay faithful.

"What's he look like?" you say, instead of goodbye.

Melinda hangs up anyway.

This time you let the glowplugs of Rory's truck warm before turning the key. The gas gauge climbs to a quarter tank, stops.

Jumper cables, you say to yourself. Jumper cables could still save you. Just lay down twenty dollars for a set, ease back to Rory's mother's house, get the Ford started, and go back to Aardvark Custom Economy Storage. Call it a day.

Except, already you're putting the diesel it took to get to Big Springs on your expense account. The diesel it took to run down your client's wife's backdoor man. Or, body shop guy—*body* guy.

You like that, are going to use it on Rory, you think. If he tries to call you St. Nick again.

Of course, you're willing to erase that expense, too. Not just because you didn't pay for the diesel in the first place, but because, really, it makes sense to take Rory's work truck instead of the Ford. If he wants you to solve the case, you have to have transportation. While the Ford's good enough for Stanton, getting all the way over to Big Springs is another story.

And, anyway, sitting high up in the supercab, you feel like a landowner.

And landowners, where do they go when the work's done?

The bar.

On a good day, you can rationalize just about anything. Sitting in the parking lot in front of the bar—Wagon Wheel, Broken Spoke, something like that—moving Rory's house key over to your key ring, you even take it a little further: because the bar is the first one you see, driving away from the prison, it's probably the closest too, the one a prison guard or two is bound to stop at after a hard day of cracking heads, just to wind down, depressurize. Remind himself that the kids he has at home aren't inmates, haven't been convicted of anything yet.

You tell the waitress you're going to be needing your receipts here, thanks.

Twenty minutes later, one guard creeps in.

You buy him his second drink, show him your badge, and by eleven o'clock, after he's sure you're going to put in a word for him with your captain, he's rolling up his sleeve to show you the work Fin's done on him.

It's a skull, a dagger in the right eye socket, a snake coiled around the handle.

"What about him, though?" you say. "He get a lot of visitors?"

The guard has to focus deep into his coaster to remember, then starts nodding, slowly. Looks up to you with a smile, says, "Yeah, that's right. That one—the teacher lady. Holy hell, man. Like to teach her some grammar."

"Conjugate a verb or two," you add.

"Get sent to the back of the class…"

Your tab, you know, is already at seventy-five. Eighty if you tip the waitress.

"He ever a discipline problem?" you say.

The guard laughs, swirls his drink. Says, "He *was* the discipline, man," then falls into a coughing fit that almost ends in vomit.

You come back to him, wait until he can hear. "What do you mean 'he was the discipline?'"

The guard takes a long enough drink that his eyes water.

"You can feel it when he's working on you," he says, touching the skull under his shirt sleeve to show what he means. "That he's like—that it's all—" He stops, starts again. "Like strong, I mean. All wound up inside."

"And he's big, right?" you say. "Like farm-boy big?"

"More like military," the guard says, rocking on his stool some. "Special...green...ranger..."

You push the rest of your drink over to him. He sips it down, has to concentrate to get his throat to go along with him.

"Never sleeps, either," he says, laughing, then staggers off to the little caballeros' room.

Fin, you say to yourself for the thousandth time.

Ex-special forces, bleeds tattoos, did eight years inside for beating a guy who maybe had something going with his ex. This is the guy whose girl you've got designs on. The one she wants you to break her up with.

You laugh to yourself, about yourself, then leave the guard in the bathroom, sign over Rory's check to the bar—no tip, just the check, slid under an empty glass—and stand in the parking lot by Rory's tall truck wishing it were cold, that there was a wind to sober you up.

Failing that, you do what you learned from your dad: open the door wide, put your fingers in, then, before you can even think about, slam the door shut.

It sobers you up so much you want another drink, for the pain. A bottle.

You don't even look at your index finger until you're up on 20 again.

The nail's purple, going black, blood seeping out on all sides, outlining it. Because the doors of the trucks your dad taught you on were old and loose and never fit that well in the first place. The cab on Rory's truck is airtight.

You laugh again, still at yourself, then stay five miles under the speed limit the whole way to the Martin County line, miss the exit for business 20—highway 80—find yourself looping over the north side of Stanton. Just to stop on top of the bridge.

From here you can see the whole town, the blanket of lights. *Napkin* of lights, you correct.

You follow the front of the truck around to the guard rail, lean against it with your shins.

The military surplus place is right below you, almost. The rocket pointed up over the fence like the Buffaloes are about to wage war on…you turn your head to follow the arc of the rocket—who?

Before you can tell, remember what's out that way—Lenora, maybe? Tarzan, if you go far enough?—Toby Garret's baby brother coasts in behind you, blue lights flashing. Up here on top of the world, they're a beacon.

"Nice out," he says, approaching.

You smile, can't help yourself. Say, as if about to zip up, "Is nice out, yeah. Think I'll just leave it out."

Toby Garrett's baby brother doesn't even flinch.

Not good. You direct your eyes down to the rocket.

"The Lawler kid, right?" you say.

Toby Garret's baby brother looks too. "Gene Lawler's been dead for thirty years, Mr. Bruiseman."

Mr. Bruiseman: worse.

"You thought I was gonna be Rory, didn't you?" you say.

Toby Garret's baby brother shakes his head no, he didn't.

"Do you need medical assistance?" he says about the index finger that won't ball up with the rest.

"Nothing I couldn't fix with the right screwdriver."

"Have you been drinking, sir?"

You don't answer, just track north on 137. Think maybe you can see the lights of Lamesa up there. Their drive-in, maybe four cars spaced out on the packed dirt.

"I guess you know I'm going to have to take you in," Toby Garrett's baby brother says.

You look back to the truck. "He won't be pressing any charges," you say.

Toby Garrett's baby brother nods that you're right about that. Then, no eye contact, because this is the part of his job he hates, he reaches back for his cuffs.

5.

THE SHERIFF IS A WOMAN named Felson. She wears her service revolver high on her hip, waits until morning to talk to you.

"I'm in county?" you say, rubbing your eye too hard with the heel of your hand.

She sits down, explains that the interstate David Garrett arrested you on was out of his jurisdiction, even though it was in the city limits.

Just to get it over with, you say it: "I know you?"

When you can see again, she's watching you, both her hands on the table. No ring.

"Trying to butter me up?" She smiles in her hard, no-lipstick way, says that she was a senior your first year of junior high. You were beneath noticing, for her. But now you've got her full attention.

"Felson," you go on anyway, like actually remembering, "yeah…"

"It's my ex-husband's name, Mr. Bruiseman. He was from Andrews."

This is where she's supposed to slap your wrist, explain that the fourteen cents a day it costs to feed you isn't worth it. That the cell you were in last night is actually bigger than the storage unit you slept in this weekend, that its thin mattress is better than the couch in the office that's usually your bed. That, if you want detox, you should pay for it like everybody else.

Instead, she leans forward with something like a question. "'Custom.' That's the part I've never understood. Aardvark, I mean, it's stupid, nothing to do with Stanton, but it works, gets them at the front of the phonebook. But—I mean, there's fourteen units, right? Each ten by twenty? What's 'Custom' about that?"

"Forgetting about 'Economy,'" you add in a salesman's bored voice. "Five dollars off a month if you pay a year in advance."

"To say nothing of the security on premises," she says.

"Speaking of that," you say, making like you're going to stand. Making like, "Thanks and all, but things to do…"

She doesn't move, though.

"Rory's not pressing any charges, is he?" you say. "I mean, he was who I was *there* for…"

Her irises are flecked with hazel, you note. Because she's staring right the hell into your soul.

She sets a silver microcassette rig between you.

You're suddenly frantic that you kicked out the side window of the patrol car last night on the way to booking.

But, no. The ride was only about three minutes after Toby Garrett's baby brother called in the wrecker for Rory's truck. All you talked about, you're pretty sure, was the one coach the two of you had shared (Baker), and his fascination with running bleachers. His fascination with *other* people running bleachers, anyway. "More of a fetish, really," you'd said.

Toby Garrett's baby brother had tried not to laugh.

You nod like this microcassette recorder is no big deal—nothing to hide, right?—study the calendar on the wall, suddenly drowning in panic. Did you *hit* something on the way back from Big Springs last night? But even in that big-ass truck you would have felt it. And…yes: parked on top of the bridge, you'd walked around the nose of the truck, traced the top of the grill guard with your palm. If there'd been blood, human, animal, or other, you would have felt it, smelled it hissing on the radiator.

"So we're making this official," you say, about the recorder.

"For the record, you are?"

"Nicholas A. Bruiseman."

"Occupation?"

"Former homicide detective, current security guard," you say. "Just the facts right?" You laugh a little about this, lean to the side as if the recorder only works when you're sitting in one place, and ask if she wants you to start over.

"You're doing fine, Mr. Bruiseman."

If this were anything serious, they'd have a detective in to talk to you, you tell yourself. Somebody trained in the delicate art of interrogation. Maybe even a tag-team: hick cop, slick cop.

Sheriff Felson pushes the recorder two inches closer to you.

"So what's this about?" you ask.

"You tell me," she says.

"It's not about that waitress, is it?" you say, both your hands palm-down on the table now. "Because that guy I was with, I told him, we had a deal. I'd pick up the tab, he'd take care of the tip."

Sheriff Felson shakes her head no. Not even close. Not even *close* to close.

You ping-pong your eyes from side to side, as if you're really having to think about what minor infraction you could be guilty of. "I guess, technically, from some severely limited point of view, you could say I might have stolen a few gallons of diesel."

No.

"It's not Thomas, is it? I mean, I don't know where they get that beer..." You lift your shoulders in defeat. "It's that I don't have a ticket, right? There's a fine for that?"

"A ticket?"

"A license."

"To practice what, Mr. Bruiseman?"

You're embarrassed to say it, do anyway: "Private investigation."

She lets herself smile about this. A real live, female smile. "That what you call it?" That the license that lets you impersonate a Midland Homicide Detective? The one that provides immunity for grand theft auto—"

"Wait. Just let me talk to Rory about that. He'll—"

"The license that lets you operate a motor vehicle while obviously inebriated, park in a strict no parking zone..." She flips her notebook open for the rest. "Oh, and hit and run parked vehicles, trespass a body shop, take unauthorized photographs?"

She's sounding a lot like the judge in Midland, ticking your charges off on her fingers. At the time, you'd had to just stand there. Now, though, now you've had some time to think about it, to prepare.

She's not going to have enough fingers.

"You forgot jaywalking, yeah?" you say. "That was the day of the body shop. I crossed way before the crosswalk. Oh, and littering, too." You shrug, caught. "I had this twenty-ounce styrofoam cup from the Town & Country, see? Just, I mean, I was even ashamed doing it, right? Dropped it right there on the ground like a common criminal. Can you make a citizen's arrest on yourself, or is that just some kind of public bondage?"

"Let me tell you what we've got," she says, leaning forward through all your bullshit. "Darryl Koenig, a cropduster out of Greenwood. He was east of town yesterday, saw you taking the back way to the old Gates place."

You don't disagree.

"You don't contest this?" she says for the recorder.

You pull it up to your lips, say it right into the mic: "No. I, Nicholas Bruiseman, of sound mind and some kind of body, don't contest this."

"And, last Thursday—correct me if I'm wrong here—you called the Gates household, here in town."

"I told you—"

"Yes or no?"

"It was probably Thursday, yeah. Sure."

"Good. Thank you. This is the Gates household of *Rory* Gates, whom you have something of a colorful history with."

"That was a long time ago."

"And a history with the wife, Gwen Gates, as well."

"Gwen Tracy," you correct. "I don't know who she is now. Anymore."

"Mr. Bruiseman answers in the affirmative," Sheriff Felson narrates into the microphone you're still holding.

"Would Sheriff Felson like the details of the aforesaid history?" you say, your lips curling into a smile. "I mean, no crime there, I don't think. We were both consenting juveniles…"

She ignores this, says, still reading, "And the truck you were driving, that according to multiple witnesses has been parked—"

"*Multiple*?"

"This truck, distinctive because of its Dallas Cowboy paint scheme, has been in your possession since that same Thursday?"

"Wednesday, actually," you say with something like a game-show lilt.

"And from Thursday afternoon until last night, you've been…" she flips through, as if the answer's in her notebook.

"Drinking," you fill in. "Trying to get my tolerance up for football season."

She's still not amused.

"Just ask Rory," you say. "Ask Gwen, too. They both hired me."

"As a private investigator?"

"As a private investigator, yes," you say into the recorder. "You want to punish me for practicing without a theme song or a sidekick, be my guest. Been feeling kind of guilty about that one anyway."

After that, it's the big stare-off. The finals.

But you're not worried. Worst they can charge you with is a DUI, and even that, it'd be a joke, since Toby Garrett's baby brother didn't make you find your nose in the dark.

Reckless endangerment, then.

It'll be your second.

"You say Rory Gates hired you," Felson says. "Why did he need your services?"

"Because Gwen kicked him out, maybe? Because he was living out in a—this haunted-ass house?"

"Where he grew up?"

"You *seen* it lately, ma'am?"

"Go on."

"Gwen was—" You open your hand before your face, close it back. "She was seeing somebody else. Rory wanted evidence. Stop me if you've heard this before. I guess adultery looks good in court."

"It's called sexual abandonment," Sheriff Felson corrects. "And Gwen Gates also had need of your services. Supposedly."

"No 'supposedly' about it. Seems she kind of caught something teaching English over in the federal pen. He's big, blue, and, well—won't go away. That a good way to say it?"

"You're saying she told you that Fin Payne was stalking her?"

"That's it."

"I don't suppose you thought to record this, get an affidavit, sign a contract?"

"I wasn't even a PI, then," you tell her.

Sheriff Felson pulls her top lip between her teeth. "And you were supposed to...?"

"She was afraid he was going to get violent," you say. "Kind of has a history of that, as I understand."

"Then *Fin* would be the one *Rory* was suspicious of?"

"Yes. Ma'am. Just like watching *Dallas*."

"Nobody watches Dallas anymore, Mr. Bruiseman. And Gwen Gates will verify this...this state of affairs?"

"I don't see why not."

"Maybe because you ran into her car?"

"Her mirror," you correct. "And that wasn't me."

"She filed a report, Mr. Bruiseman. We have the physical evidence."

"There's another set of keys."

Sheriff Felson stares at you about this.

You look away. "So we're back to me, like, im*person*ating myself again?"

"Impersonating the cop you used to be," she says. "Yeah."

"Tell me what this is really about. Or I guess I'll have to get a lawyer involved."

She closes her notebook, guides it spiral-edge first into the slope of her chest pocket. "Rory Gates is dead, Mr. Bruiseman," she says.

You turn your head to the side, towards Midland. Because it's twenty miles away from the chair you're in now.

6.

You're not real sure what race, ethnicity, or caste your lawyer is. His name is Arnot King. The only reason you have his card in your wallet is that three years ago, on a lonely Christmas day, you let him slide on what was looking to be a DUI, some statutory issues with a minor, possession with intent to distribute, and the destruction of city property. The city property was the flag in the front of the courthouse; he was shooting salt at it with a little .410 and missing badly.

At the time, the main reason you didn't haul him in was because it was downtown, where the wind wraps around the buildings, whips you in the face, and you'd left your black Walls jacket at the station house for some stupid reason. Because you'd been too worried about what your breath smelled like, probably. Whether your eyes were bleeding.

Standing there, your breath frosting, the new year almost upon you, Arnot King had offered to distribute some of what he was possessing your way, if you'd maybe let him go, yeah?

Mexican, you thought at first, then nixed that just as fast. Pakistani? Egyptian? A tall guy from Cambodia, maybe, with a whispery French *t* at the end of his name? What did people from Greenland look like? Sri Lanka?

It was something about his black eyebrows, how they wanted to be bushy but were drawn in instead. Dense, tightly woven. Manicured, almost. His eyes dancing under them, always looking to each member of the jury, telling them anything was possible, really. That there was always room for doubt.

Though he was hammered enough that his fast-food girlfriend was having to prop him up on her hip, you could tell all this.

"So?" he said, his mouth pulled up on one side, into a coyote grin.

Slowly, so he'd know this was a gift, you put the rubberband back around your clipboard, slid the whole rig into the back of your polyester pants, your utility belt creaking in the cold. You shook your head no to the baggie he dug up from his pocket.

He said, "I remember you," his accent a complete mystery. Minnesota, maybe? Something about the way he clipped his words.

"No," you told him, already casting around for any witnesses. "You don't remember me. Because I was never here."

Parting ways, he held an unsteady business card out to you, said it was worth one get out of jail free.

You took it without looking, said to the girlfriend, "You old enough to drive, miss?"

She stared at you with lizard eyes, said she was old enough for a lot of things, then asked who you were.

"Who needs to know?"

She just stared at you.

"St. Nick," you finally told her, the first time you'd even heard the name in years. Then, minutes after she was gone, "ho, ho, ho."

In the patrol car, in your coffee cup, was two fingers of brandy to steady your hands. For anybody watching, you acted like it was still hot, sipped the top off, then the rest, and didn't even look at the get out of jail free card until you were pulling away. His name, big and important, then *Legal Services. Attorney-at-Large. Professional Snake Charmer.* The 'snake' in the picture was wearing a judge's wig, was rising up over his bench, a hammer in its hand somehow.

Indian, you thought for a moment. Like from India. Except the smile, it was Indian too, no doubt—sharpened at the corners by poverty, from having to smile all the time—but the American kind.

It doesn't matter what he is, though, only that he shows up on Wednesday just before five, one day after Toby Garrett's baby brother looked him up in the phonebook for you. The number on the card was dead but there he was in the yellow pages, in medieval chain-mail, sitting on a horse, a javelin or lance standing up beside him. What the caption said now was *Cash Settlements. Insurance Specialist. Your Knight in Legal Armor.*

Toby Garrett's baby brother had held his finger on the ad, looked up to you. "Sure?" he said.

"Old friend," you said back, then pretended not to hear when he said, innocently almost, like he was just trailing a thought: "This make you a—a what, then? Damsel?"

On the third ring, Arnot King picked up, denied ever having met you.

You called him back, lowered your voice to a below-the-radar hiss, told him that if he didn't remember, then the video unit on the dash of your patrol car might help. Christmas night, three years ago? Sweet little thing he picked up in the drive-through?

For a long time he was quiet.

"So?" you said.

"This isn't about paternity, is it?" He was covering the phone with his hand for that, you're pretty sure.

Twenty-four hours later, like a fairy tale, Arnot King is there to rescue you.

The first thing he asks, staring at your file on the break room table, is for some privacy with his client, maybe? He's talking to Toby Garrett's baby brother, who's busy getting a cup of coffee drop by drop. You're in the break room because Arnot King says interrogation rooms are always wired.

"Paranoid," you say to him after the break room's empty. "I like that."

He looks up at you for a flash. "You saying I'm still using?"

The coffee percolates like thunder.

"How bad is it, then?" you say, about your file.

Arnot King laughs, does something with his eyes that everybody in his homeland probably does without even having to think about it. A gesture between humor and despair.

"About that *tape*," he says, not looking up now.

You are already thinking about spitting in the coffee, except you might want some, too. And in the pitcher, or the filter?

You come back to Arnot King slow. "Get me out of here. I know where the only copy is."

Arnot King closes the file, holds it down with both hands.

"Like, *bail*?" he says.

"You could do that?"

"No. Just asking. Because"—patting the file—"if these are the charges you want me to make disappear, you may as well go ahead and *have* somebody mail that tape. Tell your nice sheriff about it. Or that judge you've got such a crush on in Midland."

"Optimistic, too," you say, studying the far corner of the ceiling.

"Realistic, Mr. Bruiseman."

"Nick."

"Nick. Listen. Without admitting anything, yes, in my less-healthy days, I had a weakness for junk food, probably can't remember each and every, um, *wrapper* I threw away. Or under what circumstances. So, yes, it's possible that I'm in your debt. That you have me for *littering*, let's say. What this translates to for you is that if you get a speeding ticket in your new and improved life here, I can probably make it go away. But this"—the file again—"this is homicide. Not manslaughter, not negligence, not self-defense. Shooting a man in the face with a shotgun, Mr. Bruiseman. Nick. *Nabby*."

It's one of the aliases on your booking sheet. One Toby Garrett must have passed on to his baby brother. It's what Gwen called you in the storage unit, the name you still feel in your spine, even when you're expecting it.

You focus on Arnot King's face now.

"You didn't have a beard three years ago," you tell him.

"A *shot*gun," he says back, loosening his thin tie.

You close your eyes. "Please don't call me that."

"Nabby?"

It's your initials plus that time you stole the milk money. A name some parent must have thought up, because nobody in the fourth grade knew *nab*. Hearing it at school that first time, you knew in a flash that the world wasn't a fair place. That you were going to have to do what you could to compensate.

Arnot King shrugs the name away like it was never there, then says again, to prove it, to drive it home, "A shotgun. To the face. Execution-style."

You focus on the closed file, say it—"Tell me"—and he does: James Roderick "Rory" Gates was found in the second upstairs bedroom of the farmhouse he'd grown up in. It had been his room, maybe. And it seems he had either tried to cover his face with his hands, or tried to cover both barrels with his hands. It hadn't been pretty. The only part of his hands that still had skin was behind his wedding band.

"Evidence for the prosecution *one*," Arnot King says, holding a long finger up.

Next, going by the tire tracks around the farmhouse, you and Rory were the only ones who'd been there since the murder.

"How long had he been dead?" you interrupt, leaning forward, suddenly sure it happened last night, while you were in Big Springs. That you'll plead guilty to impersonating yourself, even show them the prison logbook if it'll get you out from under a homicide beef.

Arnot King shrugs. "Ever since he got shot. That's what happens with a shotgun, as I understand. Even in a place this... *provincial*."

"*When* did he get shot?"

Arnot King flips through the file. "Thursday or Friday of last week."

"They can already tell?"

Arnot King pulls up another photocopy, turns it around for you.

It's a missing persons report. Gwen Gates filed it last Friday.

The next photocopy is from the phone company, a record of your call to her the day before that.

"I was checking in," you say, pushing the sheet back.

Arnot King looks at you about this. "In the capacity of...?"

"Unlicensed private investigator," you say, looking to the door now, the one Toby Garrett's baby brother is pretending not to be standing at.

"So this"—Arnot King, reading—"this *Gwen*, wife, woman. She wanted you to use your significant investigative abilities to find him for her?"

"She knew where he was," you say. "I was working for him too."

"For the dead guy?"

Yes.

Arnot King leans back. "And the wife can confirm this?"

"He wrote me a check," you say. "They have a joint account."

Arnot King likes this. Then he sees you looking towards Big Springs. "What?" he says.

"I—it's already used."

Torn up, more like. An out-of-town check made out the first time to a 'St. Nick?' Left at a smoky bar you'd just ducked out of?

Arnot King keeps his smile but it's fake now, part of the show.

"I have proof," you say, closing your eyes to keep it all straight, "that—that she was having an affair. Like Rory said."

"Proof?"

"Pictures. They're being developed."

"The kind you—that Judge Harkness became aware of?"

You shake your head no. "Her car. In a body shop down the street."

"For damage you yourself inflicted?"

"Allegedly inflicted."

He stands up, spins away. Pours a nervous cup of coffee, his lips thin, mad.

But then you start nodding to yourself. He catches it, sits back down quietly, so as not to mess this last thing up.

"Yeah," you say, smiling. "The wrecker driver, body shop guy."

"Her lover?"

You shush him with your hand. "They're saying I called Rory," you say, "to meet him out there for whatever reason. But I talked to Gwen that day. You can ask her. That phone record. But the reason I went out there in the first place, it was because the wrecker driver told me Rory was living out there. That Gwen had kicked him out."

Arnot King processes this. Then, as he has to, he says, "This is the same wife who also reported him missing?"

Yes.

Slowly, as if already defeated, Arnot King pages through the file, finds nothing.

"And—will she confirm this, you think?"

You give him her number. He stands, tells you he's going to pretend you don't have that memorized and goes to the phone by the door, makes motions through the glass for Toby Garrett to pick up, listen, confirm.

All you hear from your side is Arnot King's polite questions, the tone you take with a new widow, but you can already tell what the answer is: Rory was with her the whole time. No, she never talked to Nicholas Bruiseman on the phone last Thursday. Maybe her husband? Had he been drinking, Nicholas Bruiseman?

Arnot King re-cradles the phone like it's made of glass and comes back to the table. "And you wonder why defense lawyers resort to narcotics."

"Drive-through girls," you add, smiling.

He laughs. "You don't have that Christmas tape, do you?"

You shake your head no, you don't, and for what feels like minutes, it's quiet. Just the coffee dripping like a metronome, counting off the seconds of your life. Your heart ticking down.

You tell yourself you understand. That this is fair. It's just the card you've pulled, somehow. It's what happens when you bet Jimmy Bones eight hundred dollars you don't have, all on the fall of a ball. You should have seen it all coming, really. And, if you're honest, you guess you kind of did, right? And now you're standing, to shrug your way out of the room, start planning a complicated escape (heating ducts, grease, a blonde wig) and then your life after that (living out in the pasture, learning to digest mesquite beans, drink water from stock tanks), but, for no reason you can name, Arnot King doesn't take the hand you offer him in farewell. Instead he just looks up at you, nodding to himself, finally shaking his head in something a lot like regret.

"This tow-truck driver," he says, his voice low, legal. "What reason would he have to lie to you about Rory living out there, you think?"

You look up to him slow. Feel a smile growing.

"I don't have any money," you say. "Judge Harkness made the fine kind of exactly match my bank account."

"Nothing to pawn?"

"They held me in temporary for two weeks that first time. Every time they'd call my name, they'd read my address out loud to be sure it was me."

Arnot King nods, seems to understand that to a tank full of accomplished breakers-and-enterers about to be released, your address had been an invitation. There'd been waves of them stripping your apartment down to the hinges and knobs that weren't even yours.

"Then you'll owe me," he says, shrugging off your gratitude. "My firm has need of investigative services from time
to time..."

"I'm not a real PI," you say.

He leans close, says, "And you think I'm a real lawyer?"
then flares his eyes wide, stands. Leaves holding the tow-receipt
from last night over his shoulder like a flag, like a pale yellow
handkerchief. Like your only chance.

7.

THAT NIGHT, BECAUSE IT'S CHEAPER, and empty, and just one cell over, Sheriff Felson puts you in the drunk tank. You ask the deputy—nobody you know, finally—for a wake-up call, maybe a chocolate mint on your pillow. He says he's got something chocolate for you, then angles the television over so you can watch the news with him through your window. You watch on the chance you're going to be on it.

By six in the morning, Toby Garrett's baby brother's there and you're in the break room, have Gwen's number punched in, the one you're not supposed to know.

Her son answers.

"...Dan," you say, having to close your eyes to pull that name out.

"*Dad*?" he whispers back, quieter, and like that you've become a ghost. Each second you don't say *no*, it's another second where Dan's world can make sense again. Where it can be a place his dad didn't get shot in the face with a shotgun, anyway.

Your first instinct is to apologize to him—but, for what? Sorry that *somebody* shot your old man, kid?

Gwen saves you. From bed it sounds like. "It's for me," she creaks.

Dan holds the phone for a breath more, hangs up slow.

"I'm sorry," you tell her, just because it was already in your mouth.

"He was—" she starts, can't finish.

"You crying?" you ask, wincing to hear it out loud, wanting to crawl into the phone line, reel your words back in.

She's crying *now*, anyway. Good job.

You don't know what to do and so you say it again—*sorry*—ease the plunger down with your index finger.

Five minutes later she calls back. It nearly shakes you out of your chair, makes you drop the phone from your head, the base from your lap. As far as Toby Garrett's baby brother in the window of the door knows, you've been talking to her the whole time. Listening anyway, the receiver pressed to the side of your head. Now she's in your ear again, saying to just let her explain, please.

"*Explain?*" You've had five minutes now to run through everything you should have said the first time, if she hadn't turned on the waterworks.

"You'd understand if... if you were me."

"Who would be me then, you think? Somebody good at taking the fall? I didn't do it, Gwen. You know that."

"Of course you didn't."

"But you told them I didn't talk to you that day. What that means to them is that I talked to Rory. Told him to meet me out at his old place. In the right light, it looks a lot like premeditation. Even in the wrong light."

On her end, for too long: silence. Her holding her phone down, saying a muffled bye over it to Dan. A screen door closing.

At least he's not on the phone.

"I just want to know why," you say. "What it would have *really* cost you to tell them."

She laughs a bit, at herself maybe. "If you were working for me, or whatever, then that means there were—that there were *marital* issues. And Dan, I can't let Dan find out anything like that. Not now. I don't know what it would do to him."

It makes you wish you had some pictures of her in bed with Fin, his blue body coiled around her.

You stand, whip around the break room table, keeping your head low so you won't pull the base crashing to the floor.

"Marital issues other than him not living there? Dan not pick up on that somehow?"

"I mean—"

"They think I *killed* him, Gwen," you say, barely controlling your voice.

It starts her crying again. She can't catch her breath, talks anyway. "...but, but they say, they think you were working for him too, Nick. See?"

You do see, or close enough. If you were working for her, then you were probably working for him too. And, because he's dead now, his jealousy gets automatically justified—Gwen *will* have been having an affair, will be that kind of widow, that kind of mom.

The moment she says yes to Sheriff Felson or Arnot King, three thousand people will hear it. Hear *under* it. Three thousand and one, counting her son.

But still.

"Good thing I came back when I did, yeah?"

"Nick—"

"Don't worry about it, Gwen."

Tick, tick, the coffee dripping, filling the room. Then, from her end, "What if I just come down there and—"

You hang up before she can finish, catch Toby Garrett's baby brother just starting to look away.

The first drunk of the day shows up an hour later. He smells like pesticide, has two days' worth of beard dusting his face, ten years of hair tangling from under his cap, and is wearing an old Greenwood Rangers letterman's jacket—the sleeves dark leathery blue, the vest-part nubbly and light.

He's ranting about how he'll do it, by God.

Inside of two minutes, he's flat on his back on one of the bunks, a forearm across his eyes, his slack jaw slipping so far back into his head that it looks dislocated.

"Hey," you say, to be sure he's asleep.

At least he doesn't have any ticks, fleas, or lice. Nothing within twenty feet of him could.

You stand at the cell door watching his thin chest rise and fall, rise and fall, and only become aware that the door behind you's open because it pulls more of the pesticide into your eyes.

It's Sheriff Felson.

In one hand she has her nightstick. In her other, the silver microcassette recorder.

You try not to smile.

"We were doing you a courtesy, you know," she says. "Just you and me, comfortable, talking."

"Lady Miranda be damned," you add.

What she's mad about is what she probably just got back from whoever the prosecuting attorney is around here: the microcassette.

If you did the buttons like you think you did, the only incriminating thing on there is your full name. And maybe not even that.

She stares at you until you shrug, say about the sleeping man, "He drink the stuff, or what?"

"Wha—?" she says, just seeing him it seems. When she does, her hand curls around the nightstick tighter, says without looking up, loud enough for any deputies behind her to hear, "What's wrong with this picture?"

Toby Garrett's baby brother is the first to get to the door, look over her, into the drunk tank.

"You're not one of mine," she tells him.

"Ma'am," he says back.

"What's wrong with this picture?" Felson says again.

"None of the sandals fit him," a real and breathless deputy chimes in, studying you—trying to *explain* the spectacle you must be here.

"The other picture," Sheriff Felson says back.

The deputy narrows his eyes at the sleeping drunk man then looks away in pain. Leads you back to your first cell, Toby Garrett's baby brother trailing behind like he belongs here.

You don't say anything, just try to listen.

It doesn't help.

What's wrong with this picture? Like it should have been obvious.

You sleep instead of eating, and then it's lunch and Arnot King is back.

This time, because the break room's off-limits—Felson's orders—everything Arnot King says he says with his hand over his mouth, his eyes flicking up to imaginary microphones, hidden cameras.

"Bad news and bad news," he says.

"Wouldn't want to break my streak."

He's wearing the same suit as yesterday. "That film you say you turned in," he says. "There's no record of it—are you sure you filled the envelope out right?"

You blow a laugh out through your nose. It's happened before, on restaurant waiting lists, radio call-ins, for door prizes: nobody believes *Bruiseman* could be a real name. So they crumple it up, throw it away.

"It was just her car in the shop, like I said."

"It might have a time index on it or something."

"Hey, yeah," you say, impressed.

"*You're* supposed to think of that, kimo. From here on out. I file motions, you see the cop-stuff. Got it?"

You nod.

"Bad news number two," he goes on, standing for the door.

Behind it is a man in thin, greasy coveralls, the brim of his cap curled into a paper towel tube, pretty much, his face squinted up like an interrogation room's the last place in the world he needs to be.

"Ronald Warrick," Arnot King says.

"Who?" you say, certain for a moment he's the sleeping man's twin brother.

"Exactly," Arnot King says, and unfolds the yellow tow-receipt onto the table.

"His name was—was Jim Martindale," you say, then, to Ronald Warrick: "You know him? Tall guy, beard, shades? Think he manages the body shop or something."

Ronald Warrick rabbits his eyes to Arnot King, shakes his head no. "I do eighty percent of the towing in Stanton, yeah? Other twenty's just, y'know, people pulling people."

"Ask Ruby, or Rubio, at the body shop—" you say to Arnot King.

"*Manuel's* place?" Ronald Warrick slips in, incredulous, and you look to him like he's not even talking English anymore. "Short little bugger of a guy?" he goes on. "Can fix anything that, y'know, has parts in it?"

Arnot King waves the back of his hand at Ronald Warrick, as if sweeping him out the door, dismissing him. It's almost Middle-Eastern—royal, like a prince might do.

"Where you from?" you say, after Ronald Warrick's gone.

Arnot King looks up to you, tries to make sense of your question.

"Monahans," he says. "Then Crane. Why?"

You study the two-way glass.

Monahans isn't even two hours away. And Crane. They were the Golden Eagles, or—Hornets? Wasps?

"Play basketball?" you ask him.

He chews the inside of his left cheek some.

You get it already: this is serious.

"I'm about out, here, Nicholas," he tells you.

You cover your mouth with your hand. "I didn't want to have to do this—" just as somebody on the back side of the two-way glass knocks three times.

Arnot King closes his eyes in pain, like he *knew* this was coming, knew they were listening, that they had lip-readers in there, and sketch artists, maybe a telepath or two, and maybe he's right: the light comes on behind the glass, and it's Sheriff Felson. Only, beside her, no make-up, her purse clutched tight to her chest, is Gwen.

"Can we?" Sheriff Felson says through the little speaker.

Arnot King stands deferentially for their entrance, offering his chair.

You sit there, watching Gwen.

For the second time that day Sheriff Felson palms the silver microcassette recorder, showing it to everyone in the room.

"Haven't we been through this?" you tell her. "It was an accident, I guess."

"You accusing him for faulty equipment now?" Arnot King says.

"What's she doing here?" you say about Gwen.

"I'm right here," she says.

"She's trying to save you," Sheriff Felson says. "Lord knows why."

You look at Gwen for a clue, but she's not playing any eye footsie today.

"What is it?" Arnot King says, about the recorder.

Sheriff Felson shakes her head in disbelief. "Looks like it wasn't all a lie."

She hits play on a muffled recording of the day Gwen hired you.

You can only stare at her about it. That she didn't trust you is the only thing on your side now. You don't know what to say.

"And—and this," she says all at once, unfolding an envelope from her purse. "Janet called me about it on her lunch."

It's the St. Nick check from the Wagon Wheel, Rory's signature down at the bottom, "for services rendered."

Sheriff Felson huffs through her nose—a true Stanton Buffalo—shakes her head.

"Services?" she says to you.

"Interested?" you cut back.

Arnot King steps between the two of you. "So?"

It's not as articulate as you think it should be for a lawyer, but it's enough.

"It doesn't mean he didn't do it," Sheriff Felson says, finally.

"Then who did?" Arnot King snaps back.

"Fin," you say, staring at Gwen about it. "Anthony Robert Payne."

She looks up to you, then to Sheriff Felson, then to the ground. "*Tony*?" she finally says.

"We know about the one-on-one, um, *tutoring*," you tell her. Then, for everybody else: "You heard how I said that, right? 'Tutoring?'"

Gwen looks to the side again. "Tony's a strong writer, yes. Was it forged checks? Something like that. But—you thought he and I, that we were—?"

She laughs a bit, brings a tissue to the inner corner of her right eye. "Nick, God. I didn't *help* you just so you could mess his life up too, just when he's putting it back together. That's not the way—Rory wouldn't want us to—"

She can't finish. Sheriff Felson guides her out.

"It was him," you tell Arnot King. "Ex-con, in the ballroom, a candlestick that goes bang."

"Reasonable doubt." Arnot King gives you that. Then he leans in, his mouth covered, but draws back at the last instant. Goes out front again.

He comes back an hour later with more bad news: Sheriff Felson can still hold you either until they talk to Fin, or for seventy-two more hours. You do the math: seventy-two hours away is Saturday night. It means you won't get out until Monday morning. Provided your paperwork doesn't get lost.

"I can't be gone from Aardvark that long," you say. "It's in my job description."

Arnot King rolls his tongue around his lower lip, says so quietly you can hardly hear him, "Unless you…you almost were going to tell me something earlier, am I right?" When you just stare at him, he palms the recorder, hits play on your voice, already cued up: "*I didn't want to have to do this…*"

You each have your fingers steepled over your noses. Any words you do or don't say will be remaining in church, pretty much.

"I must have—" you start, but he shakes his head no, as if he's feeling sorry for you here. To be losing your job and your bed both at the same time.

It might be funny if it were some other slob.

"They're sewn into the back of the couch at Aardvark," you say.

Arnot King pats your shoulder once, like he's your sponsor or something, closes the door on his way out, and—because he's trying to be quiet, because he's trying not to be grand with his exit—you just manage to catch the look on his face as he turns to the empty hall.

It's the way you watch the dogs come around that last turn when your dog's ahead by a length.

"No," you say out loud.

Because you're the dog, here. You have been all along.

You go to the door to bang on it, to insist on…what?

Instead of hitting the door with the side of your fists, you just press your forehead into it.

Before Arnot King can even be to Midland with those negatives from the couch—the fifth roll of film that Judge Harkness never knew about, that you shot for personal use—Sheriff Felson leads you to the property desk.

"Seventy-two hours?" you say to her like you've been rehearsing, the lower lids of your eyes pressing up, because you already know how she's going to answer: "Seventy-two *what*?"

You're the dog, all right.

They were processing you out all along.

The whole way to Property, you watch the door for him, know he's not going to be there to give you that victory ride across town. That he was just using you to get the one thing he would have to want worse than anything: a few clear shots of the only female judge in Midland meeting a man on the first floor corner room of an interstate motel with curtains that sighed up on the air conditioner's cold breath every few seconds, exactly like an invitation.

At the time you thought she was Jimmy Bones' friend's wife. Eight hundred dollars to you.

Instead, it cost you everything.

The property clerk—the same deputy from last night— slides your heavy brown envelope over, has you initial the log.

"So that's really your name..." he says in wonder, holding the log up to read it better.

You walk out, open your envelope in the street. Pretend not to notice that he forgot to keep your old detective shield, as evidence.

Pocket it. Keep walking.

8.

Sherilita gives you Frito pie and a plastic spoon to eat it with. When it breaks off—Frito pies are supposed to be made with chili, not yesterday's chopped beef—you reach over the counter for another. When it breaks too, you just tilt the small bag up, shake the pie into your mouth, get an eyeful of corn chip and barbecue sauce instead.

"Better than jail?" Sherilita says, wiping down a table that's already clean.

You hold the napkin to your eye like an ice-pack. "Miss me?"

"Thomas wanted to play last night," she says.

You stare at the empty bag in your hands, tilt your head next door to Aardvark Custom Economy Storage. "It was open, yeah?"

She shakes her head, her eyes wet with humor.

"Still think you're a private eye?" She stands, looks next door too. "No, Nick. Last night it was locked. Anything else?"

"You know Manuel, down at the body shop?"

Sherilita laughs to herself. "He a suspect now?"

"It's his shop there across the tracks?"

"You've been gone too long," she says. "He used to do tires down at White's?"

You just stare at her, can vaguely recall somebody rolling a tire slow along the red brick wall of the old part of White's. But that's all. And it's mostly just the tire. You thank Sherilita anyway, study the empty bag in your hands some more. Talk yourself out of going downtown, to Higginbotham's, to ask the clerk if that's where Arnot King bought the bolt cutter. The way you talk yourself out of it is that you don't have the Ford anymore, and Arnot King's already *been* to the drugstore for the film—right?—and, even if you know that's where he bought the cutters, it won't make the gate in front of Aardvark Economy Custom Storage any less open.

At least he popped the lock, you tell yourself, didn't go for the chain.

The office door should have been open for him, too—or, he's skinny enough to have reached through the payment slot, twisted the knob from the inside. And the couch, a child could break into a couch. Should be second-nature to a lawyer.

You close your eyes against it, don't want to see him there anymore. Don't want to think what you're already thinking—that, if he takes the roll of film straight to Judge Harkness, you have maybe ten hours to catch a ride out of town.

If he stops to get it developed, make some copies for safekeeping, you have a day, maybe two.

But maybe he'll just save it, for some motion he needs allowed, some search and seizure he really needs made illegal.

That'd be worse, though. Then, Judge Harkness could be sending her bailiffs or troopers or hip-pocket cons over any day. To deal with that kind of pressure, that kind of uncertainty, you'd have to steal a beer truck, hide it behind Aardvark Custom Economy Storage. Camouflage it as an RV or something. Paint a pair of old people on the windshield.

"What?" Sherilita says, wiping down another table.

"Nothing," you tell her, holding the empty Frito bag up. "Thanks."

"Family recipe," she says with half a smile, not a muscle more.

What you remember best about her from school is that once, when she was up to be the FFA's sweetheart, the way she kept acting like she didn't want it, like it was stupid, it made you follow her down the hall after she didn't get it. Not to say anything—you were fourteen—just to watch her at the double front doors. The way she looked back once, then stepped out.

"Dane Wilson," you say. When she looks up, you add, "His little brother. The one who died."

She stops wiping the table, watches you across all four tables of the water station. "What about him?"

"Wasn't he supposed to be in our grade?"

She nods, raises a shoulder like *so?*

The reason he wasn't was that his dad, Henry "Shoo Fly" Lawler, took him on the rodeo circuit with him when he was six, so he had to wait a year longer than everybody else for first grade. But then Shoo Fly died in front of eight thousand people in Denver.

Three years later, his son would be dead too, in a stock tank.

"Did you ever know him?" you say.

"Why?"

You shake your head no, no reason. Jerk your eyes away from sunlight flashing in off the side mirror of a truck pulling up next door, its no-nonsense grill guard right up against your chain link.

Sherilita leans over to the blinds, says it like the two of you have been living together for years: "It's for you."

"Miss Johnny Law?" you say, standing.

Sherilita pretends not to have heard you.

You crumple your bag into the trash, can already hear it crinkling back open before you're even out the door.

The truck next door is a three-quarter ton Ford, a new one. Goosenecked to it is a horse trailer, a thirty-foot job. For wiener-dog horses, you think. The limos of the range. Seat six cowboys at once.

Without meaning to, you say it: "Giddyup."

The woman coming back from the gate looks from the broken lock in her hand to you.

"Excuse me?" she says.

"Help you?" you say back, and on accident notice that her cheeks are freckled, beautiful in that schoolgirl way. The kind of woman who lives miles outside of town, watches the sun set every night, never has to wear make-up.

Or maybe you're just out of jail.

"Trying to find somebody here," she says.

"Hey," you say, holding your hands out to the side, presenting yourself.

She looks from you to the storage units, as if reconsidering. "How much?"

"Twenty-two a month on a one-year lease," you reel off, "five less if"—you smile, nod to yourself, should have seen this weeks ago—"if you pay cash up front."

"That include unloading it?"

You look to her gooseneck, wince a bit.

"Our insurance—" you start, unsure how you're going to end this lie, if it even is a lie, but then see she's studying the lock in her hand again, the cut metal of its thick hasp still raw.

"So, my mom's stuff," she says after you trail off, "it'll be safe here, right?"

You grin as if just tolerating this, keep your hands balled in your pockets, your weight on your heels, and can suddenly feel Sherilita at the water station window, her fingers parting the blinds.

She's waiting for you to do the right thing. Or to do one more wrong thing.

Her and everybody else.

You narrow your eyes to the horse trailer again, ask if she can leave it overnight.

"You'll unload it?" she says.

"Special bonus for cash customers," you say, your lower lip between your teeth.

"Five off a month, or total?"

"A month," you tell her after a thoughtful pause, like this is a special deal you're making just for her.

She stares at the Aardvark sign, tracks up to the Motel sign dwarfing it, and lifts her chin downtown. "I'll have to go to the bank."

You nod—anything's okay with you—and she guides the trailer through the gate on the first try, backs to the empty unit on the B-side using just her mirrors, unhitches it, cranks the legs down, the loose metal feet crunching into the caliche like the landing gear of an alien craft.

"Take your time," you tell her, and standing on the running board to climb back into the cab, she looks back at you like you're bleeding. Like you're speaking a foreign language.

You lift your hand in farewell, say it inside: twelve months times five dollars. Because the real discount for paying ahead's ten. Sixty'll almost make up for the seventy-five you dropped at the bar in Big Springs. You smile, turn around, close your eyes to catch up with yourself: Stace's parents don't even have to know that empty unit in B is rented, do they? Not if this is a cash kind of affair.

These are the same people who gave you a job, a room. Picked you over an ex-con—*fresh*-con, you used to call them.

But maybe you can make it up to Aardvark in some way. Provide *excellent* security. Stop liberating stuff from the units. Walk the straight and narrow, like you've really been meaning to get around to one of these days.

Instead of starting on the horse trailer—it's a night job anyway, a twelve-pack, midnight kind of effort—you push through the office door, roll the couch back over.

Under it is Arnot King, longways, facedown, his hands underneath him.

For too long you stand there, watching his back rise and fall.

No, you say inside, *no*, and back out, go to the fence, hang your hands high on it exactly like a prisoner in a movie. Because she knows her part, has probably been waiting in the wings for forty minutes, Sheriff Felson eases past, her passenger side window already down. If asked, of course she's just making rounds, rolling the streets up before lights out. Each of you knows better, though. She tips her hat to you, then makes her index finger into the barrel of a gun.

You try to look past her, so that her invisible bullets can bounce off you, but they pass through instead, each one a direct hit.

"Can't be happening," you say finally, and go back, look through the payment slot.

Arnot King is still there.

"How——?" You spin to the parking lot before the thought's complete.

His car, whatever he drives, it's not there. You push out through the gate, don't even know if you want a Stingray or a BMW or whatever—something slick to match his suit, something on lease because it's all for show. It doesn't matter: all the cars at the boarded-up Dairy Queen and the Sonic are Stanton cars, regulars. Town & Country, too. Franklin's, Graves, the new bank. And the carwash, it's empty, and at the water station there's just Sherilita's Sunfire, Felson's cruiser in the drive-through. There's Wheeler's, you suppose; your lawyer's car could be anything on the lot there.

More important, why wouldn't Arnot King just park in front?

Two minutes later, all the change in your pocket thumbed into the payphone, Melinda's saying your name into her dispatch headset again. Kind of mournfully, you have to admit.

"Emergency," you tell her.

"Wrong number," she says back.

"Last time," you promise.

Thirty seconds later, Arnot King's make, model and year: a bright yellow Mustang from last year. Ford. Meaning it's not with the new Chevrolets up front down at Wheeler's, anyway.

You re-cradle the phone before thinking to thank her, are studying Stanton with different eyes now, trying to filter out everything but Mustangs.

It's nowhere.

You turn back to Aardvark Custom Economy Storage, and it dawns on you slow: as far as Arnot King is concerned, you were never here.

You nod, smile, and back through the front door of the water station again.

Sherilita stops sweeping, watches you, then what you're watching: the storage unit. Through her window.

"Big stake-out?" she says.

"Commandeering this chair," you tell her, finding it with your hands.

"Just like that," she says, her fingers interlaced over the top of her broom.

"Just like that," you say back, and nod out the window, ask if she saw a man from Monahans go in there about forty-five minutes ago?

"Monahans?" she says, leaning close to the blinds now.

The two of you take the window in shifts, the other working the counter and the drive-through.

You're halfway through a second *sliced* beef sandwich—the expensive, fresh stuff—when Sherilita says, not looking away from Aardvark Custom Economy Storage for an instant, "Betsy Simms is from Monahans?"

You fall across the counter, across the tables.

Betsy Simms is the horse woman, with the freckles.

It's been three hours.

"No." You fall out the front door, the apron you've already forgot about trailing behind your hip on the right side, your thumbnail lined with barbecue sauce again.

You catch Betsy Simms just as she's about to knock on the screen door of the office.

She turns to you, lowers her sunglasses to her sharp cheekbones.

"Two ten," she says, holding out a cash envelope from the bank. "No tax, right?"

You shake your head no, or, yes: no tax. Are too out of breath for more.

"You okay?" she says, not stepping any closer than she already is.

You fake a smile, manage to resist looking through the mail slot.

Horse-woman Betsy Simms nods with you, the larger part of her expression still held in reserve, and says the last thing you want to hear: "Receipt?"

You parrot it back to her like it's a word you're not so familiar with.

She shakes her head in disbelief, hooks one side of her mouth up, her hands to her hips. "What's to stop you from just pocketing it?"

You hold her eyes for a moment, gauging, agreeing with her more or less, then slide one of her crisp twenties up from the cash envelope. On the border of the twenty, you write *190 rec'd / 12mos storage*, then sign your name over whichever president that is.

It's the *190* she's supposed to notice.

She looks up from it to you, from you to her horse trailer, then to the office door.

"This is a strange place," she says.

You don't disagree with this, and just when you think she's gone, she comes back from her idling truck with a shiny new padlock.

You tell her Aardvark Custom Economy Storage uses its own, to insure the safety of her property in case of flood, fire, or other natural disaster.

She closes her hand around the lock, narrows her eyes at you. "This is all on the contract?" she says.

You smile. "I'm here all the time, next door"—holding your apron out to show—"can let you in whenever."

Then she's gone.

You untie the apron, drape it over the seat of the riding lawnmower. Think maybe you are a PI, just like you're already a water station attendant, a security guard. A jailbird, a patsy.

You touch your chin, add one more: knot-holer. If mail slots count as knot holes.

Through it the couch is still like you put it, but Arnot King's not.

Instead of lying unconscious on the floor, he's sitting on the couch, his head in his hands.

This is what you wanted, right? For him to wake on his own, make his way outside, then either lower his Mustang key down to a door that isn't there, or not even stop outside the fence, but walk back to wherever he parked.

It was supposed to mean something, what he did, where he walked.

Three hours ago it made perfect sense, had something to do with whether you could trust him—or, yeah: it wasn't about him at all. You were going to walk up just as he emerged, say thanks for the ride, bub. That way he'd know it wasn't you who rolled a couch on top of him.

You're not so sure you care what he thinks anymore, though.

You nod to yourself for courage, close your eyes for exactly three seconds, then step into the office all at once.

Arnot King doesn't even look up. "Wondering if you were ever going to say anything to me."

You drag a folding chair over, spin it around, sit down facing him.

"You know who did this?"

He stretches his chin away from his neck like his head's pounding.

"What was that guy's name you said was the real killer here?" he asks.

"Payne," you say. "Goes by Fin."

"Big Nazi linebacker with Polynesian body art?"

"Not so sure about the Polynesian, but, yeah. Just out of Big Springs."

"The crazy house?"

"Ex-con."

"Same difference," Arnot King says, liking this even more. He tries to stand, has to start over, guide himself from the arm of the couch. About halfway up, he purses his lips in defeat. "He got the pictures."

"Film," you correct.

"Get out of jail free," he corrects back.

You give him that. "Not like you were stealing them or anything anyway, right?"

Arnot King glitters his eyes some. "Payment for services rendered. In this business I've learned to be flexible in regards to compensation. After I learned I wasn't working to get a certain VHS tape back, anyway."

"When scam artists collide," you narrate.

"Speak for yourself."

"He can't even know what they are, though."

"Except that you wanted to hide them, and I wanted to—well."

"Steal them."

"Use them as they were intended to be used," he says, his words clipped again. Meaning he's awake.

"He thinks they're of him and her," you say.

"You mean your old girlfriend, right?"

"He took your car?"

Arnot King touches the right pocket of his slacks, then the left, then lowers his head again.

"I've got to call it in," he says. "And—assault. Breaking and entering."

"Not to mention murder," you say.

Arnot King grimaces and you lead him to the payphone, ball the apron up and walk it back to the water station, hand it up through the drive-through window.

"That him?" Sherilita says about Arnot King. "Monahans guy?"

You nod.

"Don't remember him," she says. "He play anything?"

"Probably on the debate team."

"And he is…?"

"My lawyer," you tell her, hooking your eyes away like you've just admitted to gonorrhea.

Ten minutes later, Toby Garrett's baby brother rolls up, stands from his car into his flat-brimmed straw hat.

"Mr. Bruiseman," he says, nodding down to you. "Mr. King."

"So?" you say. "Does Felson believe me now? She going after him?"

Toby Garrett's baby brother rubs his forehead as if, like the story of his brother, this is too complicated to get out all at once. "I think she does believe you, yeah," he says, smiling. "But we're not going after him."

"Not going after him?" Arnot King interrupts, either truly incredulous or faking it for the jury. "Even without the homicide charge, this is a clear violation of his parole."

Toby Garrett's baby brother chews his cheek, lifts his chin to Sherilita. Says what's making him smile: "No, we're not chasing Fin, Mr. King. Mr. Bruiseman. We're not chasing him because, ten minutes ago, he walked into the station, surrendered himself."

In the silence that follows, you swear you can hear Sherilita's fingers parting the blinds in the water station, a fine rain of dust sifting down the back side of the window.

"They always come home," Arnot King says in appreciation.

"He—he *saying* anything?" you ask.

"That's just it, Mr. Bruiseman," Toby Garrett's baby brother says. "Only person he'll talk to is you."

Arnot King whistles, lowers his face to his sunglasses—isn't he supposed to be on your side?—and this time Toby Garrett's baby brother lets you sit up front.

9.

IN THE HALL OUTSIDE the interrogation room, you cover your mouth with your hand and tell Arnot King that this is a trick. That they just wanted to get you back down here.

Arnot King comes back to you from whatever stage of grief he's in (bargaining), says, like you're bothering him, "What?"

In the animated version of this running in your head, his pupils are shaped like the horse emblem of his missing Mustang. Like Felson says though, it's got to be close, just because Fin walked in. You're pretty sure she's already sent an officer to the body shop to pick through the tall careless weeds for dead horses, as it were. Or is. After that, it'll just be a matter of finding his tattoo album, his client list, checking all those people's garages and carports and places of employment. An afternoon's work, maybe. He'll be back in Midland by happy hour, on the blue bus to Big Springs inside a week.

You say it again, that this is probably all just a trick to get you here.

Arnot King shrugs yeah, maybe. You're still holding onto the brushed aluminum doorknob of the interrogation room. It feels like the pressure valve for this whole case. For your whole life.

"Sure you don't want me in there?" Arnot King says.

"I don't want me in there," you say back, and he hooks his head behind him to the high, narrow door of the viewing room.

"No worries," he says. "I'll be with her."

"Listening?"

"And you say I'm paranoid," he says, leaning close, his hand on your shoulder, his mouth to your ear. "I'll drop a stapler if she tries to hear you, okay?"

"It's soundproof."

"I'll drop a bowling ball, then. Throw myself against the glass. Push all the buttons. Turn the lights on."

Chained to the table in the interrogation room is Anthony Robert Payne. Fin. The guy whose name Felson probably wouldn't even know if you hadn't said it. The gentleman your lawyer just gave a series of statements against, statements so precise they probably include sentencing recommendations and cell mates.

If just one of them sticks, he's going back inside for a long visit, a permanent vacation. Which is where this all stops making anything like sense: why turn himself in? More important, why does he want to talk to you about it?

It has to have something to do with the film. With Gwen. Neither of which you want to talk about, really. Not at a police station.

For different reasons, Felson agrees, doesn't want you talking either. Her argument is that if Gwen keeps saying all she ever did was tutor Fin, then you'll be a potential witness for the prosecution. Meaning you shouldn't be near the suspect now, even if he spontaneously confesses to you. Or especially if he confesses. It sounded good to you, perfect. You even smiled on accident—the law was keeping you out, keeping you safe—but then your lawyer shook his head no, asked just which imaginary jury was Felson talking about here? One that's going to buy the "expert" testimony of a derelict ex-detective who smells like stale beer, lives in a storage shed, and's a suspect for the same crime himself?

He's worth every penny you're not paying him.

You step into the white room, cut a thin smile to Anthony Robert Payne.

He smiles back, lifts his wrists to show he's handcuffed to his own waist, shackled to the table legs.

"Fire hazard, wouldn't you say?" he says.

"They don't allow smoking in here." You pull your chair out, settle into it, take him in in pieces: bald head, solid chin, thick chest. Tattoos all over him that could be Polynesian, you guess, if you even knew what Polynesian was. To the prison guard in Big Springs, he's that big-ass tattoo guy in D-block. To your lawyer, he's a Nazi linebacker, a shaved Bigfoot. They're both right: even slouched down in his chair, he towers, probably goes six and a half feet in county-issue flip-flops.

The one thing you know just from being in the room with him now is that he didn't need a shotgun for Rory Gates.

"They're here too?" he says, tipping his head to the two-way glass, the ceiling, all the microphones and videotape he suspects.

You shake your head no.

He sits back. "All the same to me, detective. I don't got nothing to hide."

The way he hits hide, you know he's talking about the film.

You don't take the bait. "That why you turned yourself in? Couldn't handle the guilt?"

"I turned myself in because I tried it the other way once. Cost me eight years." He tips his head to the viewing room. "Cost them some, too, as I recall."

"You're from Stanton?"

"Cops in general, detective."

You watch his eyes, lean back as far as you can, stretch your legs so that your body's a plank. It makes room in your pocket for your hand, for a flash. Just long enough to hit the pause button on the microcassette recorder Felson insisted you take in with you.

Fin hears it, isn't stupid enough to look down.

"We probably have ninety seconds here," you say. "Maybe two minutes, if my lawyer can fake a seizure better than I give him credit for."

He smiles with one side of his face. "I could like you, you know?"

"Get in line." You lean forward, on a schedule now. "At the storage units. You were looking for me there, I take it?"

He nods.

"Needed some storage?"

He hisses a laugh through his teeth. "That your real name?" he says. "Aardvark?"

"Sure. Why not?"

"Bruiseman…" he says, breathing it in, tasting it. "Bruised man…"

"Clever," you tell him. "All my time in Midland, nobody ever came up with that one. Elementary, even. But then"—you can't help smiling—"I grew up with idiots, pretty much, I guess."

"And now you're back where you belong?" Fin says.

"This is how you want to use our time?"

He stares back, not blinking once, then shakes his head no. "You're right. I wasn't there for a storage space, detective."

"I'm not a detective."

"I know," he says. "More like a—like a rat. Or a bird. That's it. Jailbird. No, I mean songbird." This is all very funny to him. He shakes his head no again. "Pig, that's it. Yeah. Pigs squeal, right? When they're stuck? Like in jail?"

"I know you're saying something here," you tell him.

"Let me say it so even you can get it," he says then. "They came to my trailer, man. When they had to let you go. Guess I was next on the list or something, yeah?" He leans forward, his palms open on the table, the chain strained between them. "Coincidence, right?"

"Stanton PD," you say. "They always get their man."

He laughs a disgusted laugh. Can't look at you all of the sudden. "You're the only one who could have turned them onto me."

"Sure about that?"

He comes back to you for that too fast. "I'd say that means you owe me now."

You tell him you'll give him five dollars off on a storage unit if he pays a year in advance.

In return, he asks you how you've managed to stay alive so long.

"Fiberglass boats," you say, and look at the mirror in the wall, see the two of you sitting across from each other.

"More like cameras."

You stare at a spot on the table. "So where is it?"

"More like what is it?" Then, with a smile on the left side of his face, "Or, what's it worth? That's what these things always come down to, right?"

You take out all the cash in your wallet: one hundred and forty three dollars, some change.

Fin shakes his head no.

You pull out Betsy Simms' one-ninety, still in the white envelope.

Still, no.

"What then?" you say, and the "Thirty seconds..." from the speaker nearly drowns you out.

Fin stares at the money, tracks over to the corner of the table, the floor maybe. "I ran when they pulled up," he says. "Came the long way around, out by the gin. To your—the big Aardvark in the sky."

"And my attorney was present."

"That who he was?" Fin says, shaking his wide head in disbelief, looking at his right hand like he should have already washed it.

You nod, agree with that.

"...and your shark was there," Fin goes on, incorporating Arnot King. "And—you saw the rest."

"Not while you were there, I didn't."

He pulls his top lip into his mouth some, stretching the skin tight under his nose. "I knew you were the only person in town who could help me."

You look to the mirror in disbelief, then back to the tabletop. "You wanted to hire me?"

Fin doesn't deny this.

"Why?" you say.

"Because the cavalry was coming, man. Think I want to do another tour through hell?"

You wonder what exactly counts as a tour through hell. And whether this qualifies. And why hasn't Felson stormed in yet?

"But I'm the—I'm almost a witness against you," you tell him, leaning close to show him how earnest you're being. "You're the person Rory hired me to find. The one Gwen hired me to find too. The famous backdoor man from—"

You stop, the heads of the microcassette squealing a little like they're winding back up, the pause button about to pop.

Fin hears it too. Narrows his eyes for better words.

"A week ago," he says. "One week ago I could have hired you for the same thing."

You shake your head no, say, rubbing your leg to try to mask your voice on tape, "It's a betrayal, sure, but technically it's not cheating if she's doing it with her husband, I don't think. Church might even approve."

"The mistake you're making, I think, is that you—"

What stops him is your fingers on the tabletop, trying to make something like thunder on the recording. Fin smiles about it, covers his mouth. "The oversimplification you're guilty of, sir, is assuming that the person they'd both come to see you about was me."

It takes you a few seconds, but finally you nod, say through a series of painfully staged coughs, "She was cheating on the postman with the newspaper boy?"

It isn't as funny to Fin as it is to you. He nods anyway.

"Busy girl," you say.

"She knows what she likes," Fin says back. "And how."

"And what's that?"

Fin smiles, leans back. Shakes his head as if it's obvious. "Dead presidents, man. Real history buff, that one."

Money.

"Thought she taught English?" you say, flashing your eyes to the two-way mirror again, setting your fingertips to the table, like to push off, leave.

But then Fin bites his upper lip in ever so lightly. On a woman, it would mean possibility—how they say maybe without words—but on him it's more like he's reminding himself where he is. That he can't be handling things in the usual way. In his natural way.

"So…we have anything here?" he says.

You stand, lean over. "Conflict of interests, I'm afraid."

"Because you think I was framing you somehow, right?"

Yes.

"I know how you feel, detective. Exactly, you could say."

You close your eyes, don't sit down.

"Not too busy this week, are you?" he says, through a grin it sounds like.

"I—" you start, but he's right. One of your clients is dead, the other in mourning.

"I'm not what you'd call licensed," you tell him, talking for the microphone. "Or—or interested, really."

Fin waits for you to look up to him again, says, his voice clear, loud, for the tape too, "Can't help you much with the first part, I guess, but the second part, well," and then he says the rest just with a smile at the outside corners of his eyes: the film.

"Where is it?" you say, no lips again, barely any sound.

"First things first." He nods down to his forearm, the intricate Polynesian scrollwork there. "You should have seen it when it was new, detective. Best work I've ever done, I think."

He's not talking about the tattoo, you know.

That doesn't mean you get it, either.

10.

It's dark by the time Toby Garrett's baby brother delivers you back to Aardvark Custom Economy Storage. You stare through the window at the black shape of the low-slung building

"Were you there?" you ask after a few moments of not getting out of the car.

He turns his head to you slightly. "When he turned himself in, you mean?"

"Out at Rory's mom's old place."

He nods yes, like he's not proud. Like he'd rather forget.

"Did it—?" you start, can't find a way to say it, try again: "Was the shotgun still there?"

"It's an ongoing investigation," he says.

"It wasn't," you tell him.

Toby Garrett's baby brother considers this.

"All there was was Rory. Dead. I mean, it's not like it's out in the open or anything, but still. You kill somebody, don't you try to bury them or something, at least?"

Toby Garrett's baby brother shrugs again. "I never really killed anybody, I don't guess."

"We were *supposed* to find him," you say. "I was, anyway."

Toby Garrett's baby brother's looking at you now. "What are

you thinking?"

You smile to yourself, scratch your ear on your shoulder or your shoulder on your ear, you can't tell so much once you've started.

"Nothing," you lie, then tap the dashboard twice, a rimshot, and open the door, step out into the night with a name you don't want on your lips: Jim Martindale. He was the one who told you Rory was out there.

You shake your head no, though. Felson was right: this isn't your case anymore. That you're not licensed to be on any case, really. That the wheels of justice are turning now, and, for once, not against you but a real live ex-con. The one person in Stanton, Texas with both motive and opportunity to kill Rory Gates.

You say it again, to yourself, that you were *supposed* to find him dead in that bedroom, then stand in front of Aardvark Custom Economy Storage for too long, staring down 137 to the body shop. The AirStream on blocks down there, your roll of film probably stashed inside, in a cabinet, a block of ice, something.

One way to close a case is to solve it, you know.

The other way is to just step back and let things happen.

What you tell yourself on the way to the body shop is that unless an angel swoops down and stops you, this is what you're doing: jumping Manuel's tall fence, getting the film, then drinking for a few days. Nobody expects anything else. After the stunt with the pause button, too—this is what Felson calls it—she's not going to think twice about putting you in a cell with Fin. It'd be two birds, for her: You'd get beat to within a half inch of the end of your life for not springing Fin, and Fin would get another charge against him—one he couldn't shake.

And anyway, Rory's been asking for it since the second grade, pretty much. It's always been just a matter of time for him. A killer like Fin was bound to show up sooner or later, do what nobody else had the nerve to.

And Gwen, she was just using you.

You nod to yourself, that yes—*hell* yes, even—this is the only thing you could be doing, the thing that makes the most sense, but then, not even halfway to Caprock, a set of headlights flings your shadow out ahead of you. When the truck—you can hear the lifters clattering—doesn't pass on by, you turn, have to shield your eyes because the fog lights are on too. And the running lights on top of the cab.

It's a truck you know, remember: Rory's.

For an impossible moment you feel your weight shifting, so you can run, because he's about to step out of the light. Ask for his seventy-five dollars back.

You're half right: it's Dan, Dan Gates. The new Rory.

You shield your eyes, see that his pants are tucked into his boots. The way you do when you're all Billy Badass, looking for a fight. When you've got enough in you that nothing can hurt you.

It makes your scalp crawl.

"Dan," you say.

"You called my mother," he says back, a prepared line.

"We're—" you start, but don't know how to finish: old friends? new enemies?

Dan shakes his head no.

"Don't," he says. "I'm asking here."

You say it halfway on accident, before you can check yourself: "Sorry about your dad, man."

Dan laughs a bit then shakes his head no, turns away like this is over but runs at you instead, his shoulder down for the tackle-dummy sled, the moment slowed down to a series of instants, like there's a strobe light around both of you.

He's the only one moving slow, though. And—and he weighs eighty pounds less than you, at least, and can't have lost enough fights yet to know how to really win one, and besides, he hasn't ever had to wrestle drunk men down on their own lawns, with their black and blue wives watching. But then, too, it's not muscle or experience that counts at two in the morning. It's how bad you need to do what you're doing.

You slow down to his speed, let his shoulder catch you, and then let him hit you until he's crying—just patting you with his fists, more or less—then lie there while he backs his father's truck away, the stars wheeling above you on some axis you can't even begin to imagine.

For one 1978 quarter, the cold rinse at the car wash cleans you up. You spray the leftover pressure in a silver mist out towards 137, then hook the dripping wand back into its rack, duck behind the car wash when a patrol car eases by, feeling the stall out with a dummy light. You close your eyes against it like that'll hide you, and, your hands balled at your sides, have to accept the real reason you let Dan Gates go at you: it wasn't because you're a good person or anything special, but because that righteous way he was feeling, you've always wanted that.

Walking back from lock-up the first time—yesterday?—you've already stopped at the corner of your father's street once. His living room window was blue with television. What you did was hold your mouth in the shape of a word like *hello*, just one that somehow says everything else too.

You remember thinking, on accident, that maybe he'd even

kept your old bicycle in the garage. You saw again Rory Gates, your childhood enemy, shadow-boxing with his grown son on the caliche in front of Aardvark Custom Economy Storage. The way they ducked and weaved. How you had to look away.

Maybe *that's* all Dan wanted, really: the shadow-boxing, the reaching across with your fist, not to hurt.

You touch your ear where he tagged it, cock your head over in appreciation, and are glad this happened here, anyway, instead of at the funeral tomorrow. Not that anybody there would be likely to pull him off you. They'd probably start digging a second hole, even.

Stanton, Texas in the middle of July. The clown parade. You step out into it again, point yourself south down 137 and almost make it to the Caprock parking lot before the headlights come back.

You don't turn around this time, just stand there.

The truck, not diesel, eases up alongside.

It's Thomas.

"Your mom know you're out?" you say to him.

"Gonna rat me out?" he says back. "Where you going?"

You point with your chin.

"Liquor store's closed," he says. Then, looking closer, "What happened to you, man?"

You climb in.

He pulls away, going nowhere. On the floorboard on your side is a ratty phonebook, *Martindale, James* probably in there somewhere.

You look away from it, out the side window. Ease past Dairy Treat on 80, then the elementary. "So you just wasting gas out here, or what?"

Thomas trails a line of spit down to his cup. "Staying awake, yeah? My dad's coming by at five-thirty for a farm sale."

You nod, understand. He doesn't want to risk making his dad knock. Letting him down like that. It makes you wonder how long he's already been awake, trying to be perfect.

"I know him?" you say. "Your old man?"

Thomas spits again too soon, shakes his head no, and you ride with him around Stanton, play a game of slow tag with whoever's in the patrol car then finally point to Aardvark Economy Custom Storage your third time past it. He noses up to the fence and the garage doors hold the white of his headlights for seconds after he's killed them.

"That's Mark's uncle's trailer," he says, about the gooseneck still angled over to the B-side.

"Betsy Simms' mom's stuff," you tell him.

He steps out as if Aardvark Custom Economy Storage has suddenly become sacred. "Mrs. Rankin, right? Taught pre-Algebra…"

You follow him to the trailer. "Her? She's dead?"

He rests his hand on the complicated latch of the trailer gate.

"I remember her, yeah," you say, and he nods, keeps nodding, and you don't even have to ask to get him to help you unload it into what, a few nights ago, was his studio. He takes his shirt off; on the back of his shoulder, the wing bone, his football number is tattooed on.

"Fin?" you say.

He nods, balances a lamp down.

When you take your shirt off, it just smells like pesticide, from the sleeping man in the drunk tank.

"Thanks," Thomas says, seeing the shirt balled up on the spare tire of the trailer.

You keep moving, send him into the office for two beers at

three-fifteen, then two more at a quarter till four, and don't miss him until your watch beeps once, on the hour.

You say his name, but in the valley of the two buildings your voice is too large, so you carry one more of Mrs. Rankin's wooden chairs into 4-B, look through the payment slot of the office. Thomas is asleep on the couch, his face to the backrest, knees curled up. Lying on the only blanket on the property.

You close the screen door quietly then sit against the cinderblock wall across from the horse trailer, dangle your beer between your knees, promise to stay awake until five-twenty-five. It should give him just enough time to get home.

11.

You wake all at once, exactly one hour before Rory's two o'clock funeral. In the dream you're pretty sure you were having, you didn't work and live at Aardvark Custom Economy Storage, but *Aarmadillo* Custom Economy Storage. It's what Stace's parents should have named the place. Like the old Lonestar commercials—a giant armadillo coiled around a longneck. People would come from miles around.

You nod to yourself, keep nodding, and follow the bright white wall out to the payphone, find Stace's parents' number traced over and over into the back cover of the phonebook. Five digits in, though, you slow, stop. Hang up.

It doesn't matter. Aardvark, Aarmadillo. Aaunt Lily's Storage Stop. It doesn't matter, and they don't need you telling them about it.

You turn away just as the phone rings. Like always, you look around for who else the call could be for.

"Me," you say, and let it ring fourteen times before picking up.

"Nicky, Nicky, Nicky…" Jimmy Bones says in the way of hello. "This is your wake-up call. Rise and shine. Smell the good life, my man."

You hold the phone to the side of your head, watch a hot oil truck pull into the Sonic, wonder if the driver's going to walk up to one of the slots to push the button.

"I don't have it," you say to Jimmy Bones. "Them, whatever."

He laughs about this, then laughs some more, quieter. "Maybe I need to come out there, yeah? Get some storage, y'know. I have all kinds of...*items* I should probably be keeping in another county anyway..."

"Jimmy," you say. "Please."

"*Nicky*," he says back, his upper lip probably curled into a sneer.

Aarmadillo, you think, and say you have to go, a customer, your boss, the weather, a funeral, then hang up, pick the receiver up before it can ring again, balance it on top of the box.

From the water station window, Sherilita waves once to you. You nod to her, pretend to study the phonebook then really do.

There's no *Jim Martindale*, no *Martindale* at all.

But you're not on the case anymore either, so it doesn't matter.

For twenty minutes, you do some real and actual work: dig up a new lock for the one your lawyer cut; close the inner and outer gates of Betsy Simm's horse trailer, and fill out a standard 12-month contract for her; walk up and down the A and B units, slinging beer bottles up onto the roof, cupping cigarette butts in your hand, making sure all the locks are in place. They are. The silver ones are the ones the renters brought; the ones spray-painted green are the ones you've rented out over the last eight weeks, when the policy suddenly changed. If it hadn't, you wouldn't have a television in the office now, or the bench seat in your living room.

What you tell yourself about the television is that it needs to be kept limber, needs to be started every day. But, it's not like you're really stealing the stuff, right? More like borrowing. Because the rightful owners can have it back whenever they want—the knob on the office unlocks without a key if you just lift up and to the left, jerk it a bit, and the storage unit that's your living room, it doesn't even have a lock. In fact…you stop by it, studying it, don't even know why you closed it. To make sure the smell from the bench seat will soak into the walls too? That sounds about right. You shake your head in disgust, lift the cap off the up-and-down steel pipe the lawnmower's chained to and drain the cigarette butts down the concrete-splattered hole. In its other life, the ten-inch pipe was probably oilfield. As for length, it could be six feet long or sixty. Maybe Aardvark Custom Economy Storage was built around it. Maybe all of Stanton, even. The best hitching post around. It doesn't shake when you hit it with the heel of your hand, anyway. And even though it's tilted instead of standing straight up you're pretty sure that's not so much because a renter backed into it with a moving truck but because the ground half a mile down has shifted.

You picture covered wagons and Comanche Indians standing around the pipe, waiting for a pebble to hit bottom, and waiting, and waiting. You only know because you've tried. Looking back on the last week, too, you know you should have used the film canister instead of a rock. You'd be free and clear of Harkness, of Fin, of Felson. Until the mole people came up to blackmail you.

You settle the cap back on the pipe, try to blow the ash off your hands, then sling the garage door of your living room up with your head already turned against the smell, and that's the only reason you see Sheriff Felson standing at the chain link gate. Down the cinderblock wall, she's right in line with you. Has been watching.

"Mr. Bruiseman," she says, stepping forward. "Up early, I see. For you, anyway."

You nod, your eyes still narrowed from the smell, and look inside for a flash. Not so much to see the bench seat, wooden spool, and calendar, but to collect your thoughts.

It doesn't happen.

Parked smackdab in the middle of your living room is Arnot King's yellow Mustang.

You back away, breathe in sharp, then do your best to cover: narrow your eyes at the number by the door, pretend to laugh at yourself—not *this* one—and pull the door back down fast, run the post home and twist it as best you can, trying to get the holes lined up for the padlock.

Felson gets to you just as the Mustang disappears, and, instead of cueing on that bright yellow bumper housing, keys on the blue flare of your ear. Your cracked lip. "Missed a place," she says, touching her own eye, to mean yours.

You step to the next unit, a silver lock, and start cycling through all your green keys, your fingers shaking too much to settle on any one yet.

"Come by for a storage unit, Sheriff?" you manage.

She's not looking at you like you want, but at the latch for your living room. She touches the post with the toe of her boot. "Not if this is all you use to close them up, I'm not."

"It's empty," you tell her.

She pulls one side of her face into a slow smile, slides the post back about halfway. "In case you're wondering, Mr. Bruiseman. If your attorney ever finds the vehicle he was driving, we're going to have to write him up for no insurance."

"He said it was in the glove compartment," you say, every rod and cone in your eyes fixed on the post she's sliding with the toe of her boot. If she pulls it all the way out of the cinderblock, the springs on the door will jerk the door up about two feet.

"I think he probably says a lot of things," Felson says back, then does it, slides the post all the way out.

You fall back, ready to run, to fly, to explode into the sky somehow, but the door just stays there.

Sheriff Felson settles her eyes on you. "No, Mr. Bruiseman, unlike the rest of Stanton, I'm not in need of your services. Storage or…unlicensed. In fact, I don't have any use for you at all, really. That's kind of specifically why I'm here."

"To *apologize*?" you say, forcing a green key up into the silver lock, both your eyes fixed on the garage door of your living room, trying to keep it in place with the weight of your stare.

Felson smiles with her whole face now, not so much in appreciation as in tolerance, in restraint. She adjusts her wire-rim shades. "I can't imagine you'd go anyway, Mr. Bruiseman. But with you I guess that means I should expect it."

"Go where?" you say, trying to get your key back out now.

"The service," she says. "Your presence is not requested."

You stand, look past her to the carwash.

"This you talking?" you ask, "or Gwen?"

"Doesn't matter. It's me saying it. Here. Now."

"But he was my friend," you say, your voice lilting, mocking.

"Go later then."

You tap your own left cheekbone to show how solid it is. "Not like it's going to be open casket anyway, right?"

It pulls Felson in close enough that you can taste the coffee on her breath.

"And you wonder why you're not wanted there," she says. "I'll be sure to pass your respects on to the widow. It's not enough that she had to ID him from his *wedding* ring—or do you want to ask her about that too?"

You push your lower lip up with your thumb.

"So we have an understanding?" Felson says.

You swallow and your ears fill with the rushed sound of saliva. You nod, say it out loud for her: "You don't want me there, I won't be there."

She angles her head over, watches you, then looks all around at the storage units, says it like a bad joke: "'Custom.'"

"'Economy,'" you add.

She pushes her shades deeper into her face. Passing the lawnmower, she hits the handle of her nightstick lightly. It swings the butt around her hip some, into the steel post, just enough of a tap that the garage door of your living room slings up all at once.

She doesn't look back.

When you can breathe again, you lock the gate with the new lock, come back ten seconds later to make sure the key you think fits, fits. It does. One catastrophe avoided.

Next, it's Arnot King's Mustang, the gift Fin's left you.

Like Rory, he knew you were going to need transportation, maybe. Or, probably, he just didn't want to draw attention to himself—didn't want Arnot King found until he woke up on his own, walked out onto 137.

The first thing about the car is that there's no front plates. This is bad news in Texas, especially if you're driving a sports car. And if you've got dark skin, like Arnot King? Not that anybody'd be able to tell: the windows have limousine tint, are impenetrable, a solid two shades past illegal.

"Might as well paint her red," you say, running your hand over the hood, to the windshield.

Which isn't to say you don't like it.

At least now you have something to pay him with, if you need his services again. Because Felson was right: there's not going to be any insurance card in the glove compartment. A bag of something illegal, maybe, or a flask, a snub-nosed pistol, but no insurance.

You look anyway.

A scattering of business cards. New ones, apparently. No more "Snake Charmer" for Arnot King. Now, bigger and bolder, dead center, he's your "Allegator."

You slide one of the cards into your pocket, set the keys in the ignition swinging, and walk around back.

Dealer plates. This is what Felson meant by "the vehicle he was driving." She already ran whatever info he gave her, matched it to a VIN, and, from there, to a used car lot. The roundabout way of getting the Carlotta's stamped at the top of the plate. Which, obviously, Arnot King could have just told them if he wanted.

At the phonebook again, you look Carlotta's up. It's down on Florida Street, in Midland. Where you got shot, practically. One of those places always folding, rising again with a different name, repainted inventory, doctored titles.

You drop a quarter, dial the number, and a girl answers on the first ring.

"Um," you say, studying the dial pad of the phone for something to say, "just interested in a car. What do you have?"

"On the lot, you mean, or in back?"

You nod to yourself: this is Arnot King's kind of place, all right.

"Like the one I took over to Stanton, yeah?" you try.

Impersonating a scam lawyer's got to be less of a crime than impersonating a homicide detective, you tell yourself. You're getting better.

Now just to get a handle on the whole private-investigating without a ticket thing.

"Oh, Mr. *King*," the girl says, and she tells you to hold on, calls out over the phone, loud in your ear, "Mr. Jimmy?"

In what you know is the swamp-cooled office she's in, you see Jimmy Bones looking over to her from a filing cabinet, his eyes as black as his skin.

He doesn't even answer properly, just chuckles long and deep. Leans back far enough in his chair that you think you can hear the springs creak.

"Um, Mr. King?" the girl comes back, "he's—"

You hang up, cover your hand with your mouth.

Last night, because of Thomas swooping in, saving you from yourself, you'd decided to gamble, decided not to break into Fin's AirStream, grub around for the film canister.

Now things are different.

One way or another, Jimmy Bones is coming to see you. It might be best to have what he wants when he gets here.

12.

BECAUSE EVERY COP in Stanton—all three of them, you suppose—
is going to be at Rory's funeral, and everybody else too, you ease
the Mustang out of your living room, gun the engine, feel the
power coursing up through the shifter, straight into the seat of
your jaw.

You would just walk down to the body shop—were going
to, even, had already locked the gate—but then you realized that
in this copless window the funeral was providing, you could do
two things at once: get the film *and* ditch the car. Because the
body shop's where Felson expects the Mustang to be, maybe she
won't question it suddenly just being there now.

Stupider things have happened. You've got pictures to prove
it. Court documents. Scars.

It takes all of twenty-two seconds to make it down 137, ease
over the tracks. Like you'd hoped, the body shop's empty. Open,
but closed—Manuel and his helper each a quarter mile directly
to the east, watching Rory get buried.

You downshift, coast deep into the shop, where Gwen's Town
Car had been parked, and leave the keys in the ignition, take the
necessary thirty seconds to wipe the steering wheel, the dash,
the console, the door, the hood and windshield—everywhere

you might have touched—because your prints aren't just on file, but are probably already out on some desk.

On the way out through the back door, you see the tow truck Manuel uses. It's not the one Jim Martindale picked you up in.

You're not here to figure everything out, though. Just to save yourself.

Don't even cut the tape sealing the door of Fin's AirStream shut, just pull the door open (rag on the handle, not your hand), let the tape flutter.

Inside, it's a cave, and you know without wanting to that after eight years in a cell, this is the only kind of place Fin can be comfortable in anymore. That he's recreating his prison, bringing it with him.

But maybe that's why you're at the storage units yourself, too: A-block, B-block. Doing time for all your mistakes. Coming back to a place where you know nobody's going to like you, where they can remind you every day of what a bad person you are. Make sure you're back in your cell by lights out.

Where your one attempt at decoration is a calendar, though, the walls of Fin's trailer are papered in intricate tattoo designs. A gallery, almost.

You slip the pillowcase from his pillow, use it as a glove, and start opening every cabinet, every cubby, every rusted Folgers can.

Ten minutes later you give up, sit back against the edge of the stove, know the funeral's got to be winding down. You try to see the trailer from a different place, with different eyes. Better eyes.

Cans, yes. People hide stuff in cans.

You attack the cabinets with a new resolve, shaking all the peas, all the Wolf Brand Chili, praying hard for a jar of sugar like Jim Rockford used, and find instead, in the topmost cabinet, a little sawed-off, double-barrel twelve guage. *The* twelve guage? You shake your head no, back away from it, know better than to touch it. Start trying to talk yourself into believing you never saw it in the first place, just go through the motions of still looking for the film in cabinets, on shelves, then, finally, the economy refrigerator. There's only beer in it. You take one, slam it down, wipe the bottle clean. Stare at the door hiding the shotgun. Tell yourself that it justifies what you're doing. If he's stupid enough to leave the murder weapon in plain sight, he deserves what he gets.

But, if he's stupid enough to do that, the film has to be somewhere obvious too, right? What's he going to have done, hid it in a statue or something? The town cannon? This is Stanton, not the Hardy Boys. A post office box, you think. But that's hopeless, a federal crime, one more sick irony—breaking into a federal building to dispose of evidence that can put you in jail, you get caught, have to go to jail anyway.

It's not funny.

This was supposed to be easy.

You slam the side of your fist into one of the drawings and the sound surrounds you. You sit down again, breathing hard, not ready for the walk back to Aardvark Custom Economy Storage now. Not ready for *anything*. And then, right there before you, practically with a spotlight on it, is Fin's album, a three ring notebook. You open it like an ancient and fragile text, look to the door, come back to all the Polaroids of new tattoos, the flesh still risen, glossy black.

You refocus, remember what he told you: that you should have seen his tattoo when it was *new*.

It takes five minutes, but you think you find it towards the back of the album: a concentric pattern of some kind—

Polynesian, you guess—not just time-intensive, but meth-intensive.

You pull the Polaroid out. Behind it is another.

This one is Gwen. Her bedroom, it looks like.

You swallow, pull it from its plastic sleeve.

This proves the affair, anyway—what he wanted you to find? Except, he could have told *Felson* about this.

From the angle of the shot, you can tell that Gwen's probably naked, but all that's in the white frame is her lower back, up close, the intricate jewel and finials inked just above her beltline, and, just past it, her face looking back into the camera.

You study it for too long, even tilt the Polaroid like you'll be able to see into the bedroom that day, that afternoon. And at that angle, you see that you're holding *two* Polaroids.

You settle into Fin's bed-couch, because this is going to be the good stuff.

But then the shot isn't Gwen at all. From the background, you can tell that it's the same bedroom, the same afternoon probably, but Gwen's gone. In the bathroom, maybe, standing on her toes, using two mirrors to see her lower back. Fin alone on the bed for a minute or two, the camera still in his hand.

What he finds is a piece of paper, a form.

It's life insurance. On the top line, the only one even half in focus, is the insurance company's name—a logo you know, you think— and *Roderick Gates* typed in, and then the date, mid-June. It's hardly a month ago.

You look away from it, to Gwen's back again, and the whole caper locks into place around her tattoo, like it had to have that afternoon for Fin. Lure the lovesick ex-con to town, tell him he's the only one, then, after your real lover's killed your husband, use your old friend the ex-cop to set the ex-con up, because it'll look too obvious if you do it yourself. The only thing that almost messes it up—that winds up making it all look more real—is that the ex-cop, because he's *working* for the husband, lights out for Big Springs instead of discovering the husband's body, and so becomes a suspect himself for a while.

The thing is, it all hinges on one thing: you going out to Rory Gates's mom's old house by the dump. And not ever figuring out that you were supposed to.

From Fin's bed-couch, you look to the east, like you can see Gwen in black at Rory's graveside, a check probably already in the mail to her. Or to her and whichever of Rory's old running buddies are there too, being careful to keep his distance from the grieving widow.

One of his names is Martindale, you know. And that he made it up on the spot, like a joke: Martin*dale*, Martin*berg*, Martin*ville*. He was telling you it was fake, practically, showing you that he'd just read it off the Martin County limits sign down 137, in his rearview.

At the funeral, of course, he'll be clean-shaven, have different sunglasses. Not be driving the wrecker. Not be anybody you recognize.

You go there anyway.

13.

ON THE WAY, swinging back over the tracks to loop around the two big tanks, turning south again to the caliche road the cemetery's on, you slow the Mustang for just a moment, know that the *detective* way to do this is without confrontation. The *detective* way is just to wait and watch, see who Gwen starts seeing reluctantly a few months down the road, at her friends' urging. Or maybe she'll even manage to sit on the money until Dan's out of the house.

Though, like Felson says, you're not a detective.

And, anyway, if you do it like that, Fin's up the state river.

It's not that you care what happens to him so much, but that, for a few hours, you *were* him: framed, set up, your life traded in to make Gwen Gates's more comfortable.

More than that, this is the first homicide you'll have actually *solved*. Maybe it'll erase your bad run in Midland and the worse stuff it led to. You can be a hero again. In a stolen car.

This makes you ease off the gas, look around at the leather interior.

Maybe you can tell them you just found it. Walking up to the Town & Country, it was just there in the cotton field behind the tanks, keys and all. This isn't a joy ride, it's a bringing-the-evidence-to-the-proper-authorities ride. Sort of. If you happen to get caught.

You downshift when the evergreens of the cemetery roll into view, lean forward to just coast in, case the crowd, find Jim Martindale, but then—too late—realize what you've pulled in with you, high in fourth gear: a hundred-foot tall plume of white caliche dust.

You stop and it shrouds over you, settles over the cemetery, coating everything with ash, dusting the Mustang's windshield so that the mourners are all washed pale, ghosts of themselves.

Instead of stepping out and facing them, you swallow, your eyes narrowed with apology, then stall some more by leaning over the wheel to try to figure out what's a blinker, what's a windshield wiper.

By the time you find it, the thin sprays of Midland water making your windshield muddy instead of just dusty, Sheriff Felson has separated herself from the crowd, is approaching.

Over her shoulder, for the briefest second, there's Gwen, coughing like all the other mourners—like a *victim*—but then Felson's shoulder moves, raises high enough to dislodge the gun from her hip.

You want to tell her that this isn't what you planned, that this isn't how it's supposed to have gone. That you're a hero, you've figured it out. The real killer's *here*. But then, from the way she's got her face angled away...she can't see you, can she? You're a shape through glass. Anybody.

What makes you be you again, though, it's popping the clutch on accident. The Mustang paws forward, becomes, in the eyes of the law, a lethal weapon, a justification for force. A murder weapon brought to the funeral and used in front of a hundred witnesses.

Felson takes a half step back, but then her training kicks in. She fires once into the windshield.

Because you're still leaned over to decode Ford's wiper-washer assembly, the headrest just over your right shoulder explodes.

It makes the inside of the car smell new again: foam, plastic.

You lean deeper into the door panel, grab reverse, and throw the only thing at her you have: more caliche.

You're two hundred yards back down the road before the Mustang's rear tires grab anything like traction, and then you just sit there, looking at the white cloud rising into a column before you and holding like that.

Slowly, inevitably, the cloud starts to pulse red. To spread.

"And the party never stops," you say, and turn left at the tracks, *onto* the tracks. It's a thing you've always half-wanted to do, since you were fourteen and saw it in a movie. Now you think it might be your last chance.

When the Mustang finds 137 again, you smoke the tires hard past the body shop just because you can, then shift halfway through a bad fishtail so that one tire hangs in the ditch for twenty yards, leaving the plastic of Arnot King's right taillight shattered under a mailbox.

In two minutes you're out of Martin County, back in Midland County, a shotgun on the passenger seat you really should have left in its cabinet.

14.

ARNOT KING MEETS YOU at King Burger. They have the best coke floats in town.

"I know who you work for," you tell him.

He looks the place over, sits down where he can see out the front window.

"Where's my car?" he says.

"You don't want it."

"That so?"

You lean forward, brush broken glass from your hair onto the scarred tabletop.

He understands. "Just what have you stepped into, Mr. Bruiseman?"

"More like what I have *not* stepped into, Mr....*King* Burger?"

"I wish," he says, leaning back into his slick seat. "They won't even give me a discount."

"Can't win them all."

"Just the important ones."

"Speaking of?" you say, watching every muscle of his face. "You call Jimmy about this little meet-up? Should I be baking a cake, trying on suits?"

"He doesn't know about the car yet, if that's what you're

asking."

It's not, but that's good to know.

"So tell me," he says. And you do, all of it: Gwen, Fin, whoever Jim Martindale is. Your high-speed exit. The fast yellow slash through Greenwood, like an arrow Stanton shot at Midland. How that one bridge out there still smells like sewage, if he's wondering.

He's not. "So you've—you've actually and really got the *murder* weapon now," he says. "You being the last person in Texas who should *want* to have it, I mean."

It makes you cast around King Burger for who might have heard. For a terrible moment, a woman with her fingertips to the glass of the door is Judge Harkness leading a steely-eyed formation of bailiffs, DPS, and Rangers, but then she's just another redhead with a torpedo job on her chest, the men behind her just men.

Arnot King sees you looking, looks too. Comes back with a smile. "And you've come to me why?"

"Because I didn't have anybody else. I'm not even supposed to be in Midland County."

"Tonight?"

"Ever."

"Then I'll say it again. What do you think I can do for you, Nick?"

You stare at him, slurp your third coke float up through the straw.

"All this—my theory," you say. "None of it works without that insurance policy, I don't think."

"Or the shotgun."

"That kind of works the other way, I think."

"Against Payne."

"Or me."

"Accessory after the fact, obstruction, operating without a license—"

"*Okay*."

"To say nothing of your, your willful unbanishment," he sneaks in anyway then leans forward, heating his eyes up somehow, a vaguely feminine gesture you can't really track. "And you're wanting me to—to, I don't know, get that insurance policy for you with my magic wand, for *what*, exactly?"

"Because you're my lawyer."

He smiles about this. On accident, it looks like, then covers his mouth with a meaningful flourish, his eyes trying to keep yours on him, his flicking up at the last instant as a cop passes your table, back from the bathroom.

"Officer," Arnot King says to him, tapping his knuckles on the fake wood table like he was going to do it anyway, even if the cop wasn't already stopping. For a breath, it draws the officer's eyes down to the tabletop, but then he comes up, to Arnot King, then you, and all you can do, think, *be*, is a coke float drinker, your mouth clamped onto the straw, whatever it takes to keep your face at a bad angle for him.

His name is Rodriguez. The reason you don't even have to see his face to recognize him is that he was never a face to you at all, but a utility belt worn a particular way, a shirt untucked just so much—all you could see through the dry fiberglass of the boat, still sparkling down over you, your hand to your chest, trying to hold all your blood in. He was the first one to respond, didn't even stop to put gloves on. It was the last time you felt clean, really.

Seeing him here, now, doing what you're doing with the

life he saved, it's—you don't know. Almost like shame, or embarrassment, or, no: welshing on a nothing-bet, that ten-spot you know you owe somebody, and know you'll only have to pay if they ever call you on it. Which they won't.

Just don't let him see your eyes, you tell yourself.

Above you, he's already starting things up with Arnot King. "Thought you hung around the hospital this time of night, Arnie."

Arnie?

In return, Arnot King fakes a long, tolerant, open-mouthed laugh, spreads his arms to encompass all of King Burger. "The *people*, Jayme. I'm here with the people, cabrón…"

Rodriguez shakes his head in disgust, breathes out something like a laugh, and is already turning to go when you accidentally look far enough up to lock eyes with him for a moment.

He stops, angles his head over to see you better. Smiles.

You nod hey, know that if you try to run—the Mustang's just behind King Burger, two streets up, the little shotgun stuffed under a dumpster—he's going to slam you back into the booth before you've even stood the whole way, and Arnot King will just fade from the scene, never have been there.

Better to just offer your wrists, maybe. Do the six or nine months Harkness has been saving for you. Let Stanton, Texas forget you again.

Instead, Rodriguez massages his jaw in wonder. "How's the shoulder there, cowboy?"

You'd forgotten this about him, that he lives in a world of Cowboys and Indians, shoot-outs and dry gulches.

You touch the old bullet hole—*dent*, really—shrug, and Rodriguez nods like he's nodding with you, then lifts his chin to the counter. "You're paying cash, right?"

It's not a question.

You reach back for more, for him, but that's not it. He's not even looking at you anymore, is already pretending you're not there. Saying over your head, as if to the wall, "Good, cash. Nothing with that comic book name of yours on it. Let's keep it that way, shall we?"

To show you he's serious, and to make sure you know what he's giving you here, he locks eyes with you again for an instant, and you thank him with the slightest, most grateful nod in the long and colorful history of nods, and then he's gone.

The thing is, unless you live next-door, King Burger only *takes* cash.

"He's saved my life twice now," you say, once the door's closed.

"Jayme?" Arnot King says, turning in the booth to make sure Rodriguez is really backing out. "He couldn't save ten cents."

Remember to thank him inside for reminding you how much you're worth.

"We were talking payment," Arnot King says. "Compensation."

"Say I did have a tape from that Christmas?"

"Doesn't make it true."

"Your car?"

"Do you think I really want that now?"

"You're going to have to explain it being shot up to Jimmy."

"What's one more car between old friends?"

You turn sideways in your booth so that your back's against the wall. "You might be able to...to *stay* friends, if, say, you brought him something else instead."

Arnot King smiles. "Nazi boy gave it back to you?"

The film.

"He will. If you can help me here. That's the only reason I'm helping *him*, really."

Arnot King slides your cup over to his side of the table and makes a show of holding your diseased straw to the side so he can drain the last of the coke float.

Ten minutes later, the little shotgun recollected because it has a serial number, the Mustang parked on the wrong side of the street with the keys in the ignition, the window down in invitation, Arnot King eases back from Carlotta's #3 with a Lincoln Town Car. He stops where you're waiting, the street behind him red with his brake lights.

You just stand there.

"Well?" he says, opening the passenger door.

Close your eyes. Step in.

Because you're not sure you could navigate all the back roads south of Greenwood to loop you around through Sprayberry, over to Garden City, up to Big Spring, to creep back into Stanton from the east, you have Arnot King take you the north way out of Midland, up 349 to the Andrews highway. It crosses 137 a few miles north of Stanton, is a straight shot down. Like falling into the throat of the beast. Again.

"Sure about this?" Arnot King asks at the four-way stop.

You shake your head no, let him turn back south anyway. In a paper bag on the seat between you is a fifth of Jim Beam, unopened. Twenty years ago it was your father's favorite.

The receipt is burned in the ashtray. For tonight to work, it's very important there not be any back trail.

When the bridge rolls into view, the lights of the Town & Country glowing on the other side—the only place even half-awake in Stanton—you clamp your hand onto the shotgun, tell

Arnot King to slow.

He lets off the accelerator, passes beneath the hanging legs of the Lawler kid and never knows it.

You spin your head, look behind you. From his silhouetted perch on the missile, the Lawler kid doesn't wave, just tracks you with his head. Like he remembers, understands that he should have been in your grade, understands how the two of you are tied together: the day his brother Dane found him in the stock tank was the first day of your new life as Nabby. Meaning you left the child you had been behind that day. In a stock tank, it feels like now.

It didn't matter that you gave the milk money back, that your dad took his belt off and made you understand certain things, say them back to him word for word. You were Nabby. Unlike *St. Nick*, it wasn't a seasonal name, something you could wear a red hat for. To make *Nabby* fit, you had to keep stealing the milk money, pretty much. Only the milk money kept changing into other things, and other things.

"Here," you tell Arnot King, and he turns left after the Town & Country, onto St. Peters. The next turn, though, your father's, he doesn't take. Just keeps going.

"What—?"

You follow his eyes to the rearview, then through the back glass.

"It's just a truck," you say.

He shakes his head no, says, "Watch," and takes a turn right, like he's going down to the Methodist church.

Seconds later, the truck turns too, and you know it: the Ford. Yours and Gwen's, if the world was any kind of fair.

"It should be in impound," you say, your face scrunched up.

"Right?"

"It?" Arnot King watches his mirrors more than the road, then, like he's done this before, sucks the headlights back into the front of the car and accelerates hard.

The truck switches to brights, catches you by the museum.

"It's him," you say. "Jim Martindale."

Arnot King looks over to you.

"Want me to stop?" he says, nodding down to the little shotgun. You look down to it too, finally shake your head no.

Up by the baseball field, Arnot King backs into somebody's carport, lets the truck flash past, the driver just a shape hunched over the wheel, looking. Maybe Jim Martindale, maybe not.

Arnot King eases the Town Car in behind him but then the Ford sees you, slows to a crawl. Arnot King slows with it, a standoff, and then one of the truck's reverse lights glows on.

"I didn't even know they worked," you say, smiling.

Arnot King backs into another driveway to turn around. It's a slow chase, like playing tag with the cop the other night in Thomas's truck.

You let it go for three more minutes or so, the truck just following, not really wanting to catch up, then direct Arnot King up to Rory Gates's old house.

Like you hoped—she was always taking in strays—the garage door is propped up to let the cat go in and out as it wants.

"Shine your lights there," you tell Arnot King and he sweeps them around, settles them on the garage door. The rear license plate of Gwen's Town Car winks back. On cue the Ford's headlights fade down to yellow worms, then ash.

"He thought we were her," you say, patting the dashboard of

the Town Car you're *in*. "That she's got somebody else already…"

Arnot King follows the Ford east but then stops at the city limits for your decision. You watch the one dim taillight. Big Springs is that way. The dump. The scene of the crime.

You shake your head no to Arnot King.

"Your town," he says, shrugging, and it's maybe the first time anybody's ever said that to you.

You show him the insurance office on St. Peters. It's where he's supposed to meet you tomorrow morning. He finds your father's street on his own, after that, the window bleeding television light.

"Thanks," you say, your finger to the inside handle of the door. "Really, even if this—" but then, when you start to pull the shotgun over, to hide somewhere in the tomb of your father's house, it doesn't move.

You look down: Arnot King holds onto it with one finger, a napkin between his skin and the stock.

"Insurance," he says, smiling a thin smile at you, and you finally just shake your head, only light him up with the dome light for a flash before pushing the door shut just enough for it to catch, not quite enough for any noise.

He eases away, doesn't even use the brakes at the corner, and you say it again to him—*thanks*—then walk with the bottle to your father's front door, step in without knocking.

Your father looks up, trying to place you, then nods at last, lifts his hand to show you you're in the way here. That he can't see the television.

Arnot King's idea was just to have your father lie for you about having been at the funeral—because he's your father, right?

In King Burger, you'd smiled about this, looked away, could

already see this moment: you tossing the bottle down beside your father's leg then walking through the old smells of the house to the backyard, to sit on the porch and stare up at the sky while he gets drunker and drunker. Drunk enough to not be sure *when* you got there, really.

It works.

15.

THE LOGO YOU RECOGNIZED from the insurance form in Fin's Polaroid had the letter B done up like a weathervane. It was for Brock & Associates. The "Associates" part meant Cath, more or less; she had been Junior Brock's secretary for as long as he'd needed one. Standing outside their office on St. Peters, you still expect her to have cat-eye glasses, a hive of hair balanced on her head. Instead, bent over her old desk, a phone pressed to the side of his head, is a black-haired kid in a three-button suit, his socks tastefully ribbed.

"Junior?" you say, standing in the door, the cowbell above it still clanging.

He looks around to you, back to the phone, then shrugs, holds the receiver out. "It's for you, Mr. Bruiseman."

You take the phone and wonder if you ever really woke up this morning. If maybe instead of sitting on the back porch half the night, afraid to move, you went inside to the couch your father had prepared for you. Held your glass out to him, for a slug, a shot.

But then the phone, it's real—smells like the kid's cologne, even.

If this is a dream, then the last twenty years are too.

You raise the phone to your ear.

It's Arnot King. He's talking too fast, calling from lockup, just tried to catch you at your father's house. You narrow your eyes at the desk calendar (July), ask your lawyer how he got that number. He tells you it's the only Bruiseman in the phonebook.

The charge against him, like Felson warned, is driving without insurance, and as it turns out: without registration either.

"She says you were supposed to tell me," he hisses.

"Didn't think you were going to get stopped," you say. "Where'd they get you?"

"In the ass, *Nick*."

"Last night?"

"This morning. The way in."

It figures. His words as neutral as possible, Arnot King tells you there's supposed to be a call into a James Brazos, alias Jimmy "Bones." A name supposedly connected by paper to the car. According to Felson, he's a small-timer who runs a few used lots in Midland. *And plays pool*, you want to add, for the kid—Junior's son?—pretending not to be listening.

"I was just test-driving it, though," Arnot King says, his words clear, for whoever's monitoring his call.

"I know," you say back just as clearly. "This Jimmy Brazos called back yet, to clear it up?"

"More the kind of thing he'd like to handle in person, I suspect," Arnot King says. "Being an upstanding citizen and all."

"What about the sheriff?"

"That's what I'm calling about, she's—" he starts, but then you catch the kid's eye watching something, some*body*, behind you.

"—here," you finish, and hang up.

In the doorway, her hand up in the cowbell, padding the clangor, is Sheriff Felson. She lowers her face to you, her eyes so dead you want to smile, just as counterweight.

It's not like she's the first woman to look at you like that, though.

"Sheriff," you say. "We keep running into each other."

"Small town," she says back, dismissing you almost instantly, nodding once to the kid and saying his name as hello: "William."

You turn to him again and he offers his hand, and you nod, look for evidence of his father in the cut of his jaw, in his hairline, but never knew Junior when he wasn't already an old man.

"Your place?" you say to him, about the office.

"Ever since Junior cashed his policy in," Felson answers for this William the Kid, and William, shaking your hand in both of his, nods once, agreeing with her.

You rescue your hand, rub the side of your eye. "You're here to inform me my lawyer's going to be late, right?"

She smiles. "Twenty-four hours late, I'd say," and you do the math in your head, the same math that was stacked against you before. Twenty-four hours from now will be the weekend, officially. Meaning Arnot King will be in until Monday morning.

Unless Jimmy Bones shows up with bail in one hand, a lead pipe in the other.

You smile back at her, *with* her, everything a game, and open your mouth to say something smart when it hits you. In her car, or in a locker at the station, is what Arnot King had on the seat beside him: the shotgun.

"What?" she says, stepping in.

"That Lincoln," you say, and look around, trying to think of some filler. "He was just test-driving it, you know? That a crime?"

"Kind of what I'm here about, Mr. Bruiseman."

"At the insurance office."

There's a new glitter in her that you think is swallowed laughter. "Can you account for your whereabouts since the last time we spoke?"

"You told me not to go to Rory's funeral, if I recall."

"Kind of what I thought."

You start to say something back, reevaluate. "You're using past tense. *Thought.*"

She prunes her chin out in appreciation, nods.

"Meaning?" you lead.

"Your attorney's cute little sports car finally turned up," she says, watching your face. You try to keep it as slack as possible.

"Where?" you say, your tone either dead-on or absolutely fake—you're too close to tell.

She hooks her head west. "East side of Midland. I need to ask you if your prints are going to be in it."

"Like you said," you tell her, "he's my attorney."

"But you walked back to your—to the storage units, I thought. After your stay with us."

"He picked me up on his way out of town?"

"After he left before you? I presume this would be when he had already looped into Midland, to test-drive the Town Car."

You shrug. "Stanton is the test, yeah. Car can make it here, it can make it—"

"Mr. Bruiseman."

"Didn't know I was going to need to keep notes, Sheriff." You keep staring at her. "What are you thinking I did, though? Drop Fin off to you, hide the car, then have somebody dump it in Midland?"

She shakes her head no. "I don't think you dropped Fin off at all."

It almost makes you smile.

"I was at my father's house," you say. "Went to ask him for some life advice, all that."

Felson likes this, has to cover her mouth with the side of her fist, like she's about to cough into it.

Your face still as slack as you can get it, you pick up William the Kid's phone. "Ask him," you say.

She takes the phone, lets you dial it. For an uncomfortable moment, your eyes and William's get tangled up, and still the phone's ringing.

Finally your dad picks up. You can hear exactly what he says into his end: nothing.

"Mr. Bruiseman?" Felson says loud into the phone, turning away.

Thirty seconds of questions later she hangs up, holds the phone down, thinking of what to say next, and how to say it. "Your father says you were there long enough for him to drink this much out of a quart."

"How long is that?"

"You tell me," she says, and shakes her head no, as if abandoning this already. "Your attorney—"

"—just called."

She nods, waits before speaking, to see if you're going to be interrupting again. "Your attorney says that he was coming into Stanton to meet with his client. You."

"He was," you tell her. "We had an appointment."

"For thirty minutes ago."

You look back to the clock above the door to what must be William's office, nod. "For eleven, yeah. Guess I overslept."

Felson studies a stapler or paper clip holder on the reception desk. Says without looking up, "He told us everything, Mr. Bruiseman. Gwen Gates, Fin, this imaginary third party."

You watch her, are nodding with this.

"…an insurance policy," she adds for William Brock.

He comes to life, pushes off from the cheap seats—the wood-veneer coffee hutch—and says, "Gates, is it?"

"Rory," you say, and follow him into his office.

The policy, it turns out, was for a hundred and twenty-five grand with Gwen as sole beneficiary. Serious money. The worth-killing-for kind. None of the cases you tried to work in Midland were like this. Your first was a man on Front Street, beaten to death with a tire-iron. Your last was a man changing his tire on the side of the road, some truck or car clipping him just as he was rolling the spare into place. This insurance stuff, though—the follow-the-money trick, instead of follow-the-tire—if you'd just pulled *one* like this in those two dry years in Homicide, then you probably never would have leaned down over a pool table with Jimmy Bones. Never would have seen Judge Harkness's breasts through a telephoto lens.

Not that you regret that part of it, mind.

"Either of you care if I record this?" Felson says, setting her silver microcassette recorder on the leading edge of William the Kid's mahogany desk.

He looks to it, opens his mouth, then finally gets it out with as much tact as he can manage: "Actually, since none of the beneficiaries are here, it might be best if—"

Felson saves him the trouble. She hits the stop button with the ring finger of her right hand.

You don't need this. Especially now that you *can't* be involved—now that this insurance form can be entered into evidence. With it in hand, you're just another of Gwen's victims.

"Pay it out already?" you ask William.

He looks to Felson for permission, then nods yes.

"Hundred and twenty five *thou*sand." You lean back. "That's a lot of reasons, right, sheriff?"

"For suicide, maybe," she says. You pull the document across the table, William's hand following it. Felson stops him, shakes her head. "He needs to see."

You hear yourself fake a single laugh that sounds like a cough.

"He—he…" you say.

"Signed it," Felson says. Then, to William, "You wouldn't have mailed it to the widow if he hadn't—am I right?"

He nods, makes a face as if he's about to apologize for policy, but she holds her hand up, goes on. "Insurance companies tend not to release funds until the investigation has cleared their payee."

William the Kid nods. "It's not like we didn't trust Mrs. Gates, Mr. Bruiseman. Please understand. It's just that—"

"You can't be too careful," you add, still studying Rory's signature, trying to match it up with what you don't remember from his check.

"It's real." William pulls the paper back to his side of the desk. "Cath notarized it."

Hearing her name, you jerk your head around, and there she is, in her same place at the desk. Same glasses, same hair.

She smiles an embarrassed smile, waves her fingertips to you. Might even still have suckers in her drawer.

You come back to William.

"He couldn't have," you say. "The copy Gwen—"

"The one she had for her files was incomplete, I'm afraid."

"Not valid?"

"She paid a year's premiums in advance, Mr. Bruiseman. All done in good faith."

"But—"

"She said Rory would be in to sign it later."

You probably could have guessed this: that of *course* that's what she'd say. And even if the policy turned out not to be wholly valid, Stanton's got three thousand people, would Brock & Associates really argue details with a grieving widow, when it might cost them 2,999 clients?

"Well?" Felson says from some other dimension.

You wade back, focus in on her, on William. "And you—you actually *saw* him sign it. Rory Gates?"

Felson shakes her head, reaches forward for the silver recorder, its tiny heads turning silently.

"Must have a voice-activated mode," Felson says, doing her eyes like *Oops, forgot*.

She knows about Fin, then. That you're working for him without a license. That he's *making* you work for him.

You close your eyes, try to just see now, here. Finally you say to William, "He *signed* it?"

William looks to Felson about this, like you're a joke they're sharing. "He came in to get liability for a truck he'd bought for his son at an auction, Mr. Bruiseman. I told him I had something else he could sign while he was here."

There's more—he's a salesman, after all, has to give you the whole scene, reel you all the way in, sell it to you—but you lose the thread of what he's saying, like he's distant again, on tape.

The Ford.

It all starts with the Ford.

16.

THE FIRST PLACE YOU LOOK for it is in all sixteen storage units at Aardvark Custom Economy Storage, even the ones blocked off by Betsy Simm's horse trailer. Ten of the units have numbered green padlocks on them; the other six you have to cut with the shiny new bolt cutters Arnot King left in the office. They're better than the ones that came with the place.

The truck isn't in any of the units.

You stand in the alley between them all, looking to each one in turn, then go to the one that's your living room, drag the wooden spool and bench seat out to the center again. The tractor on the calendar for January is a double-wheel, four-wheel-drive job, the tires beautiful and black. You flip through the rest of the months, don't like any of the other tractors as much, so leave it on January.

Of the six storage units you haven't been through yet, four of them are a wall of broken appliances, exercise equipment, and mismatched cardboard boxes—the clear tape on them just decoration now. The other two units are a surprise: one is walled with cages, still smells like animals, has a pallet of forty-pound concrete bags directly under the light; the other, the one just before Betsy Simm's mother's new unit, has a coin-drop little pool table in it, old skin magazines folded under the legs to level it out, beer bottles on every flat surface, the sticks leaned in the corner, their blue tips bunched together like they're talking about you.

You shake your head in wonder, either smell stale smoke drifting up from the green felt or remember it. You feel in your pocket for two quarters, come up instead with a handful of Polaroids: Gwen's tat and the incomplete insurance form.

You hold them for a long time, telling yourself what Felson told you before dropping you off: that this isn't any of your concern anymore. That even if Gwen was sleeping with Fin, which her sweet spot tattoo doesn't *legally* prove, that still, Rory signed the insurance form. William the Kid *saw* him do it, even.

The part he left out, though—the part he would have left out, because he didn't know to look for it—is the way Rory had to have hesitated when William said there was something else he needed to sign. How it must have felt seeing that insurance form, how it must have felt standing in a strange office, having to keep a smile on your face while it dawns on you that your wife has been unfaithful to you. That she's planning to kill you. That you're worth more to her dead than alive. That you're in the way of everything she seems to want.

What you want to ask Gwen is how it felt for her seeing Rory's name on the dotted line of that policy. His note to her from the grave. How much it might be worth to her for you not to say anything. Five percent? Ten?

Maybe it'll be enough to get Jimmy Bones off your back.

Your only other choice is to actually solve the case somehow, figure out who Jim Martindale is. Really, it's what Rory hired you to do.

You toss the Polaroids onto the pool table. They fan out, stay there, and you pull the overhead light, shut the door, then shut the fifteen other doors, dig up six new locks and go inside to wait out the heat of the day.

Four hours later you walk out into the glare coming off all the white storage unit doors, think for a second you should paint them, that they're too bright. You remember your sunglasses, thread them onto your face instead.

Like Stace's parents would *pay* you to paint them.

Nod once to Betsy Simm's horse trailer as you walk alongside it. The one she wasn't able to get since the gate was locked.

There's no way to both leave the gate unlocked *and* keep anybody from driving off with the riding lawnmower, so you drift over to the water station instead. Sherilita sets a chopped beef basket and an empty styrofoam cup on the counter for you. You take them both, jerk your own tea, want her to call you a gumshoe or ask about the private eye racket. Instead she looks to you once, then away.

"What?" you say.

"Shouldn't you be working?"

"What?" you say again, not playing.

She's doing something with the pickle jar. Doing nothing, really.

"Thomas told me about the other night," she says, her lips thin.

"He helped me unload—"

"—Mrs. Rankin's stuff, yeah."

"He wasn't late, was he?"

She smiles about this, is still looking down at her hands. "No, Nick. He wasn't late. You did good."

"For once," you add, giving her your best smile. But then she looks up to you and you see she's about to cry. That what she's doing with her hands behind the gallon pickle jar is folding a napkin down smaller and smaller. Like everybody else, she's human, has her own story, her own shit going on. Her world doesn't revolve around you coming in for chopped beef sandwiches.

You lose the smile, say the first part of her name.

She shrugs her left shoulder, keeps folding the napkin. "Thomas. He's—the other morning, when you sent him home—"

"To go to the farm sale."

"To meet his dad to go to the farm sale." Sherilita composes herself. "He sat there in the kitchen waiting for him, Nick. Until I came up here at nine."

"He didn't show. The dad."

"I don't know why I thought he would. They'd only been planning it for three weeks." She laughs about this. It's not a real laugh, or a comfortable one.

"I'll talk to him for you," you say, standing.

She looks up to you from under her hand. "You can find him?"

"What's his name?"

She lowers her hands, uses her folded-up napkin to clean an already-clean spot on the counter. "*Thomas*, Nick. What are you...? When I came home that day he wasn't there."

You nod about this. "The father, I mean. Your ex."

"*Talk* to him?" It's funny to her. "Have to find him first."

"It's what I do."

Now she's laughing, holding her hand up to you in apology, trying to keep her next few breaths in because she's about to cry, and you look back down to your chopped beef sandwich, rotate it around for the best bite. When it's to your mouth, a windshield flashes on 137, the car turning in from the north.

Or not on 137 at all, but in the ditch, the caliche lot that bleeds over to Aardvark Custom Economy Storage.

The car is a black Town Car. The one Arnot King was driving.

It's moving too slow to be him, though. Too deliberate, like a shark hanging in the water, its sleek body full of purpose, of patience, of confidence.

Jimmy Bones.

He got the car out of impound already. Wants to take care of some other business while he's in town.

Over the counter you're suddenly sitting under, you hear his voice through the drive-through window. He's asking about the gentleman who manages the storage facility next door, his voice syrupy and benign.

"You want to rent a unit?" Sherilita says down to him. You close your eyes, realize that the kickboard behind you—the base of the counter—is just paneling, isn't any thicker than the hull of a fiberglass boat.

Jimmy Bones's reply is muffled and amused, and it ramps up into a question at the end.

"Just missed him," Sherilita says, a new flatness in her voice.

This time Jimmy Bones's voice come through loud and clear, like he's leaned out of the window now: "That his drink?"

From under the counter you can see it: your styrofoam cup of tea, and, beside it, the chopped beef sandwich, its paper still uncrinkling around it, blooming in the heat.

"Excuse me?" Sherilita says.

"Forget it," Jimmy Bones says. "Think he always cleans his plate anyway, that one. He say when he's due back?"

"He was going to the liquor store, I think."

Jimmy Bones says that sounds about right, says he could use a beer too, blowtorch of a day like this.

Sherilita directs him south across 137.

When he's gone, you're standing on your side of the counter. Sherilita turns, shakes her head to you, *at* you.

"How can you help Thomas?" she says. "You can't even—"

You don't hear the end of it. You're already moving.

Standing in front of the office door of Aardvark Custom Economy Storage, Jimmy Bones two miles up the road, maybe— two miles of five, meaning ten minutes for a roundtrip—it comes to you, how to leave Betsy Simm's horse trailer available and not get the lawnmower stolen: take the mower with you. *Drive* it, like Rory was saying. Pull a George Jones. That way, when Jimmy Bones gets back, the chain link gate will still be open. He probably won't even notice the chain at the base of the steel pole, the extension cord still leading to it.

You would put them up, hide them too, but the clock's ticking.

You leave both lights in the office like they were (overhead off, lamp on), take a beer for each pocket and find that your hands are shaking.

The lawnmower starts on the third try, and you don't even mess with any of the low gears, just make your fast getaway up in the sixth, the throttle pushed all the way up the rabbit's ass. At first the PTO's still on, a helicopter too close to the ground sending up curling plumes of caliche on each side, but you finally find the toggle, click it off and pop the clutch, spin the small tires out through the gate.

It's not a yellow Mustang, but it'll do.

Your plan is to jump across 137, pull in behind the carwash and make two beers last the afternoon, until Jimmy Bones creeps back to Midland.

Instead, coming south down the turn lane, Toby Garrett's baby brother flashes his lights at you.

You pull over as far away from Aardvark Custom Economy Storage as you can, wave back to whoever it is driving by, cheering you on with their horn. It dopplers away, leaves you with Toby Garrett's baby brother. You keep both hands on the wheel, stare straight ahead.

"So," you say.

He hooks his left boot up onto the painted diamond plate under the clutch.

"I'm supposed to be watching you," he says, turning to look down towards the tracks. It's the direction you're already looking.

"If you're tailing me," you say, "I don't know. I'm not on the force anymore or anything, so could be everything's changed, but is this really how it's done? So up close and personal?"

He nods down to the lawnmower. "What are you doing?"

"Little freelance landscaping?" you say. Before he can answer, you lift your chin to the carwash. "Can't bring water to the horse, then bring the horse to the water, right?"

Toby Garrett's baby brother shrugs like that's good enough, he guesses.

"You'll want some bags, though," he says.

"Bags?"

"For the air filter," he says, then steps back to his cruiser, comes back with three Town & Country shopping bags.

You take them, lift them to him in thanks, and the beer in your offside pocket slips out, clatters on the fender, thunks into the gravel at the side of the road.

This would be a good place to cough into your hand. Or run away.

Toby Garrett's baby brother keeps his eyes up and far away, says, "Serious about that landscaping?"

Two minutes later his mother-in-law's address is scribbled on the back of one of Arnot King's Allegator business cards—the only piece of paper you could paw up.

You tuck it into your shirt pocket like you're thankful for it. "Ever heard of a Jim Martindale?"

"That's the guy you say…Mrs. Gates's backdoor man?"

"Twice removed," you add. "But, yeah."

He purses his lips, shakes his head no then looks over you. "Madelyn'd know, though. If he ever went here."

You follow his line of sight to the pale brick of the high school, nod. Of course. Madelyn, the Sherilita of your father's generation.

"Yeah," you say, nodding thanks for real this time. You hold your hand to the key of the lawnmower until Toby Garrett's baby brother has reached down under his dash to engage the autopilot installed in every law enforcement vehicle in Martin County. It delivers him down to the Town & Country.

If he's lucky, four kids won't be walking out with their faces lowered to 44-ounce drinks. Or, no: if he's lucky, four kids will be, and they'll run like water for the safety of some other street, and their motion will be so beautiful that Toby Garrett's baby brother will just sit there behind his wheel, not give chase, not make them shoot him.

If this case is ever over, you want to sit at the Town & Country again with him, look through his binoculars at the Lawler kid. Ask him about his big brother Toby. What ever happened to him? What ever happened to any of you?

You turn the key on the lawnmower, see the black Town Car just as it crests the railroad tracks, too close now for any more fast getaways. So you do what you can: toggle the PTO back in, let the dust and grass rise on either side of you like pale, smoky wings.

They carry you to the high school. To Madelyn.

17.

SHE CATCHES YOU tucking your shirt in, *tsk tsks* her way over.

"Nicholas," she says. "Catherine said she saw you."

"That was this morning?" you say, having to study the floor to dig Cath from 'Catherine'—Brock & Associates; cat-eye glasses under a beehive do.

"Along with that boy from Monahans," Madelyn adds, leading you by simply not breaking stride. "He's trouble, you know."

You nod, have a pretty good read on Arnot King, yeah.

"You hear about the excitement at the funeral?" she asks, touching the side of your right arm with the back of her fingers, and you keep nodding. "That was his car," she whispers, as if this makes her case about Arnot King.

"He was in—" you start, meaning to say *Midland*, but then don't. Because what she's probably getting at anyway is that, at the cemetery yesterday, through the mourners, through the dust and grief and roses, the twenty years since you've skulked these halls, she recognized you. She'd never say it straight-out, though.

"So," she says, at her desk again, in front of the principal's office, "what can I help you with today, Nicholas?"

Suddenly unable to make eye-contact, you say, "Just looking for somebody, I guess."

"From your class, I take it?"

"I think so, yeah."

"Name?"

"He—he said Jim Martindale, but I don't think that's it."

Madelyn tilts her head over in thought, shakes it no. "There was James *White*, Standford's oldest son, but—Martindale?"

"I think it was a fake name."

"And you didn't recognize him?"

"He had a beard, glasses."

"But he recognized *you*?"

You nod, hear what she's trying to tell you, to make you see: he recognized *you*. From where? If he needed you to wind up out at Rory Gates's mother's old house, then he needed to talk to you at some point, sure, lie about Rory living out there now. But—but maybe he *didn't* recognize you. Maybe it was just that he knew jolly old St. Nick was back in town, and because he *didn't* know you, you became the best contender?

You rub your eye hard with the heel of your hand, look at your hand afterward.

"Thanks," you say to Madelyn, and start to stand, except now that you've asked her a question, she's not letting you leave without an answer.

Five minutes later, you're in the library with her. She sits you down at a table, brings two copies of your yearbook over.

In one series of nightmares you think you might have had, or are definitely going to be having now, this is what you're doing: looking at your old yearbook, then looking out of the yearbook too, at yourself. Signing it: *Better luck next time. Watch out for the 8-ball.*

But then you smile, look up to Madelyn. "I'm not in this one. It's the year I left."

"Your senior year," she says, nodding like this is obvious— like the mistake you're trying to call her on isn't one she'd ever make—"but we're not looking for you, right? But for somebody who might have had access to the annuals you are in. Somebody necessarily *forward* in time from then."

You raise your eyebrows about this and push your lower lip out. "Ever tried police work?"

"I don't know how to use a camera so well," she says back right in step, licking the pad of her middle finger to page through the yearbook.

You're seventeen again. Mute. Pretending to do what she's doing for real: running your finger up one row of names and down the other. You try not to stop at *Tracy, Gwen*. Madelyn doesn't say anything about it, about her. To you anyway.

Soon enough the two of you are back to prom night, and the next part of this happening nightmare is Gwen and Rory, king and queen.

This time Madelyn can't help herself, reaches over to touch Rory on the face, "The first picture he would be in that night," and then leaves her finger there but turns her head to the side, thinking. Is about to let you in on it when the door behind you opens. It changes Madelyn's expression completely.

"The queen herself," she says, rising from the table, and suddenly, more than anything, you're afraid to turn around, not because it's Gwen, but because it's going to be Gwen in her senior varsity cheerleading outfit, her black pom-poms drooping in front of her, and then you'll be helpless. She'll lead you out to the Ford probably waiting in the parking lot, and it'll be night, the sound of the band still ringing in your head, the smell of October in the stadium lights, and—

You'd be helpless. Unable not to get into that truck, even though you know what she is, what she'll become. It doesn't change the way she looks, the way she can look *at* you.

"Ms. Tracy," Madelyn says curtly. It doesn't match how dismissive her eyes already are. She knows about Fin.

"Madelyn," Gwen says back, her voice tea-party sharp. "I didn't realize you were still up here."

Somehow, Madelyn keeps the smile on her face. "I believe you, um, *know* Mr. Bruiseman here…"

"Yes," Gwen says, holding her purse in front of her with both hands. "Sherilita said he might have gone this way."

"Sherilita," you say, closing the yearbook, hiding the prom picture.

"She told me she thought you were going to mow a lawn or something?"

You smile, look up to Madelyn, let her hold your eyes long enough that you understand she's telling you she can save you here, if you want. She can kick you out of the library, escort you down to some made-up appointment with the principal, *some*thing.

In return, still with just your eyes, you ask where she was three months ago. Where she's been all your life.

"Thanks," you say, and pat the yearbooks. "I'm sure they'll be enough."

She nods once to you, once to Gwen, and leaves you there.

For thirty seconds after you're alone, Gwen doesn't sit, just stands there, her hands crossed over her purse, her alligator sunglasses still on. They go with her widow weeds: the tight black skirt, the charcoal blouse with billowy sleeves like a veil.

"I know what you think of me," she says, finally.

You stare down into the cover of the yearbook. "Doesn't matter. Felson doesn't believe me. Not like I have proof, anything like that."

"Look at me, Nick."

You do, again, then focus on the spines of all the books beside her, their labels all at random places on the spines, no progression at all, no carryover from one year to the next.

"Ask me how I know," she says.

You catch her eye again, and she tells you. "William called me. From the insurance place."

"Junior's son," you say.

She nods, her mouth hard, painted. "You're better than I thought, Nick. Better than I planned."

"I hear that a lot," you lie.

She shakes her head. "You don't get it, do you?"

"Get what?"

"That you're right. The life insurance. Fin. All of it."

"Jim Martindale?"

"Who?"

You close your eyes. "What'd William tell you?"

She takes her sunglasses off, doesn't have any eye-makeup on. "That you were telling Felson that it was a plan. To get Rory out of the way. Collect the money."

"Except?"

"It came yesterday. The check."

You look back to the yearbook. "Did you even cry at the funeral, Gwen?"

"Because you ruined it?"

"You don't know that."

She shrugs, gives your words back to you. "Not like I have proof, anything like that."

"Why'd you even come here?"

"To tell you you were right, I guess. And that I didn't do anything wrong."

You lower your head now, close your eyes to get this part right. Both parts can't be true—either you're right or Gwen's innocent.

You tell it to her like that. Add that either way, Rory's not around anymore.

"That picture Fin took," she says.

"In your bedroom."

"In my bedroom, yes. It was insurance, he said. For if—"

"If he wound up in jail, without you."

"Yes."

"Then he's making it up to—frame you back, for framing him. Making it up about Jim Martindale."

"Jim Martindale?"

"The other man, Gwen. The other backdoor."

This purses her lips, gets her cheeks sucked in, and for a fraction of a second her mask slips, and you see that she's scared here. That she's barely holding it together.

"I don't have to listen to this," she says, already straightening her mask.

You lean back in your chair. "That's just the two I know about, too."

If she were closer, she'd be slapping you again. Instead, at her distance, all she can do is stare.

You rub the side of your nose as if you can't feel the weight of her eyes. "But we're not here to talk about your love life, are we? I mean"—looking at your watch—"I don't have all day here."

She comes to the table, sets her purse between the two of you, sits in Madelyn's wooden chair.

"You recording this?" she says.

"Are you?" you say back.

She rubs a spot on her forehead. "We thought of it in Big Springs. Fin and I. He even wrote a paper on it. A hypothetical situation. It sounded too good, too easy. I guess I was in love or something. Or out of love enough with Rory. You can understand that, I think."

"But."

"But then—I don't know. It's not as easy as it is on *Matlock*, right?"

"Killing somebody?"

She nods. "I told him that we weren't going to do it, that I would try to pay him or whatever. That it was over. And then"—she laughs about this part—"and then guess who swoops back into town?"

"You wanted—"

"Just to make him feel watched. It was supposed to be enough to—to get him to leave, I guess. I don't know."

"But he didn't."

"He wouldn't."

"And he went through with it, too," you add.

She nods.

"And you can prove this somehow?"

In reply, she opens her purse, pulls out a Polaroid.

It's a sister to the one Fin directed you to: the insurance form, blurry, matted against a bedspread, is supposed to prove her story—that the Polaroids *were* insurance for the insurance scam.

"So," you say, studying the Polaroid for longer than you need to—is there a way to tell one from another, by camera, by cartridge?—"so you're here to—to assure me that Fin's in the right place, is that it?"

She shakes her head no.

You lower the Polaroid.

"What then?" you say, your face turned half away from whatever answer she's got.

"I want to hire you again," she says.

You have to smile, then can't stop. Finally manage to shake your head no. Thanks, but no, no. You tap the yearbook in front of you. "Already got a hot case."

"Working for Fin?"

"For Thomas Howard," you say.

She has to focus her eyes deep inside to place him. "Thomas?"

"I'm supposed to find his dad."

Gwen stares at you like you're not making any sense, takes the yearbook, doesn't even spin it around, just flips through it upside down, to the senior portraits, the H's: *Howard, Tom.*

"Sherilita's ex?" you say.

"You don't know him?"

"Tom Howard?"

"He's from—I don't know. Lamesa? Tahoka? Maybe it was after you left."

"Tom," you say.

"Sherilita's dad's land?"

You nod, remember. The stock tank the Lawler kid drowned in was at the corner of one of Sherilita's dad's pastures. "He ran cattle, though."

"It's cotton now," Gwen says. "Tom started poisoning the mesquites before Mr. Jamison was even in the ground. It's his now, I guess. I don't know. You should go see him, though. Sure

you two'd get along great. He's never there when you need him
either."

"That's kind of what this is about."

"Case solved, then. Now you can take mine."

"I don't—" you start, but then her purse is open again. The
bank notes she had that first day in the storage unit are in the
form of a cashier's check now. One-hundred and twenty-five
thousand. She turns it over, signs it, and pushes it at you with her
palm, like she doesn't want to leave fingerprints, doesn't want to
be associated with the blood money.

You stare at it, stare at it, then say just what does she need
here?

She shakes her head, her eyes fixed on you. Disappointed,
maybe. Shrug it off. One-hundred and twenty-five thousand
dollars. A cool eighth of a million.

"Find Dan," she says.

"Dan?" you say.

"My son?"

"I know—"

"He's didn't even come to the funeral. I haven't seen him
in—" and then she starts crying, has to put her sunglasses back
on.

"Dan," you say again.

Gwen has to look away, tighten her lips.

One-hundred and twenty-five thousand dollars, you say inside and
reach for it.

Gwen's hand beats you by little enough that your skin rubs
hers.

On the edge of the table, she rips the check in two, gives half
to you.

"It was made out to you anyway," you say.

"Just find him," she says, "please. We'll cash it together. He's—he's all I have left of Rory. I have to make it all up to him."

It chokes her up too much again and she hustles out, leaving you not with sixty-two thousand and five hundred dollars, but nothing, a worthless piece of paper.

It's the story of your life.

18.

It doesn't take an ex-homicide detective/unlicensed private investigator to guess that Thomas and Dan are together out at Rory's mother's old house with a few cases of beer, a growing pile of cans, maybe a .22 to plink them with. What you do have to be a professional to figure out is that maybe, just maybe, Jim Martindale was Rory Gates in his best Hank Jr. getup, playing you in some elaborate game that backfired, got him shot in the face with a shotgun. By Fin, who's playing you now, trying to get you to set Gwen up?

Maybe. Except you can't trust Gwen, either.

What you want to do is lock yourself into a storage unit with a cooler, let all this play itself out without you. But then Aardvark Custom Economy Storage is all the way across 137, on one of the streets Jimmy Bones is trolling up and down.

If he bailed Arnot King out, too, then he has the little shotgun that was probably used on Rory, is looking to make a trade that involves the cartridge of film you can only get back by springing Fin.

You sit in the library of your old high school and think about it all until you can't think anymore, then decide to take out some insurance yourself. Madelyn lets you use the phone in the nurse's office. You call Stanton PD, ask for Toby Garrett's baby brother.

"You mean David?" the dispatcher says back.

Four minutes later, his voice uneven through the static, Toby Garrett's baby brother answers.

"It's me," you tell him.

"Still at the high school?"

"You don't know that."

"Forgot, yeah. What can I do you for, Mr. Bruiseman?"

"I'd like to report a reckless driver. Maybe he's drunk. I just saw him bouncing off the yellow line on Main."

"From the high school you saw this?"

"That's how bad he's driving."

"Jet-black Lincoln, just out of impound?"

"I saw him coming back from the liquor store."

"You'd sign an affidavit about this."

"In blood."

"And this isn't just to get me bogged down in paperwork?"

"Think of the revenue for a DUI," you tell him. "I know—this driver, he keeps his right hand on the neck of his beer at all times. Calls it safety first."

"So you saw an open container?"

You stare at the wall. "It was like he was showing it off, officer."

Toby Garrett's baby brother laughs about this. "No disrespect, but isn't this like the pot calling the kettle drunk?"

You close your eyes, give him that. "I'll wash her car too, you want."

His mother-in-law. The one who's now getting her lawn mowed for free.

"She has two," he says.

"Lawns or cars?"

"Cars."

"Both, then," you say. "I just don't want any—I'd feel bad if he hit some kid because I didn't report him, y'know?"

"Yeah," Toby Garrett's baby brother says. "Got to keep the streets clean, I suppose."

"I'll meet you later," you tell him. "Explain some stuff. Town & Country. Say, midnight?"

"Midnight," he says back, and breaks the connection.

"That all?" Madelyn says from the door.

You hang up, don't look back to her. "Just doing my duty," you say. "Responsible citizen, all that."

"Yes," Madelyn says. "I remember that about you. So socially conscious. What was your government teacher's name again?"

"Coach Baker," you say with a smile, like that explains everything. Head still down—only way you know to walk these halls—you ease through the door past her, lift your hand in thanks.

"Be careful," she says after you.

Round your shoulders forward. Don't look back.

What you tell Sherilita through the drive-through, from the seat of the riding lawnmower, is that you need to borrow her car.

She smiles through the screen, looks behind you to 137.

You follow, sure that what she's going to be looking at are the headlights of the Lincoln you've been watching for from the carwash all afternoon.

It's nothing, though. Just dusk falling again, pulling night down over Stanton.

"Chopped or sliced?" she says.

"Just for a few hours," you tell her, nodding to her Sunfire parked in what was the shade.

She passes a chopped beef sandwich through to you. You take it.

"What?" she says. "That thing doesn't have headlights?"

Your lawnmower.

You hook one leg over the steering wheel like it's a saddle horn, bite into the sandwich. "Tea?"

She passes a cup over. "Why?"

"The car?"

"Yes, Nick. My car."

"Because I think I know where Thomas is."

This tightens the muscles around her mouth. She gives you her keys, all of them, all at once.

You chew, thank her with your eyes. "That gentlemen from earlier. Was he alone?"

"Your friend from Monahans was with him," she says. "Thought you knew."

You nod like that's that. You have approximately until Jimmy Bones finds you to solve this case enough that it springs Fin. Whether he did it or not. Otherwise, no film. After that, it's hazy, is either Jimmy Bones, you, and the silhouette of a pipe rising and falling, or Jimmy Bones, presenting the murder weapon with your prints on it to Judge Harkness. That way she'll owe him one, at least.

"Midnight," you say to Sherilita, rattling the keys at face-level.

The last thing she says is to bring him back, Nicholas.

You swallow, ease the lawnmower back to Aardvark Custom Economy Storage unit, chain it up, plug it in. Don't notice Betsy

Simms' horse trailer is gone until you have your back to the space it had been in.

It's definitely gone, though.

The reason you're sure is that something else is there now, crunching the gravel.

"Reach for the sky," a voice says.

Arnot King. He steps forward, pulls the toothpick from his mouth, the shadows around him dancing.

"You smell like pesticide," you tell him.

"Yeah, well," he says, throwing the toothpick down, stepping on it like a cigarette, "company I've been keeping, I guess."

The toxic man asleep on the cot in the drunk tank.

"He's still there?" you say.

"Man-shaped roach trap," Arnot King says. "All the rage at your better detainment facilities."

"And the distinguished Mr. Brazos?"

"His second distinguished DUI. An anonymous tip, I think. CrimeWatchers, the officer said."

"The Town Car?"

"At your father's house."

"You?"

He shrugs. "I'm your lawyer, man. Where you go, I go."

"Until you make bail for Jimmy."

"Seven in the a.m."

"It's a one-seater," you say, about the lawnmower.

Arnot King smiles. "I'll run behind."

"I'm on a different case now."

He hooks his head to the side, asks what this town did before you showed up?

You'd kind of been wondering that yourself.

Sherilita's Sunfire is turquoise with faded pink pinstripes, the exact opposite of Gwen's car. Because the plan had been to go out to Tom Howard's place—where Sherilita grew up, north and west of town, if you're remembering right—you head east instead, towards the dump. When Arnot King asks why, you say you were lying about that different case. That you're still trying to get that film back for Jimmy Bones.

"It's out *here*?" Arnot King asks, peering into the darkness, already not believing you.

"The truck," you say. "Guy tailing us the other night? I know where he was going, I think."

"Scene of the crime," Arnot King says.

You nod what you hope is a cop-nod of sorts, start practicing the surprise it's going to be to just find a couple of underage drinkers at the old house instead. Maybe confiscate their beer in the name of law-and-order then back the rear tire of Sherilita's car over a sharp brown bottle.

It should keep you busy until midnight, maybe. Keep Arnot King from your discussion with Tom Howard, which needs to be private. That still leaves seven hours, though.

"Where's the shotgun?" you say, when it's the only thing left to say.

"Safe," Arnot King says. Just that.

You pull onto the first caliche road after the dump-sign and turn the Sunfire's headlights off, like this is a stealth mission. Like there's really a killer out there in the darkness ahead of you.

Arnot King places both hands on the cracked dashboard. "You can see?"

"Shh," you say, and drive slower than you need to.

———

The story Arnot King tells you for the next few minutes is the chicken and the egg one. How it's funny to throw eggs from a moving car, let them splat against a speed limit sign or whatever. From this more than anything, you can tell he's really from Monahans, where the sand hills stretch for miles and miles.

"Fun if you're not hungry," you say.

"No," he says, using both his hands to talk, "listen," and then pushes through to what he was really saying: that, while maybe it's funny to throw *eggs* at signs on the side of the road, let those eggs incubate a few days instead, hatch, then sling a handful of baby chicks at a yield sign at sixty miles per hour, and bam, you're a stone cold killer, an outlaw, a bad man, living in a world of hurt.

"If anybody sees," you add.

"They do," Arnot King says, and smiles, narrows his eyes out to as far as the Sunfire's headlights are reaching. "They always see, man. That's what I'm saying."

"That you—you threw those baby chickens?"

"*Timing*," Arnot King says. "Aren't you listening? Five days earlier, and it's just eggs, just nothing."

You give him that for whatever it's worth and click the headlights up for the next landfill sign. For just a second, before the caliche you've raised drifts in and becomes a nimbus in the Sunfire's brights, it's there, pointing you on.

"Sure it's out here?" Arnot King says.

"Gotta be somewhere," you say back, and lower the lights back down, go with just the parking lights now.

Arnot King shrugs, looks out his window. "You don't get it, man."

"About your chickens?"

"About timing," Arnot King says. "When you called that day, when you were locked up. I was already outside the door, yeah? I mean, if I would have left ten seconds earlier, or if you'd have waited one minute to call—"

"Then none of this would be happening."

Arnot King shakes his head no. "It still would be, I think. I just wouldn't be in*volved*, man."

"But you work for Jimmy. And Jimmy wants those pictures."

"I didn't even know who you were until I went by to borrow a car. Honest. I was just coming over—"

"For the tape I didn't have."

He nods, and you drive, think about it all. "Apology accepted."

Arnot King turns to you in wonder but you just smile, lift your chin to the darkness ahead of you, a second-story window glowing down to black.

"He saw us," you say.

"*What?*" Arnot King says again, turning forward just as you accelerate, and you don't tell him what just happened: with the Sunfire's parking lights on, Thomas would recognize his mother's car.

Less than half a minute later, twin brake lights flare in the front yard of the old Gates house—a truck with an automatic transmission, dropping down into gear—and then the truck starts to move steadily away.

You pull the Sunfire's headlights all the way on and lean forward over the small, plastic wheel. When you cross by the old house after the truck, driving straight into its dust plume, you try to hit as many bottles as you can. The second way you know Arnot King is from Monahans is that, after Sherilita's front tire pops, skidding the Sunfire towards the living room of the old house, he already has his arms locked against the dashboard, his teeth set, both eyes wide open.

19.

WHAT YOU WANT TO BE the tip of an angel's finger coming down to touch you on the back of the head turns out to be the runny yellow dome light that you thought was broke. It flickers on moments after the Sunfire's front bumper plinks into the railing of the porch, a layer of moths drifting up from the contact. Not the afterlife, you tell yourself, watching them rise into the night sky. Even if it should be. But at least the front of the house hasn't fallen down on top of you. Yet.

Arnot King massages his knee. He's grinning thin, happy just to be alive.

The moment he opens his door, the dome light fades out, doesn't come back.

Yes, this too was stupid. You pop the trunk, rummage through Sherilita's junk for the spare.

Soon enough Arnot King is there with you, leaning down so that his fingers, if the trunk were to fall, would be gone.

"Learn that at the academy?" he says, moving back and forth with his shoulders to show he's talking about the stunt-driving.

"Glad you enjoyed it," you tell him, your arm suddenly slipping down below the floor of the trunk, to the factory tools.

"What if that had really been him, though?" Arnot King says, same tone, same voice, everything.

You pull the toy jack out, make no eye contact with him.

"What do you mean?"

He laughs, looks up to the old house the Sunfire's front bumper is resting against. "The truck that followed us the other night," he says. "It was a Ford. I used to have one like it."

You roll the spare out, aim it for a beer bottle by your foot. It hits the bottle, just pushes it deeper into the ground.

"Oh well." Arnot King rolls another bottle over with the toe of his leather shoe. "Try again?"

What he's saying about the Ford is what you didn't expect him to catch: the tail lights of the truck that just pulled away were too low, too square. From the right decade maybe, but still, Chevrolet. Thomas's truck.

"If it had been it," you say, picking your words, "then we'd still be here, I guess. Rocket science."

Arnot King just watches you, disappointed, then tears himself away, looks up to the second floor window. "Scene of the crime," he says. The next time you look up, he's gone. Either peeing or in the house. Maybe both.

You stare out across the pastures, down the dirt road Thomas took out of here.

What Arnot King hasn't guessed is that one truck blasting out of here doesn't make sense—What about Dan Gates? Or, even if him and Thomas had decided to just use one truck, why Thomas's, when they had Rory's tricked-out three-quarter-ton?

It doesn't make sense, but maybe it doesn't matter either. They're kids, were just supposed to do what they've already done: strand you out here, burn some time until you can lose your lawyer on grounds of serious conflict of interest. You crack the lug nuts loose as slowly as possible, acting like they're tighter than they are, then take too long figuring out the magician's wand that, if you fold it just right, say just the right words, will become a jack handle for a few turns at a time. Still though, it hardly takes fifteen minutes to get the tiny wheel off, roll it out into the darkness as hard as you can. Right as it crashes into some dry weeds, you remember it's Sherilita's and notice all of the sudden that you're holding your breath, like you're waiting for something. The tire to roll back? No, but…nothing on the ground. Something else.

The belly of a yellow cropduster plane, banking up from the field. That's it. You track what its course would be, what its course was.

Arnot King interrupts you with your full name. "*Nicholas.*"

He's calling as if from far away.

You pull your eyes from the empty fields, focus on the house. Say it to yourself again: that there should have been *two* of them out here—Thomas, driving away already, and Dan.

You keep the tire iron by your leg, follow Arnot King's voice up the stairs. In the first tiny bedroom, the one that was glowing ten minutes ago, is a dull, upturned hubcap, a bed of coals still smoking in it, beer steaming off them, all the glass in the room swept up against the baseboards.

The next room is the one Rory used as a kid. The one he died in. There's still yellow tape fluttering around the doorframe, meaning the window's gone in there too.

"Check it out," Arnot King says, rolling the wheel of his lighter.

This is the room you were supposed to have stumbled into last week.

It smells like nothing now. The same as outside.

"Not bad, yeah?" Arnot King says, the lighter flickering out, stranding you with the afterimage of all that's left of Rory: kitty litter, to soak up the bloodstains. An evidence flag used once for a photograph then forgotten. A leg-sized hole in the floor, where the pellets from the shotgun punched through, because Rory's head wasn't enough to stop them. His head *and* hands. And whatever he was saying at the end. To—who? Fin? Gwen? Jim Martindale?

Except Rory *was* Jim Martindale. You just didn't see it. Weren't looking for it, didn't know what you were getting into.

It wasn't a suicide either. Because there was no shotgun. Because he signed the insurance form, and everybody knows the insurance doesn't work if you off yourself.

Arnot King strikes his lighter again and you look through the window hole, still waiting for the yellow plane to strain up into the sky, barely clearing a power line, its twelve nozzles still blowing, blowing—

Pesticide.

You focus again on the kitty litter, look up to Arnot King, and then he interrupts you. "There's no glass."

You keep your mouth open, look down to the baseboards.

He's right.

"They swept it up," you tell him. "Evidence."

There's still bottles though, the fingerprints on them twenty years old. Yours, maybe, chalk still trapped in them from the hash marks of whatever town you'd played in that night.

Arnot King runs another toothpick into his mouth. "You were going to say something, detective?"

You look out to the field again. "I have to meet somebody in town at midnight, I think."

Arnot King hooks his head down to the Sunfire. "Your girlfriend?"

You smile one side of your face. "One of my old friends' little brothers. I think I know who did it."

This time, instead of pulling blindly across the packed dirt around the old house, you have Arnot King walk ahead of you to kick beer bottles out of the way. You wind up on the side of the house opposite the road you came in on. You look back to it long enough that Arnot King says, "What, kimo?"

"We don't have another spare," you tell him.

He hooks his chin up the road you're half-on. "Where's this go?"

"The long way."

"Long enough you can explain this-all to me?"

You nod, take the road Thomas already took, and tell Arnot King what you should have seen all along, when Felson got you moved from the drunk tank back to your cell: it was the cropduster. He was committing the perfect crime. The reason there was only your tracks and Rory's at the old house was that he'd set his plane down in the road, or the field, then walked in, walked out. That he was the main and only witness against you, *that* should have been enough. But, if not, there was more: not only had he committed the perfect crime, but now he was hiding in the perfect place: jail. Probably for disorderly conduct or public intoxication, some nothing-misdemeanor he'd been just asking for.

"So he's this—this Martindale character?" Arnot King says. "The one who's real and not made up?"

You hadn't taken it that far yet. But, maybe. Probably. Yes.

"And you didn't recognize him?" Arnot King says, more delicately.

For the third time in a week, you say it: "He was—he had a beard, glasses. A hat."

"His voice, though?"

"I never heard it. In jail, I mean. He just, like, yelled once, maybe."

Arnot King sits back, shakes his head, says like a punch line, "Timing."

You turn to him.

"You could have figured this out a long time ago," he says. "The world was trying to tell you."

You slow for a turn, accelerate too fast out of it, the dump spread out below you. "Maybe it was all a plan," you say. "How else was I going to get Fin to give me that film, if it wasn't in payment for saving his ass?"

Arnot King smiles, isn't buying it for even a moment.

Two seconds later the cab of the Sunfire is flooded with light.

A truck behind you. Right on you.

Arnot King looks at you, his eyes hot. "I thought he wasn't out here?"

"You tell me," you say, and jerk the Sunfire over into a berm and stand on the brakes. The truck flashes past, just a shape in the risen dust.

You kill the headlights, back up, sling the nose around, and take the road you just came up. At the last possible moment, though, the road plummets down into the dump, the incline so sharp you can't even see the packed ruts coming up to meet you.

Arnot King has his hands on the dash, his head turned sideways for the coming impact.

Halfway down the hill you lock the front tires, turn them sideways, plowing up more and more dirt. The one time they catch, threatening to shoot you off into rat-nest refrigerators and cable spools, you whip them back, hit the brakes again, and finally come to a stop, the one thick chain of the gate stretched tight against the Sunfire's windshield, its thin metal No Trespassing sign flipped upside down, tapping the glass.

Neither of you laugh, or breathe.

Across the dump, a pile of trash lights up suddenly: the truck, cresting the hill behind you.

It creeps down at a sane speed, its lights on bright, so you still can't see anything but them.

Dimly, you become aware of Arnot King already out of the car, trying to pull the rusted padlock from the post, the chain scratching across the paint of the Sunfire's hood, Sherilita's antenna already snapped off.

You stand from your side of the car with the tire iron, have to shield your eyes from the truck.

If you're right about the cropduster, then the bad guy's already in jail, and the only person who could have been driving the Ford the other night was Dan, the one Rory bought it for in the first place. Meaning this is either him, in the Ford, or Thomas, in his Chevy.

Twenty feet out, the truck goes down to parking lights, to a square Chevy grill.

Thomas.

He steps out, sees you but doesn't say anything. Says instead, to Arnot King, hunched over the chain, "Mom?"

Arnot King stands, looks to you for an answer.

You let the tire iron fall down into the Sunfire's driver's seat. "Thomas," you say.

He steps to the trunk of the Sunfire, a tire iron in his hand too.

"She's going to be pissed about her car," he says, pity in his voice.

"Happy to know where you are, though."

"That's what you're doing?"

You nod, hope Arnot King isn't about to question this.

"Why out here?" you say to Thomas.

He shrugs, looks away, and you fill your own story in for him: his father was supposed to drop everything, come looking for him, right? It makes sense. If he'd wanted Sherilita to find him, he would have camped out at Aardvark Custom Economy Storage, or the old motel, or on the roof of the high school, or at a friend's, or just in his truck, always moving. Out here, though—farmland—only a farmer would know it. One like Tom Howard, who runs all of Sherilita's dad's old fields. They're checker-boarded all across Martin County. Probably a couple within dirt-clod distance of here, even.

You don't make Thomas actually say any of this—or make him listen to it, either.

"Got enough to eat?" you say.

"Liquid diet, yeah?" he says. "Learned from a pro, you could say."

You lean back against the Sunfire, your arms crossed.

"I told her I'd bring you back," you say, looking at the dump instead of him.

"She paying you?" he says.

"She's a friend."

Thomas nods at Arnot King. "Him too?"

Arnot King lowers his face, waves two fingers' worth of hello.

"Lawyer," you explain. "Never leave home without one."

Thomas shakes his head, chews his gum loud. He comes back from his truck with a beer for each of you. This close to the dump, it's the most right thing to do. Halfway through, he throws his can out into the piles of trash. "Sucks out here anyway."

"Burrito?" you say, tilting your head to town.

"You buying?" Thomas says.

"Who said anything about *buying*?" When Thomas smiles, you add, "I didn't even know you and Dan hung out."

Thomas stops on the way back to his truck, looks to you, then Arnot King. "Dan *Gates*?"

"It's his house," you say.

"Just because his dad died in it?" Thomas says, and then, after you can't think of the next question, the follow-up, he gets into his truck, backs all the way up the hill, leaves his headlights on so you don't drive his mother's Sunfire into an old washing machine.

"What was that about?" Arnot King says, his eyes locked to the mirror on his side, his large hand cupping it, keeping it steady.

You don't know.

20.

THE DREAM YOU HAVE in the last booth at Town & Country lasts, you think, about two seconds. The bite of burrito in your mouth is still warm when you wake back up anyway, but now you have a feeling you didn't have before: that you're sitting in a fiberglass boat in a stock tank that stretches for fifty yards around you in each direction. Standing at the edge of the tank, on the toolbox of a truck you can't see, is the Lawler kid. He's still six years old. You lift your hand to wave to him just as you notice the boat's filling with water, that the water's seeping in through a .38 caliber hole. Slowly, deliberately, like it's a puzzle piece you're placing, you lower the hand you were holding up to the Lawler kid, point your finger like the barrel of a gun, and force it into the hole to stop the water, but then jerk it back out fast when something fine and silky like hair brushes over the tight skin of your fingertip.

"You're one to talk," Thomas says. He's sitting across from you. Evidently.

You rub the dry skin around the corners of your mouth, have no idea what you might have just said.

Standing in front of the coffee machine, waiting on it, his eyes glazed into marbles, is your lawyer. By the register is a beef jerky jar, the plastic kind with a hand-sized hole angled up from the side. If you have a business card, you can drop it in, maybe win a tank of gas. In the forty minutes the three of you have been there, Arnot King has slipped six cards into the jar. He doesn't even have liability insurance, doesn't even have a car.

You take another bite, wipe the bean juice from your mouth and tell Thomas his mom's going to turn into a pumpkin if he's not home in T-minus five minutes.

"What about you?" he says, balling up his burrito paper.

"Meeting somebody," you say, and slide the Sunfire keys across the table. Thomas catches them, looks out to the parking lot. You tell him you'll leave his truck at the water station.

"You just don't want to be the one to give it back to her like that," he says, nodding out to the Sunfire, it's plastic underbumper hanging.

"Tell her to take it out of my expenses."

Thomas shakes his head in what you hope is a total absence of faith in the adult world, but stands anyway. You wave away the two dollars he offers for the burrito.

"Rich man," he says, walking away.

Sixty-seven thousand five-hundred dollars.

Five minutes later, on military time, Toby Garrett's baby brother rolls up in a minivan, parks where you can't see without turning your head. You don't have to, though. You can tell the law is there because one moment your lawyer's watching the coffee drip, a seventh Allegator card palmed in his hand, and the next moment he's faded back to the funnels and lubricants and Brodie knobs of the trucker wall, is keeping his back to the parking lot.

Toby Garrett's baby brother sits down opposite you. "That Thomas I saw?"

You say in your most everyday voice, "It's what I do."

Toby Garrett's baby brother toasts you with his coffee.

"Double shift?" you say about him still being in uniform at twelve when he was in uniform at noon, too.

"Personal time," he says back, and nods out to the wood-panel minivan, his patrol car already checked out to another officer.

You slurp the top off your coffee.

"You said you were going to explain—what?" Toby Garrett's baby brother starts off with.

"My eternal gratitude. For picking up that Brazos character. Keeping the streets of my hometown safe."

"Glad we could be of assistance. Anybody else it would be convenient to you for us to detain?"

You look to Arnot King. He's reading the ingredients or directions off a tube of oatmeal. You remember when they used to have coke glasses buried in them.

"I know who did it," you say, come back to Toby Garrett's baby brother all at once.

He smiles. "Was that supposed to be dramatic?"

You let your head continue its motion past him, settle your eyes on a rack of abridged audio books.

"If you don't want to know…" you tell him.

"I thought you already figured it out once, though," he says. "You were wrong then?"

"I was right then."

"So it's still Gwen and—whoever, that other guy?"

You nod once.

Toby Garrett's baby brother shrugs, leans back in his seat. "So tell the Sheriff, then. Get her to release—"

He stops himself, pulls his bottom lip into his mouth.

"Release Fin?" you say.

Toby Garrett's baby brother nods.

"What?" you say. It's not really a question.

He stalls with another slurp of coffee, grimaces like it hurts, what he just almost told you. What he shouldn't have told you.

You say it again, "*What?*"

He pulls up one side of his face. "You'd have found out anyway. What you and him are talking about on Felson's tape—"

You feel all the blood leave your face, are pretty sure you taste it going down.

"The film?" you whisper.

Toby Garrett's baby brother nods, shrugs again, and says like it's obvious. "He had it on him when he surrendered. It's in his property basket."

"Still?"

"Felson doesn't—it's on the report, but she doesn't know. It doesn't matter, though. Legally, we can't touch it."

You breathe out through your eyes, it feels like. "But, legally," you say, "you could, say, step out for a sandwich down at the water station." He shakes his head no, like this is a joke. "On me," you add.

"Just get him released, you're so sure it's not him. Then everything's above-board."

"I don't have that kind of proof yet."

"Like last time."

Even the people who are supposed to be helping are working against you.

"That was you out at the dump?" Toby Garrett's baby brother says.

You angle your head, catch his eye. "The landfill?"

He laughs without smiling much. "Just hope you weren't fooling around with the crime scene."

"That'd be obstruction."

"Tampering, at least." Toby Garrett's baby brother shrugs. "In addition to offering to bribe a peace officer. A two-dollar seventy-five cent bribe, last time I looked at Sherilita's menu."

"You were there, though," you say, leaning forward, your hands cupped over your coffee like you don't want it to hear the confession he's about to make.

"The dump?"

"The house."

"So?"

"You should have seen it too, then." To explain, you ramp your hand up from the edge of the table, bank it over the napkin dispenser.

"Darryl Koenig?"

"That cropduster?"

Yes.

"Think about it," you say. "One truck out there, the Ford. That *I* left. But, after you eliminate me, who does that leave? You can't *walk* out of there—"

"But you *can* fly," he finishes.

You shoot him with your finger gun, blow the smoke off.

Toby Garrett's baby brother shrugs, doesn't seem to *not* believe you, anyway. It's a start.

"What's he in for?"

"He tried to charge a fifth of vodka to somebody else's account. Out at the liquor store. Made a scene, all that, then assaulted Lan—another officer."

"He only did that to be sure you'd keep him a few days. So he'd be, like, not on the radar. Above suspicion."

"It's a serious offense."

"His first, right?"

"Yes."

You lean back, shrug like it's obvious. It'll get busted down to, at most, resisting arrest. Maybe even just drunk and disorderly, depending on how much shame he can muster up for the judge.

"And that's when he told you about me, right?" you say. "In trade?"

Again, yes.

All so obvious. Look at Toby Garrett's baby brother like you're daring him not to see it. "So I can talk to him? Now that he's not a witness against me?"

"You his lawyer?"

"He doesn't have one?"

Toby Garrett's baby brother follows the tilt of your head to Arnot King, inspecting the baby food now, moving his lips with the ingredients.

"No, please."

"Pro bono," you say. "We'll be there—ten?"

"I come on at eleven."

"Then it's not your concern, is it?"

"Nick—"

"He did it, David. Not just to Rory, but to Gwen, to Dan— to *me*, and Fin."

Toby Garrett's baby brother looks out at his minivan.

"So you're saying Koenig and Gwen Gates, that they—?"

Toby Garrett's baby brother laughs. "Maybe I'll come in early, see the show."

"What are you saying?"

"She's not his type."

"Her type is whoever she can use."

"But—you saw it, Mr. Bruiseman. I mean, Rory Gates. Put him and Darryl Koenig in a room, Koenig isn't the one walking out."

"He had a shotgun. Maybe the element of surprise."

Toby Garrett's baby brother shakes his head. "Surprise? They both just happened to be in that old house?"

Give him that. You'd forgotten the meeting had probably been arranged. But, still.

"And, Rory," Toby Garrett's baby brother goes on, tilting his head over in appreciation, "I mean, he used to be a scrapper, yeah? You don't get a piece of—a girl like Gwen Gates without busting a few heads."

"In *high* school."

Toby Garrett's baby brother leans back. "Felson told me she had to lock him up for it her first year, even. Rented tuxedo and all."

"She should have left him there," you say. "Been safe from her. From Gwen."

"So you really and truly think it's her?"

You nod.

"And all you have to support this is?"

You shrug.

Toby Garrett's baby brother shakes his head in pity. "Felson'll, well, you know."

He doesn't quite manage to swallow his smile. Or cover it with his coffee.

"What would you suggest?" you say. "As a duly sworn officer of the law?"

"Corroborating evidence," he says back. "You say Koenig was wearing a fake beard, right?"

"We'll never find that."

"What *can't* he hide, though, right?"

You study the tabletop between your fingers, finally get it. "The wrecker."

Toby Garrett's baby brother raises his eyebrows in appreciation.

"But Ruby says—" you start. "Manuel, I mean."

"You should talk to Tom Howard," Toby Garrett interrupts. "He's at every auction, tracks every truck, implement, and piece of junk in Martin County, like, I don't know. Like how scientists track all those nuts and bolts in orbit."

"Tom Howard," you say, your eyes losing focus, blurring your hand. You look up to Toby Garrett's baby brother. "That Ford I left out at the house that day. Where is it?"

"It's not still there?" he says back.

You catch yourself. "I wouldn't know."

Toby Garrett's baby brother appreciates this.

"You're not going out there now, are you?" he says. "To Tom's?"

"Sherilita's," you correct.

He doesn't disagree. "You can probably catch him out at the Davidson place in the morning."

"Auction?"

He drains his coffee. "It's Friday now, isn't it?"

"Just barely, yeah."

"If Felson asks—" he says, standing.

"—you were never here," you finish, already looking away, north and west.

The cowbell above the door jangles him out, Arnot King's eyes flicking after him, his head nodding, mouth curling into a smile.

"What now?" he says.

"Ever been to a farm sale?" you say, peering up for his reaction.

On the way out, you fold your half of Gwen's insurance check down to the size of a business card, slide it into the beef jerky jar.

21.

BECAUSE HE'S ALREADY been let down by his dad, doesn't need
you to let him down too, you leave Thomas's truck parked by
the water station before stepping over to Aardvark Custom
Economy Storage for a pocketful of beer.

"I see you're strapped," Arnot King says about the longnecks
angled out of your pants.

"I'm going to get the Lincoln."

"You're what?"

"Want to get it yourself?" you say. "Drive it back without
getting stopped?"

He just stares at you, slides the keys across the coffee table to
you. "You're coming back, right?"

"Like a boomerang." You flip the keys around so they slap
your palm. "Seven, right?"

It's when he's supposed to bail Jimmy Bones out.

Arnot King nods, leans back onto the couch, his eyes already
closing.

From the door, just before it closes, you say, "Got you another
client, too. Ten o'clock." You walk away smiling, knowing that
Arnot King's eyes are open again.

Fifteen minutes later you push the Lincoln's key into the hole in the door, straighten your back when a voice comes up behind you. "I could have had it towed. You think about that?"

Your father. He's sitting on the porch, his hand cupped around the end of his cigar, his legs coming through the wrought iron railing. You, plus thirty years.

"I just—" you say, your eyes closed tight. "This case, I mean. I'm on a case now. We needed to park—"

"I'll have to put a meter up," he says, then laughs at his own joke until it turns into a smoky fit of coughing.

"Remember where the Davidson place is?" you say when he's better.

"Freddy or Nate?"

"The one who farmed."

"Out by the Rankin place, as I recall."

"Up eight—?" You close your eyes for the road number, and he supplies it: 829. The faded two-lane that ghosts 137 for a few miles.

You nod thanks, pull away before he can say anything else. Go faster than you need to with a beer in each of your pockets, your name not on anything in the glove compartment. Back at 137, by the Town & Country, you sit for too long. One way is Aardvark Custom Economy Storage. The other way, north and then west, under 20, is the Davidson place, nestled in that tangle of pastures and houses deep behind the John Deere House.

"Boomerang," you say out loud, like Arnot King should have known better, and duck under 20, close your eyes the whole way past the military surplus. Twenty lost minutes later you park in the tall weeds out by an old stripper basket at the Davidson place. From inside it, behind the steel mesh, a possum watches you. All you can see are her eyes catching the little light there is. The way you can tell she's female, a mother. Moments after she looks towards you, eighteen smaller eyes glow open all along the ridge of her spine, each of them settling on you.

You raise your beer to them, nod once, and, with the bottom of the bottle, lock the Lincoln's door.

You wake clutching the dash, the last half of your second beer splashing into the floorboard.

It's light out, bearded men in mesh caps milling all around, a man with a bullhorn wired to his hip calling out prices in a voice high and plaintive.

On the windshield of the Lincoln, in yellow chalk, is the number 302. It's a joke; the auction crew had to have been working off a list the bank gave them. While they might have to talk to each other to tell a 1978 4440 John Deere from one five years newer, by no stretch is a Town Car with faded dealer plates a farm vehicle.

On the hood of the Lincoln near the headlights are styrofoam coffee cups.

You stare at them until you're pretty sure you're awake, then stand into the farm sale, lean on the roof of the Lincoln to get your feet beneath you. Nobody looks back at you when you close the door, spilling three of the twenty styrofoam cups on the hood, and nobody looks when you surprise yourself with a phlegmy cough that goes on and on, but the moment you bring the heel of your hand up to rub your eye, one of the spotters sees you, raises his finger, and now you're bidding, and everybody's smiling back at you.

"Number—" the spotter leads off, holding his spread fingers

out to you, waiting for you to show him your yellow card, the one all the farmers have poking up from their chest pockets.

You shake your head no, back away to the other side of the cotton trailer the stripper basket's on then keep walking, pushing off from barrel to barrel, truck to truck.

The auction moves on without you, down a row of shop-made trailers, and for a few steps you're lost in the junk, are having to see it as Toby Garrett's brother said it: space debris orbiting Stanton, random pieces giving in to the seduction of gravity, falling into town.

"Not the model you were looking for?" a woman mostly behind you says, her voice curled into a smile.

It's Betsy Simms, still so beautiful without make-up that you have to look away. She's sitting on a rusted toolbar, eating a breakfast burrito. Her mouth full, she points south. "Thanks for leaving the gate open."

You follow, see her horse trailer cocked behind her tall dually.

"Yeah," you say, still waking up, it seems.

"What you're looking for's more blue and silver, right?" she says, tearing off another bite.

The Ford.

She knows its history with you somehow. With you and Gwen. "You should talk to Sherilita's ex, Tom—"

"—Howard," you finish.

She comes back to you impressed, and you look away, to the farmers easing from implement to implement now, nodding to themselves, making jokes too quiet for you to hear, too subtle for you to ever get. You have been gone too long.

"It's his?" you say, not understanding, really.

"For about five minutes," she says. "He bought it two weeks

ago. In a lot of four, I think."

"How do you know?"

She adjusts her flat-brimmed hat lower onto her forehead. "It used to be our hay truck."

"Your—?" you try, not sure at all what the question should be now.

"My dad's, I mean." She squints when one of the auction crew fires up a front-end loader, black diesel smoke billowing up in a thick column.

Her dad. You watch the smoke, finally catch up with what Betsy Simms is telling you: her mom's stuff is in your storage unit, her mom was Mrs. Rankin, the math teacher, so then her dad had to be *Mr.* Rankin, the farmer. The spread next door, practically. The farm sale that happened two weeks ago.

"Rory bought it from Tom," you say. "For Dan."

All these first names. You do need a flip-notebook.

"I'm sure Tom made money on it, though. Knowing him."

You don't need her to explain how it works. You buy a lot of four junk trucks only if you think you can turn around, sell them for more one by one.

"Not that Rory's ever got cash on him," she adds.

You flash on the *St. Nick* check, have to agree.

"What else was in that lot?" you ask.

"You should talk to Tom," Betsy Simms says.

"Which one is he?" you say about the farmers bunched together at the front-end loader.

Betsy Simms rubs the corner of her mouth with the ball joint of her thumb. It's a man's gesture, what you do when you're used to wearing gloves, but it looks good on her. Perfect, even. She angles her head to see through the sea of caps and hats, then opens her mouth, closes it again. "It's late July, isn't it?"

You nod.

"Late July for him means Kansas. They always have a big sale up there about now. He usually makes a week out of it, I think. That beer up there's three-two, right?" She laughs to herself. "Makes him feel like Superman."

You fake a silent laugh, like you know what she means. "No offense here, but you know his business pretty well, yeah?"

She loses her smile, settles her eyes on you.

"What are you saying, Mr. Bruiseman?"

You shake your head no, nothing, understand in a flash why Sherilita recognized Betsy Simm's truck and trailer so fast through the mini blinds of the water station: she was the reason for the divorce. Or one of the reasons—probably the last. Tom Howard, the ladies' man.

You wonder if Thomas knows and lose yourself for a moment thinking of Betsy Simms walking across a freshly-plowed field, towards a tractor, then come back to her as she is now, to ask her about the other three trucks in that lot Tom Howard bought. Whether her father had had an old wrecker, maybe. Whether a certain cropduster might have been looking under the hood that day.

The way she's looking at you shuts you up, though.

"Thought you were supposed to be providing security in town?" she says. "That you were there all the time, keeping our stuff safe?"

"I am," you say. "I'm just—" but then, in the silence after the front-end loader's sold, you hear a more familiar sound: the Lincoln, turning over.

They're selling it too.

You look back to Betsy Simms and she just raises her

eyebrows, takes another bite.

Maybe one mile across the pasture and the field is the husk of her father's farm. You try not to look at it too much when you ask her where she got that burrito.

Halfway through the field, walking at right angles to go straight, because it's easier to stay in a furrow for a few yards at a time, Nate Davidson's large barn between you and the auction, a memory wells up in the back of your throat: hay.

You've been across this field before, when it was just pasture land, a horse trap. You were eleven, maybe, on a cotton trailer mounded with bales of hay. It was a Halloween ride Sherilita's dad had rigged up for the fifth graders.

You track the narrow field west to where Sherilita's house was—*is*—where her dad had been pulling you. It's Tom Howard's now. Not all the way, though. He doesn't know about the hay ride, never had that part of Sherilita that turned her head to watch the tall tires of her dad's tractor turning, turning, his hand on the fender so he could sit sideways in the seat, make sure no one fell off his cotton trailer, got left behind.

It takes ten more minutes to touch the barn of the Rankin place, catalogue the leftovers of the auction two weeks ago: the cab of a model A, rusted so far into the ground that it would crumble if you tried to winch it out; tractor tires rotting on their sides; a cotton trailer that somebody bought, tried to pull away, but the front set of wheels stayed in place, let the floor of the trailer slide over them. The grease caps on all its wheels on the side you're on are Diet Dr. Pepper bottles cut in half at the shoulders. The few sand fighters and breaking plows that haven't been picked up yet still have yellow chalk numbers on them. It hasn't rained for weeks. You keep your hand to the side of the barn, step around it, watching the windows of the old house the whole time. It's empty, though; the last person in it, probably, was Betsy Simms, loading her mother's cardboard boxes into the horse trailer.

You make your way to the end of the barn, holding your breath for what you hope is going to be *some*thing, and get more than that: the Ford. It's nosed under a broken-limbed peach tree, behind the three gas tanks.

You touch the keys in your pocket. "There you are, then."

This would be the best place to hide it, after all. The place it would be least out of place—the place it's been the last fifteen years, probably, since Gwen's dad retired it to be a work truck.

On its windshield again, the best camouflage: *43* in yellow chalk. As if Rory never picked it up, never paid Tom Howard for it. Which, according to Betsy, you guess he probably didn't. Or, according to him, it was *Dan* who didn't.

Either way, it's here, isn't it?

You walk across to it, touching everything on the way over, finally stop at the bed. In a direct line from the Ford, over its steering wheel probably, is the wrecker you've already ridden in once.

It's pulled up to a pop-up camper trailer with flat tires.

For ten minutes, maybe, you just watch it, don't want to look away.

This is where it came from. The wrecker. Tom Howard bought it in a lot of four, traded it off to Darryl Koenig. Not for cash, even, but services. Cropdusting. A line of ownership nearly impossible to follow, but you have. And you didn't even need to dig Tom Howard up to do it, either, which is better— now you won't owe him anything, can talk to him straight about

Thomas, about Sherilita.

But that's all later.

Felson will have to believe you now. The wrecker *exists*. There are prints in it, even, if she wants to go that far.

You edge your way up to the wrecker like it's a skittish horse, like if you can just touch it—

It doesn't explode, is just an old truck with a flatbed, and an arm bolted onto that bed. You look through its rusted cables and chains to the Davidson place, Betsy Simms still sitting on her toolbar maybe, and then, unasked-for, you see all at once what the missing glass in Rory Gates's boyhood bedroom has to mean: the window fell out the *other* way, from the inside.

Shot out, maybe?

Again, you're standing on the wood plank floor, looking down through the ragged hole, kitty litter crunching under your feet.

You only come back when the stunted door of the pop-up camper opens.

For a few long seconds, you and Dan Gates try to make sense of each other, and then he's running hard, jumping discs you have to skirt, one-handing fences you have to hold the wire down to step over.

You chase him out into the pasture on the other side of the house, then lean down on your knees just to breathe, watch his bare back until it drops into a draw you didn't know was there, and he's gone, a rabbit gone to ground.

What you want to tell him with your hands cupped around your mouth is that it's okay about the other night. That you're sorry. That his mother, she's—

It's better that you didn't catch him.

On the way back to the wrecker, you stop at the stock tank,

cup water up to your face, finally just push your whole head under, open your eyes. Wonder if this is what it's like, then. Five minutes later you open the door of the camper, wait for your pupils to adjust.

It's what you expected: grocery sacks, magazines, a battery-run little television still on at the foot of the stubby couch mat Dan's been sleeping on during the day. The mat of his night bed is crossways at the front of the trailer.

You turn the television off so his batteries won't be all the way gone by the time he slinks back and almost have the door closed again when you see what isn't there, what Thomas had out at the old house, what any sixteen-year old kid's going to need: beer.

Does Dan, Rory Gates's *son*, not drink?

It's not the kind of question you can ask Gwen, really.

Just in case it disappears, before you leave, you copy down the license and VIN of the wrecker, then find yourself watching the stock tank again, know that if there's beer anywhere on this property, then it's there, hanging on a wire deep underwater.

You don't want it that bad, though.

The Ford starts for you on the fourth try, but you have a better idea.

22.

DURING YOUR INITIAL HOMICIDE ORIENTATION two years ago , the detective you rode with to learn procedure—an old man named Sanders, who claimed to still remember Midland ranchers storing hay in the office buildings along Wall Street during the Depression—told you that every investigation is a math problem: all you do is add the numbers together, carry the one, and then look at the bottom of the page for the answer.

Because you were still a hero, and because he'd probably done all twelve grades in one classroom and never had a Mrs. Rankin to test him on the quadratic formula, you'd asked him where algebra fit in?

In answer he'd rubbed his nose in the shameless way of old men, shrugged, and said that that kind of fancy arithmetic was what you might call a *murder* investigation—the kind of problem where you already have the answer, a dead person, then all this evidence bunched up on the other side of the equals-sign. Your job as a detective, then, is to arrange the evidence in such a way that only one variable will work with them to produce a dead body. And that variable, that x, that's your killer.

"What if there's two or three x's?" you'd asked.

"Then the second x is y, the third's a z, and it's conspiracy, as long as it all adds up right."

It had made your head hurt. And you'd never learned the quadratic formula like Mrs. Rankin taught it anyway. For some reason, it makes you feel guilty about stealing the wrecker and the Ford from her husband's place.

The deal you make in your head with her is that if you can just get the wrecker primed, jumped, then figure out the lift enough to tow the Ford, you'll look at one of Thomas's algebra books.

It's the least you can do.

And it's not like you promised to *open* it or anything.

You might be disgraced, an outcast from the police, a reject in your own town, going through drive-throughs on lawnmowers, but still, you're not low enough yet for tenth grade math.

Because Betsy Simms might still be watching from the Davidson place, you don't take the cut-across to 137 but pull the Ford all the way back to 829 instead. Its tailgate pops open going over the cattle guard but doesn't drag sparks on the asphalt, so you keep going, the wrecker wrapped up high in second gear, and you only realize you're touching the steering wheel with bare skin when you're back by the military surplus.

You try to wipe your prints off with the rag from the dash, leave just Darryl Koenig's, then drive with the heels of your hands past the Town & Country, your heart slamming into the walls of your chest because this is like coming back from the ocean with a thirty-foot killer shark strapped to the side of your rowboat. If you can keep it straight in your head, you might even use Sanders's algebra to explain to Sheriff Felson that Koenig the cropduster is the only variable that can make Rory's death make sense.

With the evidence of the wrecker, it'll be obvious to her that you were set up to finger Fin for the murder. Then, like a series of gears, she'll have to let Fin go, and you'll be waiting for him at the property desk, and then you can carry the film back to Aardvark Custom Economy Storage, where Jimmy Bones and Arnot King have to be waiting. Maybe you'll give it to Jimmy Bones or maybe he'll buy it, you're not sure yet.

Either way, you'll be back in the game.

You swing wide for the final turn to the sheriff's office, and see at last what you probably should have seen a quarter of a mile ago, if the Ford hadn't been in the wrecker's rearview: a dark Lincoln Town Car shadowing you.

You swallow, look back to the road, weave the wrecker to see the Lincoln in your side mirror now.

No auction number. It's Gwen.

You straighten back up, bite your lower lip, and grip the thin steering wheel with your whole hand now: it's a parade. First the wrecker, then the Ford, then the second variable, the real killer. The one too pretty, too grief-stricken to suspect.

By the time you park longways across the four handicapped spaces of the court house, she's coming at you across the road, her purse clutched tight to her side.

The first thing she says is about the Ford. "It's already broke down?"

For a moment you don't understand, but then look back to it, its front tires hanging, the bumper knuckled under from the tow straps you know you didn't quite figure out right.

"Thought you'd be more interested in this—in the evidence?" you say, nodding down to the wrecker.

She shrugs like she doesn't have time for this. "You're saying you found him?"

"The cropduster?"

"The—*what?*"

"Mr. Darryl Koenig," you announce, both hands in your pockets.

Her eyes behind her alligator print sunglasses track across the name letter by letter, and then she nods to herself, ducks her head forward, unsure. "That Future Farmer of America from Greenwood?"

"You've got this down good," you tell her.

"Listen," she says, cupping her forehead in her hand. "You have Dan's truck. This means you found him, right? Is he all right? Why isn't he with you?"

You try to process at least some of this—that she's interested in the gimme-case, not the one that's going to put her away.

"Yeah, I found him," you say. "It's what I do, right? Last time I saw him, he was"—you nod to yourself, as if confirming this in your head—"yeah. He was crossing Mrs. Rankin's north pasture."

"*Janey* Rankin?"

You had never considered that Mrs. Rankin might have a first name, but shrug sure all the same. "He's been sleeping in a little hideaway camper thing. You want, I can move him into town, a little efficiency unit I've got..."

When she doesn't smile, you do. But have to look away from her, too. She touches you light on the bicep. You turn back to her, your mouth formed around a word you haven't even thought of yet, but before you can say it her forehead is against your chest and she's crying. Saying she's sorry for getting you involved, that it was never supposed to be like this, that—

She finishes with the fingers of her other hand stuffing her half of the insurance check into your chest pocket.

You spread your pocket to see it, and then she's pushing away from you, the kind of push you always imagine one person would give another if they were both standing in a road, a pair of headlights coming fast.

You try to say your word again, still don't know what it was going to be—what did you say to her in the truck, that first time, when it was done and neither of you knew whether to laugh or kiss, cry or get married?

It doesn't matter.

In four long scrapes of her slingback heels she's across the road, behind the dark windows of her Lincoln. Her right rear tire breaks free a bit, spits a handful of gravel up into the afternoon.

"Display of acceleration..." Toby Garrett's baby brother says from behind you.

"You'd write *me* up for it," you tell him.

"You're not a grieving widow."

You look at the wrecker one more time and ask if the good sheriff's in.

Toby Garrett's baby brother smiles wide, nods like this is an inside joke. Before you can turn to go inside, he points with his chin down the block, toward your lawyer.

He's waving his arms wide like you're landing a plane.

If you were, then what he'd be telling you is *pull up, pull up. Don't land.*

You lift your hand back to him and hold it there, trying to tell him that it's all right, that everything's fine now.

Deep in the shade of the awning is another more compact figure: Jimmy Bones.

From across all this distance, you can feel him watching you.

It makes you feel like—like a South American president, your arm up to the crowd, the crosshairs settling on you.

You bring your hand down to the back of your neck, to your chin. Pull at the loose skin of your throat.

"What's that about, you think?" Toby Garrett's baby brother asks.

You look at Arnot King still trying to signal you away. "As my lawyer, I guess he doesn't want me to park in an illegal fashion."

Toby Garrett's baby brother tries hard not to smile. "Remind me to write you up for that later." He holds the glass door open for you, the refrigerated air of the sheriff's office rushing out, making you look away at the last moment to the squat, black form of Jimmy Bones, Panhandle-division 9-ball champion for three years running. The cane he's walking away on is painted like a cue, has an ornate bridge-rig for a handle. Moving beside him, the lanky, raggedy shape of your lawyer, looking back to you the same as you're looking at him.

"Coming?" Toby Garrett's baby brother says, stepping aside.

"Of course," you hear yourself say.

Of course.

23.

At the tall front desk, Toby Garrett's baby brother peels off, nods ahead to Felson's office.

Through her open door you can see one side of her desk, part of her left arm.

This is the beginning of the end of your first case as an unlicensed PI. She won't like that you've solved her murder for her, but, hey, what did she expect? If she wanted all the glory, she should have kept you locked up when she had the chance. Even then, you probably would have broke out somehow.

Live-in security guard for a storage facility? That's just a cover, ma'am. One of many.

You pause before you're in her office, knock lightly on the wall.

She leans over, narrows her eyes at you, lets her face twitch into a smile.

"Mr. Bruiseman," she says, very formal, waving you in with just her hand, "we've been waiting for you."

"We—?" you start and then forget how to breathe. In one of the two conference chairs is Judge Sheila Lynn Harkness.

"Detective," she says, angling her head over, her metallic red hair spilling down across her not insignificant left breast.

You manage to say, "Your honor."

"Sit down," Felson directs.

You guide yourself into the chair.

Felson and Harkness sit watching. By degrees, you learn to breathe again, are even able to fake the smallest possible smile. "This about me?"

"You could say that," Harkness says.

You keep your smile, swallow, the saliva loud in your ears.

"Nice of you to drop by like this," Felson says. "Saves us some footwork."

You nod as if accepting her gratitude, have to consciously make yourself stop.

"I was—I was bringing evidence," you say. "Math."

Felson leans forward so you can say it again.

You close your eyes, start over. "I found that wrecker I told you about. It's real."

"I know," Felson says, and for an instant you forget about Harkness, are only aware of Felson. "Dan said you were messing with it when he left."

Dan, Dan. It takes saying his name a few times to attach it.

"He's *here*?" you say.

Felson stands to wave him in.

You turn awkwardly, watch him rise from the chairs on the other side of the glass door you walked in. He's wearing clean clothes, has his hair plastered down to his skull, must have had Rory's tall truck parked in the bottom of the draw he was running for.

"Mr. Bruiseman," he says, and holds his hand out.

You look from it up to him, then back to Felson.

She explains: "He said you were probably going to—that you were going to accuse him of trespassing, stealing, loitering, something like that."

You shake your head no.

"Show him," Felson says.

Dan unfolds a yellow receipt from his pocket. It's from the auction two weeks ago. The item paid for with a check was one camper, lot 14. The buyer was Rory Gates.

"We were going to fix it up for the lease down at Robert Lee," he says, not looking at any of you.

"And the—the wrecker?" you manage.

Felson answers for him: "It's not his, Mr. Bruiseman."

"It's not supposed to be. It's Darryl Koenig's."

Felson leans back in her chair, studies you.

"He's the one who did it," you say.

It sounds more like a question now than it did on the drive over.

Sheriff Felson smiles, likes this. "And he did it because...?"

"Because Gwen—" you start, but Felson interrupts, stands to usher Dan Gates out, shut the door behind him. She stares at you all the way back to her chair.

"He did it because Gwen Tracy told him to."

"Gwen Gates," Felson corrects. "This isn't high school anymore."

You squint, knew that. "It was her, ma'am."

Felson shakes her head back and forth, her eyes never leaving yours. "So we're back to that again?"

You settle the plate number and VIN onto the edge of her desk in response.

She doesn't even look at it.

"Why not Dan himself?" she says. "Since you're accusing everybody and all."

You stare at her paperclip-holder, consider it.

"He had access to the tow-truck, right?" she says.

"It wasn't—he's not Jim Martindale."

"But Darryl Koenig *is*?"

"Was, yeah."

Harkness pops a bubble with her molars, makes you think about her breasts.

"And your little…" Felson says, motioning out front to the wrecker, "your little grand-theft auto today. It's supposed to somehow prove this beyond a reasonable doubt?"

"It's Koenig, ma'am. The cropduster."

"And you'd bet your life on this, Mr. Bruiseman?"

You collapse a little inside. "I've bet it on less."

Ten awkward minutes later, most of which you spend in the bathroom hiding from Harkness, Toby Garrett's baby brother props Darryl Koenig up in the door of Felson's office, then takes a step back.

"Mr. Koenig," Felson says.

He peers out at the office like he's been underground for days. He's wearing a jumpsuit now, has his hair washed. It spills down across his shoulders.

Felson introduces you and Judge Harkness.

Koenig keeps his eyes on Harkness until Felson asks him if he bought or found himself driving a tow-truck at any time in the last seven to ten days.

"Gonna pin that on me too?"

"Just answer the question, Mr. Koenig."

He leans forward to trail a line of spit into Felson's planter. "What'd it do, this tow-truck?"

"Were you at the Rankin farm sale two weeks ago?" Felson says.

"I don't even go to Rankin anymore," Koenig says, his upper lip raised at the idea.

"It was an auction here in town."

"They selling planes?"

Felson shakes her head no.

Koenig flashes his gap-toothed smile, and you ask him if he didn't buy the truck from Tom Howard, maybe?

"Howard?" he says, shaking his head with disgust. "You see him, give him this from me," and then he brings his hand up to your face, extends his middle finger.

"It's okay," Felson says, staring at Koenig now. "This would have been…Thursday, Mr. Bruiseman?"

You nod, your teeth set, Judge Harkness smiling at you the whole time.

"Thursday," Koenig says, smiling again, waggling his eyebrows. "Got to say, sheriff. Thursday's a little cloudy to me."

Felson stares at him for one moment more, then nods to Toby Garrett's baby brother to take him back to his cell. After Koenig disappears she punches the intercom on her phone, asks for Darryl Koenig's logbook.

Two minutes later an officer you don't know brings it in. It's creased and stained from living in Koenig's back pocket, smooth on one side like he keeps it behind his wallet.

Felson keeps the palms of her hands as far from it as she can and flips to the last page Koenig filled in, the day before the night he was arrested at the liquor store. She spins the book around for you to read.

"Go on," she says, when you don't lean forward.

Harkness leans forward with you. Her hair smells like it would taste of fruit.

"Cloudy," she says, leaning back into her chair.

What the logbook has Koenig doing Thursday until 9:22 is spraying, flying, cropdusting. You flip back a few days and see that in spite of his attitude and appearance, Darryl Koenig's logs are meticulous. As if he's had them called into question once or twice before.

You pretend to read the logbook longer than you really do, try to focus on the words and numbers and *think*.

Nothing's coming.

Felson lifts the phone to the side of her head. "Should we confirm this, Mr. Bruiseman?"

You stare at her stapler, don't answer. Koenig has long hair. Sitting across the seat from you in the wrecker last Thursday, he couldn't have hidden long hair from you, even if you weren't looking for it. And his voice, the nasal way he sounds, like he wants you to hit him—

It's not him.

Then, who?

Dan Gates, like Felson was joking?

"Detective?" Harkness says from her comfortable chair.

Back in her throat, Felson chuckles, settles the phone back down onto its base.

You shake your head no about Dan Gates. Not just because Rory was his father, and not the *guilty* one anyway—the one stepping out with an ex-con—but because he's sixteen, seventeen, not smart enough to have orchestrated it all—Jim Martindale, the guilty shotgun in Fin's trailer, his mom hiring you. And, anyway, you know from the way he hit you over and over last week that he's really grieving. He didn't want this to have happened. It's not about guilt with him, but unfairness. He's tasting it for real for the very first time, and in the worst way.

If not him, though, and not Koenig, and not Fin, then *who*? Gwen? Did she do it herself?

You raise your face back to Felson.

"What?" she says, but you shake your head, haven't thought it through yet. How Gwen could have walked, drove or hitched home from the old house.

It would explain why it was an execution, though. Toby Garrett's baby brother said it: Rory Gates could fight, *would* have fought. Unless it was his wife, and he was daring her, on his knees, saying she'd already taken everything else, why not this too?

"I've got—" you start, your arms cocked back on the armrests of your chair, but Felson opens her hand, stopping you.

"There's still the matter of..." she starts.

Instead of finishing, she sets her silver microcassette recorder up on the desk. From the way Harkness looks over to you, you know she's heard it—heard you and Fin in the interrogation room, talking all around the film that's not supposed to exist anymore. As if to hide it, you lift the recorder from its perch, study it in your hand.

"Obviously that's not the only copy," Felson says.

You pretend not to have thought it might have been.

"Detective," Harkness leads off, finally getting around to why she's here in the first place. "If memory serves, you swore, promised, and vowed that you had surrendered all of the... incriminating evidence. That you were starting over."

"It's something different," you lie. "What we were talking about."

She smiles. "And that would be why Jimmy Bones is out on the sidewalk? Isn't he the one who requested your services back then? For his friend's...*wife*?"

Don't say anything here.

"Look at it from my bench," Harkness says, leaning forward, one hand in the other. "You were supposed to deliver certain products to him. Now, months later, after the heat's died down, he's come to retrieve them."

"I gave them all."

Harkness restarts her gum, shrugs to you. "I'm confident you're telling the truth, Detective. Because, if you weren't—"

She nods to Felson, who finishes: "We still have you for impersonating an officer in Big Springs. That's a federal facility. So, federal charges. And taking Rory Gates's truck for a joyride. And distributing alcohol to minors. Driving an unauthorized lawn maintenance vehicle on public roads." She smiles about that one. "Not to mention attempting to obstruct a murder investigation, hiding evidence, breaking and entering—"

"Breaking and—?"

"We found your prints in Fin's mobile home."

You look down to the leg of her desk.

"As well as in your lawyer's stolen Mustang," she adds. "There's even unofficial reports that you were back in Midland County for a night, Mr. Bruiseman."

"All of which can become an issue," Harkness finishes.

"What about today?" you say.

They both look to you, wait.

"Another auto theft," you say, "right?" You nod out Felson's window for her, to the wrecker, the Ford. "To say nothing of parking in four handicapped spaces at once."

Felson shakes her head in something like disbelief.

Harkness laughs, tells you you're digging a hole here.

"More like a grave, right?" you say, pushing up from the chair now.

"I don't need to tell you that if a fifth roll surfaces—" she starts.

You look up to Felson.

"Can I return the trucks, at least?" you say. "One less charge, I suppose."

Felson narrows her eyes at you, considers this. Finally shrugs what the hell.

You give her the same shrug back, nod once to Harkness, say, "Judge." It means goodbye.

"Detective," she says back. It means see you later.

As you're walking out her door, Felson asks what you're really up to here?

Where she can't see, you smile.

Because you're on a holy mission, the wrecker starts for you without the jumper cables. It would have been complicated anyway, dropping the Ford, pulling it around to the front of the wrecker. Felson and Harkness watching.

What you've got to do, you've decided, is get Gwen to confess. It's the only way. Otherwise she's pulled off the perfect murder, pretty much. She's even given away the money from it. Maybe she even *feels* bad about it now, a week after the ugly fact. But that doesn't make her innocent. Not by a long shot. The rub, though, is that there's not any physical evidence tying her to the murder. The only thing that can convict her now, get Fin out, get you the film, either save you from Harkness or fry you with Jimmy Bones, is if she confesses. And if you can record it on the silver microcassette recorder Felson hasn't missed yet.

You think you can make this happen, too. She's stressed, close to the edge, ready to spill it all. More than that, the way she grabbed your arm, how it felt protective, it cued you into something else—that she *does* care about something, about some*one*.

Dan.

The way to get her to confess is to tell her what Felson said when she was illustrating for you how ridiculous all your theories were, trying to one-up you: that Dan shot Rory.

Maybe she'll get all maternal, take the blame that's hers in the first place.

And where she's going is where you're going, where she thinks Dan still is. The Rankin place. Never mind that Dan's already in town.

It's beautiful.

You go over it again, try to keep it straight in your head, and steer with your knee, both hands fiddling with the recorder, looking for the voice-activated mode.

The next time you look up you're almost to 137, by the Town & Country. On the side of the road, his cane lifted, flagging you down, it's Jimmy Bones.

You brake with reluctance, the wrecker's ancient drums barely enough to stop it and the Ford both, even ten yards past Jimmy Bones and, stepping from behind a dead tree, Arnot King. The Ford swings forward on the straps, its nose clinking against the arm of the wrecker, and then it falls back, pulling you a couple of feet back, closer to Jimmy Bones.

Arnot King opens the door for him.

"Gentlemen," you say, and feel suddenly like Jim Martindale, not picking somebody up off the side of the road because you want to—because you're nice—but because you have to.

Jimmy Bones works his way over to the middle of the bench seat, plants his cane into the hump of the floorboard like a second gearshift, and Arnot King pulls the door closed.

"Guess you'd be looking for your car, right?" you say, groaning onto 137.

Jimmy Bones's chest rises and falls in what you think is a laugh.

By your best guess, he's sixty-two years old, five-seven in boots, but still: the reason he could raise a pipe over you, let it fall, it has nothing to do with size or strength. With him it's more about demeanor. And that, if you resist the pipe he's known for, he'll extract the famous .22 from his shoulder rig, rest the barrel between the back of your jaw and your ear.

Three times he's been up for homicide, and three times he's skated. It's made him a legend, the big fish Homicide never could quite reel in, the math problem Sanders could never add up right.

He's not somebody you can pretend you didn't see on the side of the road.

Instead of closing your eyes as you pull under the missile angled over the fence of the military surplus, you hold your breath, hope that's good enough.

"I supposed to say something here?" you finally ask, because, for once, even Arnot King is quiet.

Beside you, Jimmy Bones lifts one shoulder in answer. "The lady judge doesn't know you have it."

"Maybe I don't."

"Then keep driving," Jimmy Bones says, nodding to all the empty pastureland ahead, past 829. "I should imagine we can settle this now."

You turn onto 829. "I was just saying maybe."

Jimmy Bones doesn't look over.

"Where we going this time?" Arnot King says, leaning forward to catch your eye for a flash, like he's on your side here.

"To get your car," you say. "I left it out here. To keep it safe."

Arnot King doesn't call you on this.

"Is the film in it?" Jimmy Bones says.

You rattle over the cattleguard to the Rankin place, shudder up into third. "In a manner of speaking."

Jimmy Bones looks over, waits for you to explain.

You hand over hand the wheel to swing around Mrs. Rankin's house and tell him that if you can just get the woman who's out here on tape saying the right things, then the ex-con who's come into possession of the film will get cut loose, hand it over.

"Hmn," Jimmy Bones says, switching hands on the end of his cane so that the left one is under now, the right on top. "So this is what you do now, solve other people's murders?"

"Better than my own," you say, and slide to a sudden stop when Gwen's Town Car is on the other side of a rusted tank.

"That's not it," Arnot King says. "Mine's black, as I recall."

You're already stepping down, the wrecker still running. You point to the Davidson place for him. "It's over there. Number three-twelve, I think."

"Three-*what*?" Arnot King says, but you're already walking away, the sharp, dry weeds cracking around your thighs, grabbing at your fingertips.

The pop-up camper looks naked without the wrecker nosed up to it.

You hear Arnot King grind into second behind you and pull around Gwen's Lincoln, but you don't look back. Maybe the Town Car with *Carlotta* plates will be there, maybe it won't. Either way, you have to talk to Gwen, have one single conversation with her where she says real things, where she's not the one with the angle.

Because she has to be in the pop-up camper, out of the sun, you knock twice on the door and step back, the right corner of your lips pulled between your teeth, the recorder high in your pocket, mic facing out.

After thirty seconds you knock again, then step inside saying her name.

She's not there.

You stand in the doorway and survey the Rankin place, consider that she could be in the house but decide not. That would be real trespassing, would be you going into somebody's private space, not just their boxed-up junk.

She is a murderer though, you remind yourself, and then study the barn, finally nod about it, that it would be cool enough for a woman with make-up, maybe. The concrete floor, the shotgun doors front and back to pass the wind through. A good place to wait for Dan, to watch.

To have a final showdown, you add, liking it.

And the acoustics are probably decent in there too.

You walk to it with your eyes half-closed, because she might have a gun now, somehow, but she hasn't read the script you've already written for her, doesn't know where she's supposed to be.

From the tractor-wide doorway you look back to her Town Car, pan all around again, not real sure what to do.

Was there some *other* vehicle here she could have left in?

You shrug, realize what a good idea it would be to make sure her keys aren't in the ignition, and then see her again an hour ago, taking her four skidding steps across the street, right after stuffing the partial check into your pocket. Past her, you think— *know*—was Rory's tall three-quarter ton that you definitely should have clued in on, if you were any kind of real PI.

You walk slower, to be sure, to see it again in your head. Tell yourself that just because *you* didn't register it at the time— as far as you knew then, Dan was still out here, in the draw— that doesn't mean she wouldn't. The prize truck of the man she killed? The one her son's been driving, her son she's hired you to look for?

She would think every truck was that truck, would be looking twice at anything tall and white.

But still, she came out here.

You shake your head slow back and forth, open her door, have to sit down to be sure the keys aren't there, that she can't strand you.

Satisfied—with that at least—you plant your hand in the seat to climb up, back into the heat, but are heavy enough that the Town Car rocks the slightest bit, and you see what the sun's been trying to tell you: dangling from the cigarette lighter is a simple wedding band, worn thin on one side, dull everywhere else. The one Gwen had to identify Rory with.

You take it, hold it up, try to make sense of the barely-there 5, 2 or *N* etched into its underside, then smile, see that you can look through it like a telescope, can pan across all the derelict cotton trailers for Gwen.

This isn't how the real private eyes do it, you know.

This isn't how anybody does it.

You hang the ring back onto the lighter knob, drop it, and scrabbling on the floor mat for it—probably the kind of thing she wants to hold onto—find Gwen's alligator skin purse instead.

You open it with the back of your fingers, like it might be rigged to blow. When it doesn't, you let the gum wrappers and lipstick tubes and credit cards spill out, roll towards the backrest of the passenger seat.

The last thing is light enough that you have to pull it out, by the corner: a white cash envelope from the bank, the flap tucked into the body, not licked shut.

You lay it on the seat like a thing that was once alive, might still be, and look all around for Gwen. Because you don't want to get caught in her purse like this. But you have to know, too.

Slowly, with the edge of one of her credit cards, you lift the flap, pull out the only thing the envelope has for you: the invoice for Rory's headstone. A photocopy of it. You set it down on the seat, dig through the rest of the stuff that's spilled from her purse. Why *photocopy* it? A scrapbook or something? For Brock & Associates, maybe? Wouldn't a real live death certificate be more legal?

Crumpled, stuffed, and hidden in the rest of the trash are six more photocopies, some of them weathered, it looks like, dried in the sun. Like the headstone guy thinks she's going to leave town or something, or needs her confirmation, or keeps wanting to remind—

That's it.

Somebody *else* knows what she's done, that she killed Rory. Has been leaving these under the windshield blades.

It would explain her nerves in the library the other day. And why she doesn't want the money anymore.

You shake your head, put the envelope back, put it all back. Getting Gwen to confess is going to be easier than you thought. She might even already think it's you whose been leaving the invoices.

And maybe for the purposes of a certain recording you've got plans to make, she's right.

You finally find the ring, hook it back on the lighter then push on the steering wheel with the heel of your right hand, stand all at once from the seat, sling the door shut.

Yesterday, the high was 111 degrees. Kid stuff compared to today.

You wipe your forehead with the back of your arm and walk a straight line through the weeds to the concrete stock tank, for the beer you know has to be there, for the beer the world *owes* you. Tell yourself that if you can't find the wire or string it's hanging on, you're going to ram the tank with one of these old trucks, push the side in, let the water out. Then it'll see who's boss here.

It never comes to that.

Running your hand around the rough lip of the tank, you see something that makes you slide your hand back: Gwen's alligator-print sunglasses bobbing in some green sludge near the surface.

The world rotates around you, the clouds wheeling overhead, trees living and dying and living again, the sun shooting overhead like a tetherball, and even though it's the last thing you ever thought you'd do, you peel your shirt off and slip over the edge of the tank, into the water, the moss slick on your face, caressing your shoulders, the world perfectly silent under there.

At the bottom, a chain across her chest, is Gwen.

You stand with her in your arms, fall twice getting her to the side before balancing her on the edge. When you can breathe again you try to breathe into her, but it's been too long, and finally you just hold her by the upper arms and lower your face to her left collarbone, hold her as close as you once promised yourself you would when you were sixteen and none of this was ever going to happen.

24.

W HEN THE PHONE in Mrs. Rankin's stripped kitchen doesn't work you start opening drawers for a book of matches. If you can't bring Felson and the rest with a call, you'll bring them with smoke.

Pawing through the odd spoons and bits of string, though, you find your hand moving slower and slower, finally stopping altogether. The only thing you can see anymore is the pop-up camper framed in the kitchen window.

Two beds. There were *two* beds in it, *both* being used at once, not Dan going back and forth from one to the other.

And—and Rory's three-quarter ton, hidden out in the draw.

Why hide *that* truck, instead of the Ford, when the Ford was the one the police were missing? And why drive the Ford to town at all, even? Why *two* trucks?

Out at Rory's old house, two trucks is what you'd expected: one for Dan, one for Thomas.

But, here, there's just Dan, just one driver.

How would he even have *got* both trucks to the Rankin place?

You lower your eyes, stare into the white of the sink, and see it again: the envelope secreted away in Gwen's purse. All the invoices, the lines filled up with the names and numbers the headstone guy's going to carve.

Is *that* what the real message was? The names and numbers?

But—but then *who*?

So far, the only person in her life that's left her even one note was Rory, and that was his name on the insurance form. But, Dan? Does Dan know what she did? Is *that* why he's been hiding from her, because he's still loyal to Rory? To the memory of his dad?

The only other person who could leave the note, who *knew*, would be her other backdoor man, Jim Martindale. Whoever that is. But unless she's double-crossing him somehow, he shouldn't have to be leaving notes, could just tell her.

You rub your lips. After Jim Martindale and Dan, then—and you, and Fin, but he's in jail—the only person left who knows for sure what happened is Rory himself.

And then you stop smiling, look at what you know for sure: in that old house out by the dump, Rory was blown away in what the papers want to sketch out as a small-time gangland-style shooting, a single shot to the face.

Except maybe that's not what it was. Not at all.

The glass blown *out* of the window of Rory's old bedroom finally makes sense a little bit: there *wasn't* just one shot. There were three. The first, however it happened, had turned his head into ground meat, killed him for sure. But still, his head probably kept most of the pellets. Didn't leave enough to go through the *floor* and leave that kind of hole. It probably wasn't a straight-down shot either, because who'd want to lie down there in the rat shit and faded rubbers?

No, the hole in the floor was from the second shot, when the shooter, Jim Martindale, stood on Rory's arm to steady it, nuzzled the barrel into the palm, looked away to pull the trigger.

But then that left a hole that was unacceptable, made it look like he was *trying* to erase the fingerprints. For the third shot, he held the other hand up to the window, so the pellets and glass and meat would fan out into the dirt. Presto, no second hole in the floor, just one person standing up to shoot another person made to lie down and that lying-down person holding both hands in front of his face. It made sense to all us types not there to see it happen.

The problem, though, is why go to all that trouble? Why lure Rory into his childhood home only to shoot him enough that fingerprints wouldn't matter, that dental records wouldn't matter, that his DMV picture wouldn't matter?

"Because it wasn't him," you say out loud. Slowly, the colors bleeding into each other against the faded wood of the old house, Rory changes places with his shooter, holds the gun now. He's the one leaving invoices on Gwen's windshield, reminding her over and over that the name on them is wrong. Daring her to turn him in, to cash that check, become the criminal you've been saying she is all along.

From the moment Gwen stepped into the room with the body Felson had told her was her husband, she had known all this, known just by looking at the wedding band that Rory was out there.

The reason that *5* or *2* or *N* doesn't mean anything is because you were trying to make it fit with her somehow. But it doesn't, it won't. And she'd have seen that immediately.

Why else give away the money?

Or, to look at it another way, who else would have reason to drown her now?

You back away from the sink, sit down into the space where

the stove used to be and just stare up at the ceiling, your elbows on your knees, arms straight.

Gwen didn't come out here to find Dan at all, or to wait for you to trick her into a confession. What she came out here for was to confront Rory. To apologize, or to tell him to stay away from Dan, or to threaten that she knew he was a killer, that she was going to turn him in. Maybe even to tell him that you had the insurance money now, that she wasn't a part of this anymore.

Whatever she'd said, it didn't matter. Rory hadn't been in the listening mood. Not after being dead for a week.

You close your eyes, ball your fists, know you should have seen this all earlier somehow. You should have guessed it, listened to your gut. Should have had a better gut.

All week you've been toying with the idea of applying for a PI license, for kicks and grins.

Now you're not so sure. Of anything.

You open your eyes when you have to, when you can't hide anymore, when someone in boots is coming down the stairs half a house away.

You wait, wait, and then Rory walks in, his mouth full with spit, eyes unable to settle on anything for long. He crosses to the sink, trails a brown line down into the drain then scoops his dip out into the curve of his right index finger, flicks it after the spit.

He's wearing the same clothes he was the last time you saw him.

In his left hand, clinking against each other, he has two longnecks.

He takes a long step forward, holds one out to you, and you take it, drink half down in one gulp. It makes your eyes water.

"You a ghost?" you say, looking up at him.

He nods yes, tips his beer up.

You hold yours up to the light. "You don't let Dan drink, do you?"

"I'm a good father," he says back.

It's why there was no beer in the camper.

He leans back against the counter, crosses his boots, stares out the back door.

"I really liked her, y'know?" he says, running his eyes along all the counters.

"Gwen?"

He laughs a single laugh through his nose. "Mrs. Rankin."

You nod, liked her too, you guess. Have all her stuff down at Aardvark Custom Economy Storage, even. For some reason it makes you feel like crying.

"So what now?" you say.

"Does it matter, really?"

You study the lines in the linoleum, can see from your seat that there are three layers of it, really, each about an eighth of an inch thick. Mrs. Rankin, aging, standing at the stove, probably never noticed her ceiling getting closer. Because it was coming down at the same rate her vertebrae were compressing.

"Did that check clear?" Rory says, bringing you back to him.

"Check?" you say, not even sure what the word means anymore with Gwen lying dead fifty yards away.

Rory smiles big, sets his beer on the edge of the sink, and says, something final in his voice, like he's about to try and joke his way out of the room, "St. Nicholas..."

You smile a little.

Rory looks away. "You know, it would have—if you just would have dropped it, yeah? Just let him go to jail, do his time like a good little tattoo guy."

Fin.

"It wouldn't be his time," you say. "It would be yours."

Rory spits a grain off the end of his tongue. "He wanted my wife, he should have been ready to take the fall too, I think. Fair's fair."

"Maybe you should have shot him too, then."

"I wish—yeah. That would have been better."

"Putting the shotgun in his camper was the next best thing?"

He shrugs like that's all in the past already, doesn't matter.

"I couldn't drop it," you say. "It's what I do, I guess. Now."

Rory rubs a spot on his forehead, looks right at you for once. "You carry a gun, Detective Bruiseman?"

You shake your head no.

"You *have* one, though, right?"

You keep shaking your head no.

"Gonna be hard to shoot you" he says, pushing up from the counter.

You finish your beer. "You can always drown me, I guess. Throw a chain on top of me to keep me down."

Rory smiles, even laughs a bit. Rubs his nose.

"What about Jim Martindale?" you say.

He stops with his index finger right at his tear duct. "Who?"

You shake your head no, nobody. That must have been part of Gwen's scam, not his. Jim Martindale was her third man, the one who was supposed to have shot Rory out at the old house.

"I thought it was the cropduster," you say, rubbing a dirt dobber nest that's under the lip of the counter. The dust sifts down onto your shoulder.

"Cropduster?" Rory says back.

"He's the only one who could have—who could have got out of there without leaving any tracks."

Rory tongues his lower lip out. "Not the only way, hoss.

You've been gone too long."

"Dan picked you up," you say, when you figure it out.

Rory stares at you hard. "In what? You had his truck, as I recall."

Open your hand, give him that.

"It wasn't Gwen," you say. "Was it?"

"Let it go already, man. It's all—it was stupid."

"But you're going to shoot me anyway."

Rory shrugs.

"With what?" you ask, peering up at him.

He puckers his lips out in something a lot like regret, you think. "It's upstairs."

"The shotgun?"

He steps forward to have another angle out the back door.

"The Davidson place?" you say, watching him.

He nods.

"It's my lawyer," you tell him. "And the other guy who wants to kill me."

Rory covers his mouth with the web of his hand. "I know how you feel," he says. "You'll wait here, if I, y'know, go upstairs?"

"Of course," you say, playing along.

He smiles wider, with his eyes even, and says, "She told me about you, you know that? You and her, after that Colorado City game?"

You nod, remember, could never forget the thirty-four lines her hair made in the window glass. How deep they were.

"So you're just, just taking care of everybody she ever—that she?"

In answer, he thumps his can of dip into the side of his wrist, packing it. He leans forward to get it into his lip. Holds the can out to you. You shake your head no.

"Never too late to start," he says, fitting the chrome lid back on.

"Got enough bad habits," you say back, and he nods, his eyes watering with the rush of nicotine. His mouth too full of spit for words, he points upstairs, that that's where he's going. You nod that you understand, yes. And goodbye. Like two people passing on a road, he lifts his finger to you, slips past, becomes a sound on the stairs.

Two long steps later you're through what's left of Mrs. Rankin's screen door, scrabbling through the dirt and weeds for—

You don't know.

Easing back from the Davidson place is the black Town Car, but at the careful pace Arnot King's picking along the grain-drilled road, they're two minutes away. For you, now, that's a lifetime. Maybe more.

You crouch as low as you can, look back to the house—no Rory, yet—and step behind a rusted tank, almost fall over the hood of Gwen's Town Car. You start to go around it but then stop, look back to it.

Ten seconds later, you're low in the driver's seat, waiting for the lighter to pop back out, hoping that fuse doesn't feed off the ignition.

It doesn't.

You roll out of the car cupping the red coils in your hand and curve as much of your body as you can over the driest weed you can find, blow gently and desperately on the thin yellow arm you hold the heat to.

Just as the coils of the lighter go from red-hot to ash-grey, a

going sixty, anyway.

The 5 on the back, though. It's the first part of a date, has to be. May. You need to find out who-all from your graduating class—maybe two years in either direction—who-all got hitched in May. And which of them's a widow now, even if she doesn't know it.

Each box you open in your mind, there's a smaller box inside it.

Maybe this is something all storage unit security personnel eventually have to face at some point of the job.

"What?" Felson says about whatever's funny here.

You shake your head no, nothing. Snug the blanket around your shoulders a bit more. You're sitting at the back edge of one of the two ambulances to respond, are a victim. It's not yet five o'clock.

"Rory," Felson says. "So you say."

You shrug yes like you've been doing ever since she got here an hour ago, but this time, instead of explaining it all to her, you feel something purring against your chest, raise your hand to it.

The silver microcassette recorder, in voice-activated mode, its heads sluggish with water.

You pull it up from your pocket, shake it out and rewind it all the way, set it on the bumper for Felson.

She pushes the play button but there's too much emergency personnel milling around and she has to retreat to her cruiser, close the door.

What's on the tape, you know, is your and Rory's voices—yours louder, his distant, like he's dead.

But he's not.

And he's not here, either.

For a while after you handed Gwen over to Toby Garrett's

baby brother, you'd watched the horizon for Rory's small form moving away, but he never was. Or he already had.

Felson comes back ten minutes later with the recorder in her hand, a new flatness in her eyes.

She's listened to it twice, you know.

"So?" you say.

Without looking at you, she nods.

Any other day, you'd make her say it, that you were right. Make her apologize, make her understand that if she'd just listened to you, then maybe Gwen would still be alive.

On this day, though, it doesn't seem worth the effort. Isn't going to change anything.

"What about Fin, then?" you say.

Felson sucks her cheeks in, purses her lips out in thought, and nods once, her eyes flashing to you for a fraction of a second. She knows Fin has whatever it is Judge Harkness is looking for, and that, whatever it is, it's probably going to ruin you, to keep on ruining you. And that you're lucky now to not already be in jail or in the coroner's van with Gwen.

"When?" you say, still talking about Fin.

"Depends if your attorney presses all his charges or not," she says. Then, nodding out to the pastures, "You think he's still out there somewhere?"

"Rory?"

"The tooth fairy, Mr. Bruiseman."

You smile about this, how comfortable it's getting to be with her.

"Thomas's dad lives over there," you say, pointing with your chin to the southwest. "Right?" And the way Felson nods without even having to think about it pulls you back twenty-four hours, to the library in the high school, when you'd said nearly the same thing to Gwen—that you were working for Thomas Howard.

Her response had been different, though. She'd had to think to bring *Thomas Howard* to the front of her mind. When he was in her own son's grade, had probably been playing with him since diapers.

Even Felson, years older, from a whole different generation, knew Thomas Howard right off. And his dad, who had graduated with Gwen.

Why the charade in the library, then?

Felson doesn't give you time to follow it through. "Tom's not there."

"His house is empty?"

"Rory would know where Tom keeps all his keys, though. And clothes, I guess."

You look across the pasture to the idea of Tom Howard's house, *Sherilita's* house, and ask when's he back from Kansas?

"That where he is?" Felson says, coming back to you.

"It's—it's late July," you say, shrugging like that's an explanation, then narrow your eyes at the ground. "But...but you knew he was gone anyway?"

"I'll send a car over," Felson says, and starts casting around for an officer.

You say it again, more insistent: "You *knew* he was gone?"

"We called him twice the night you were arrested coming back from Big Springs, Mr. Bruiseman."

You squint, trying to catch up mentally here.

She shakes her head in wonder at you. "A dead man was found in a house on land he farms, get it? A house he *owns*? And then, your cropduster. Whose account do you think he was trying to charge that vodka to?"

"I thought it was—that he—"

"Tom," Felson fills in, impatient with having to explain what, to her, is so obvious.

"Tom Howard," you repeat. "Why?"

"He said Tom owed him."

"For what?"

"That field he was spraying when he saw you? It was the third day in a row he'd sprayed it, according to his logbook. Didn't you see it in there?"

"I was looking at—I was looking at times."

Felson shrugs one shoulder. "All Darryl Koenig wanted was payment for three applications of whatever he was laying down. For boll weevils, I think. He said Tom's new wife had been calling him at all hours, telling him he had to spray it again, over and over."

"She was calling for Tom," you say.

Felson nods, is the one trying to catch up now.

"What's Tom's new wife's name?" you ask then.

Felson starts to say it, to say something, then looks down, searching her own brain. Comes back up to you all hangdog. "Guess Koenig just assumed it was a wife," she says. "Or maybe she told him. He probably won't fuel up just for a girlfriend, right?"

You breathe out through your nose, close your eyes. It had been Gwen calling.

"You said—you said Rory would know where Tom Howard kept his keys, right?"

"I thought you were in their class?"

"He came here—" you start, then hear it again, from Jim

Martindale: *I moved here my senior year in high school.* "He showed up after I left," you finish.

Felson looks over at you now.

"What?" she says.

"They wear the same size clothes, right?"

She nods, just as aware as you that the thing neither of you has been saying is that if Rory's out here starting fires and killing wives and not letting his son drink beer, then who's in his grave?

"Toby Garret's little—*David*." you start, trying to remember it right. "David says you had to arrest Rory one night back then."

Or was it Madelyn who said it? Something about the prom picture—the prom picture not being his first picture of the night.

Both, then. They'd both been trying to tell you, not even known it.

You wait for Felson to tell you too: "Him and Tom both," she says. "For fighting, yeah."

"Over Gwen," you say.

Felson looks away, at all the new blackness.

"Rory's the only one—" you say, then start over. "He's not the only one who would know that Tom Howard's fingerprints would be in the system, the same as his. From that night. But he *would* know that you'd be able to identify him that way, right?"

Felson shakes her head like this is too much. "Tom was his best friend."

"That would kind of make it worse, wouldn't it?" you say, covering the wedding band on your finger. The wedding band Tom Howard must have never stopped wearing. The *5* on the back wasn't "May," it was an *S*. For *Sherilita*.

Jim Martindale was Tom Howard, and Tom Howard is

buried in the cemetery now, a headstone on order for him, *Rory Gates* carved deep into it. And maybe he's dead now too, like the Town Car. Burned up in the fire. But you know better.

In the long, rambling statement Felson has you write down before she lets you go, you figure out what Rory meant when he told you you'd been gone too long to figure out how he got away from the old house.

He didn't walk, didn't hitch, didn't fly. He *drove*. You'd even stood in one of his tracks, chipped a dirt clod up. It was shaped like a tractor tread, was what Tom Howard—Jim Martindale— had driven *to* the house that day. It was part of his and Gwen's perfect murder plan: nobody would question that he was plowing his own field, so the tracks wouldn't even be considered, would be like the fingerprints you already know at a scene, the ones that get eliminated. And since he wasn't going to be the witness, nobody would even know he was there, really, as long as he didn't drop his plow into the ground.

Maybe that was what had cued Rory in that Tom Howard wasn't meeting him there for whatever reason he'd said— probably to finally *pay* for the blue and silver Ford; maybe Rory'd seen Tom Howard's tractor coming across the field, its plow lifted. What it would tell Rory, who'd grown up farming, was that the meeting wasn't about convenience—the old house sitting in a turnrow Tom Howard was going to be using anyway—but isolation.

It was why Rory had killed him so violently, probably. Where he'd been expecting Fin to be orchestrating the whole insurance scam, all at once his best friend from high school was involved. The one guy he was supposed to be able to trust, the guy he was supposed to have *already* won Gwen from.

And then he walked into the house he'd grown up in, felt the ghosts rise all around him.

You almost feel sorry for him.

After your statement—three legal-size pages, the yellow pad left on Felson's back seat—nobody notices you walking to the Davidson place, and nobody hears the Ford crash down from the wrecker's tow straps, and nobody sees the smoke when it starts, because there's smoke everywhere.

One more grand theft auto isn't going to break anybody, you tell yourself.

And anyway, the rightful owner of the truck is a fugitive now. Unless it's still in Tom Howard's name, in which case the rightful owner is dead, meaning you're just taking back what's yours, by deed if not by title.

Because you're not ready to face Sherilita yet—to tell her that her son's father, you found him all right, his ring anyway— you take the Ford downtown, to the drugstore, belly up to the counter.

"Cheeseburger?" the same kid in an apron asks, and you nod, watch it cook. Hope Felson doesn't question that the shotgun Rory said he had was the one he shot Tom Howard with.

If it is, or if she believes it is, that'll be one less thing Jimmy Bones has on you, at least.

Your cheeseburger pops and hisses, the kid balancing it on his chrome spatula like a trick then arcing it back down into its own grease.

After he slides it over to you he leans against the counter behind him, crosses his arms, and opens his mouth like he's going to say something but pushes back off the counter instead.

What he comes back with from the office is a packet of

photographs.

"They finally turned up?" you say, wedging them under your plate, chewing gloriously.

"You can only fill out a form so wrong," the kid says.

You nod, would like to agree, then don't open the green-on-white envelope until your plate's empty. Because you already know what the snapshots are going to be: Thomas taking smeary pictures from the window of the Ford, Gwen's car twice, then you, screwing around in front of Aardvark Custom Economy Storage, in the daylight.

You're half right.

The first of the middle shots you flip to is of nothing—a misfire when you fell down off the railroad tracks, probably. Then the next two, the ones you wanted, are inside Manuel's body shop.

But it's the ten before that that make you close your eyes: they're of Gwen and a man you think is Rory at first, but finally isn't. They're in the parking lot of the IGA afterhours, arguing, glaring at each other. It's more intimate than anything you've ever seen, you think. They're all you needed to have given Rory to have stopped all this.

And you didn't take those pictures, you know. Not even twenty cans into a case.

At first you think what you thought last week, when you saw the camera advanced ten shots: Thomas, a joke.

Now you know better.

It was Dan Gates. He was the one who took the Ford that first night, the one who grazed his mother's Lincoln with it, trying to strand her, keep her home. The one who, after that didn't work, had tried to take all his disappointment out on you with his fists. Because *you* were the one who could have stopped it all. *You* were the one who should have seen those pictures, should have told his dad what he couldn't.

The next ten pictures are the ones you took of the Motel sign. Only there's nothing there, just sky.

You lay them down in a row the kid behind the counter has to look at.

"What?" he says, finally, watching your eyes.

"The—the Motel sign," you say. "The big one, like a truck stop. For the Bellevue."

"Bellevue like the Church of Christ?"

"Before your time, I guess."

"No, I remember the sign," the kid says. "It's gone, though, man. Up in sign heaven."

You shake your head, tamp the black tube of negatives into your chest pocket and snap your pocket over them. Tell him you've been gone a long time, you guess. Maybe too long.

He smiles one side of his face and you leave twenty dollars for the burger, take the long way back to Aardvark Custom Economy Storage. The way that loops through all the roads you chased up and down on a bike as a kid—then, later, in old trucks.

It spits you out by the Town & Country, like always.

Toby Garrett's baby brother is there, his window down, binoculars fixed on the underpass.

You look through it, maybe see the dim shape of a boy sitting on a missile, swinging his legs.

He can see the Motel sign, you know.

Maybe that's enough.

At Aardvark, every light is on.

You coast the Ford in, turn the headlights off.

All fourteen doors are open, the locks cut, the boxes and

exercise equipment pulled out.

Through the open window of the Ford, you hear the distinctive crack of Jimmy Bones breaking a tight rack.

He found the quarter table, then.

You step down, nod to yourself that this is good. That you would have showed it to him anyway.

On the pale caliche outside that unit, you can see his shadow leaning over the edge of the table. Arnot King steps into the doorway, his back to you, the butt of his cue planted between his feet.

You can take him on a short table, maybe.

And Jimmy Bones?

He *is* used to playing regulation, you tell yourself, then almost smile when he steps out, running one of the sticks through the chalk in the web of his hand. He nods to you, his face and neck a sheen of sweat, and steps back in.

An instant later, he shoots too hard from the other end. It sends the three-ball spinning out through the caliche and boxes, leaves it against the yellow grass shield of the lawnmower.

Without ever breaking stride, you jog after it, have to step around to the other side of the lawnmower to get the right angle, and see at the last instant not Jimmy Bones, the .22 by his leg, or Arnot King, his pool cue raised, but the battery charger. It's been hooked up wrong. Instead of clamping onto the two little terminals, the jaws are biting down on the hood panel, scratching the paint.

"Gonna rust like tha—" you start to say under your breath.

It's something your father used to tell you.

When you place your hand on the hood to brace yourself,

lean under for the three-ball, the current running through the metal throws you back, leaves you awake but unable to move.

Jimmy Bones stands above you, leaning on his cane with both hands. Laughing without any sound.

26.

IT HAD BEEN DUSK when you'd pulled up to Aardvark Custom Economy Storage. By the time you can stand again, after the lawnmower, it's full-on dark. You're pretty sure that you've either slept or passed out. It only felt like a blink, a long blink maybe, but when you open your eyes again, things are different.

First: Jimmy Bones and Arnot King are gone.

Second: all the lights of all the storage units are turned off. *So nobody would find you*, you tell yourself. Lights draw attention. Bodies in the caliche draw attention. Even yours.

Third—and you're not sure if this different or not—under your left arm is the pistol grip of a shotgun. One with a shimmery walnut stock, with…with ebony tips and mother-of-pearl accents? What the hell? Who puts a high-dollar weapon like this in storage? And just behind a *single* padlock? More important, how'd you miss it when *you* went through that unit?

Answer: you're pretty sure you didn't.

But what other explanation is there?

You pull it close to your side, try to be quiet about standing but then cough like you're going to throw up, end up dry-heaving on your hands and knees, your eyes watering.

So much for stealth.

You flip the shotgun around so its butt's to the ground and use it to push yourself up, careful to keep your face away from the business end. Not that it's loaded—even in Stanton, Texas, nobody would put a loaded gun in storage. You look at the stuff spilled out of unit 4, on the off-chance it fits with the shotgun, but instead of duck decoys or hunting photographs or more guns or bricks of cash, there's just three identical lamps, a cardboard box of old letters, and a pair of skis that probably haven't been to Colorado since Cadillacs had fins.

Still, maybe you weren't thinking right. Weren't *looking* right. It was dusk, you tell yourself. It was dusk and Jimmy Bones had just hit the brightest ball on the table into the white caliche, so that even you could track the flashing orange over to where he was leaving it for you: the lawnmower.

Your eyes had been looking for round things, not gun-shaped things.

And, anyway, you'd just spent thirty minutes holding your dead ex-girlfriend up out of the water of a stock tank so she wouldn't burn up. Give yourself a break already. And maybe you did see it, even—the memory of it just got electrocuted out of you.

By the lawnmower, yeah.

You look to it again, to the storage unit with the pool table in it, then touch your chest pocket.

The black tube of film is gone. All the pictures you didn't take of the Motel sign.

"Have at them," you say out loud to Jimmy Bones, wherever he is, and cross to the pool table. In the corner with the cues is a brush. For ten minutes, like therapy, you brush the table down until it's perfect, until all the glass from the broken bulb is gone, and then a car or truck streaks past on 137, the driver leaning on the horn, the sound dopplering away to the south, like they're going to hit the hump of the train tracks, just blast off.

It's over, you tell yourself.

Rory's not dead, but he's known, is living in barns now. Maybe trying to make Mexico in one of Tom Howard's old trucks. Or—

You narrow your eyes at 137.

Or he's here in town again. For his son, for Dan. To try to explain it all, maybe. To apologize for calling him from his truck the day he had to shoot his best friend, Tom Howard. Calling Dan and telling him to meet him at the far end of the field out by the old house, where the rows would spit a tractor up, where a tractor could sit for weeks and nobody would care.

It almost was the perfect murder.

Except Tom Howard was going to have been missed eventually. Kansas isn't that big.

You pull the door down over the pool table. To keep the birds out, you tell yourself. This is what you do, this is your job. So you did a little moonlighting. But it all worked out. At least you got a fancy shotgun out of the whole deal, right? On permanent loan now, for security purposes. The shotgun'll help you keep the shotgun safe, something like that. Anyway, how bad could the owner need it if he was keeping it in storage, right?

You raise it to the roofline of Aardvark Custom Economy Storage, sight in on the full moon, make the sound once with your mouth then pull the trigger.

The sound is what you imagine a cannon would make in a small room, the kind of sound that you associate with pressure, with visible sound waves.

You tilt your head—your right ear canal—over maybe five degrees, all you have time for.

The shot pocks the top corner of the B unit, the pellets leaving little grey craters in the painted-white cinderblock, the gun itself falling from your hand so you have to fumble it back to your chest.

It's loaded.

You look left, to where a few houses are, then right, west to 137. Lean the gun up against the chain link before stepping out by the Ford, to see if the sound's drawn anybody. To act for Felson like, yeah, you heard it too—some fool's shooting inside city limits?

There's nobody, though. Some kids down at the Sonic, a truck or two at the Town & Country. All the shiny new windshields at Wheeler's, a parts truck or something at Blockers—*Franklin's.* It's Franklin's now. You nod to it in apology, the gas station. The only other vehicle even slightly out of place is the front-end loader from the Davidson sale this morning. It's pulled into the carwash across the street. But it's not out of place, either: you buy something as high-dollar as that, you want to clean it up before taking it home to the wife. Right now the farmer driving it back to his place—who has a lowboy trailer that big?—is dodging carhops down at Sonic probably, treating himself to a vanilla coke.

Nobody's heard your shot. Nobody cares.

You ease back through the gate and pull it shut, chain it down tight, pick the shotgun up by the barrel and say it to Rory in your head: You've got a gun *now*, sir.

It's supposed to be funny.

Two beers later, you finally smile. When the payphone outside rings, you just let it, even tip a third beer to it in appreciation. But then it won't stop ringing.

You go out in bare feet, press the receiver to the side of your head. "Ring My Bell Male Escorts, will you be paying cash or cash tonight?"

The person on the other end laughs a bit, then says back, "Think I have some credit, actually, Mr. Bruiseman."

You close your eyes: Jimmy Bones. Arnot King finally pulled the roll of negatives from the black tube for him, held them up to the dome light of the Lincoln. They're in Midland somewhere. Carlotta's, probably, or one of the other lots.

"Jimmy—" you start, wincing inside, but he's already gone.

Twenty minutes, then. Twenty minutes for the twenty miles of 20 between you and him. You hang the phone up, pull your lower lip between your teeth, and shrug. It's not like you haven't seen this coming, not like you didn't ask for it. All there is to it now, to save yourself, is to tell Jimmy Bones the real and true score: that the film is in the Property desk of the Sheriff's offices, in a brown envelope only Anthony Robert Payne can sign for. That, if Arnot King chooses to drop all his charges, chalk it up to mistaken identity or heat of the moment or whatever, then Anthony Robert Payne should be released Monday, sometime. Knowing Felson, at 4:59.

And, anyway, it's not like you ever *told* Jimmy Bones that the film in your chest pocket was the last of the Harkness rolls. If he hadn't run 110 volts through you, then he could have saved himself forty miles.

Once he gets the actual film, though, and tries to use it to get Harkness to look the other way on something, that's when Stanton isn't going to be far enough away from Midland for you anymore. That's when nowhere with DPS is going to be far enough away. Nowhere she can touch with radio.

And now your keen detective senses are telling you it's *past* time for you to steal away in a stolen truck. Try to change your name to something even less probable. Disappear until even you forget who you are, who you were, who you could have been, had things played out differently.

And maybe it'll be better that way. Maybe Madelyn at the high school can somehow change the yearbook, even, so that your picture is like the Lawler kid's, the year he drowned: the silhouette of a person, the shape of a life; a placeholder.

At least now, for your next life, you have some experience to put on an application, you tell yourself. You're a security guard.

It makes you want a beer for each hand.

You lean the shotgun against the payment slot, step into the office, to the compact refrigerator, and stand with your beers clinking together, then just stand there some more, staring into the darkness, something undulating just under the surface of your thoughts, trying to rise.

When it finally doesn't, you step back outside, shake your head at the mess Jimmy Bones and Arnot King have made of Aardvark Custom Economy Storage. You drain the first beer down, sling the bottle up onto the roof and set the second carefully on the seat of the lawnmower. Chances are you could unclamp the two jaws biting down on the rear flange of the hood, stop the current. Even safer, though, is just pulling the extension cord from the socket it's plugged into under the air conditioner in the office. Next time you go for beer.

Tonight, judging by the mess you've got to clean up, that should be about every four minutes. You lean into it with what little energy you've got, start picking through the boxes spilled from the storage units, end up shopping in the dark like always, wheeling stuff over to the concrete in front of your storage unit.

The first two things you get are a cream-colored exercise bike that uses a brown fan for resistance. The second is a television set so old the glass looks like a bubble. The third is a large painting in a brass-colored plastic frame. It's a seascape, one wave of a thousand rolling in. You'll hang it on the nail the calendar's on now, you think. The nail Rory drove in for you.

Masonry nail—was that what he said it was? Can you buy those single-serve, or you got to spring for the whole box?

Like you're going to be here long enough. Furnishing your office like this, it's—it's standing outside, a comet blazing down out of the sky for your side of the earth, and nodding up to it as you angle your water hose over to the tomato plants you've been coaxing up their sticks for two months already.

Not like you have anything better to do, though.

You keep the television on your hip under one arm and duck under the mostly-open door of your unit, stand into the inky blackness, your free hand automatically grubbing above for the pull chain of the light. It just rains glass down. You look down to the sound, realize how barefoot you are, and then what's been just under your thoughts rises all at once: the glass on the pool table that you had to brush into a pile, sweep up onto a piece of paper.

The reason you did it was because a table shouldn't be treated like that. It's one of the few standards you've got left. But—

But Jimmy Bones didn't do that. Jimmy Bones *wouldn't* do that. And he wouldn't have Arnot King do it either. To a pool player, trashing a table like that's inviting bad karma, missed shots, balls that the banks will hold onto for a moment too long, soaking up all the English on that most important shot.

If not Jimmy Bones—

You don't get to finish. In a flash of heat, the television under your arm explodes and the storage unit is full of sound, and, for an instant, light. Standing in the back corner, at the other end of the stab of flame, it's Rory Gates.

Slowly, time pieces itself back together around him, spins you around by the arm that you're only now realizing has caught a pellet or two. And—and the side of your face, under your jaw: the glass from the television screen is embedded there, a thousand tiny slashes.

You fall down in the door, look to your other hand still holding the pull chain of the light, and then Rory racks another shell into the chamber, lowers the gun at you and steps forward to show that the light at the end of *this* tunnel, it's going to be coming through at fifteen hundred feet per second.

You shake your head no, pleading, and roll back, roll again, the caliche rock sticking to the blood already coating your face.

Rory steps forward again, all the way into the half-light. He's holding his shotgun in one hand, one of your beers in the other.

The beer he throws down on you. It's empty, clatters away.

"Brusha brusha brusha," he singsongs. Meaning he watched you clean the pool table. He was there the whole time, probably could have reached over and tapped you with that goose barrel.

You follow the beer with your eyes, realize too late that that's the wrong move, and when you come back to Rory again, he fires. Not right at you, but right in front of you, gouging caliche dust up into your face.

Two shots, you count in your head, rolling again, holding your eyes.

If that shotgun has a plug in it like it should, he should have two more, maybe. If that first shot was already racked.

Rory takes another step onto the concrete skirt in front of your storage unit. He looks over to the exercise bike and smiles about it. "Finally joining the human race, Nabby?"

You clear your eyes, rise to one knee. "Anything to be more like you, Rory."

It stops the smile he had building, brings the gun up to your face again.

"Be careful," he says. "I might just—"

"Do me like you did Tom?" you interrupt, standing now, a handful of caliche in your left hand, down by your thigh.

"He was my friend," Rory says, leaning away from the gun to spit.

"I'd hate to see what you'd do to somebody you *don't* like, then."

In answer, Rory fires again, the pellets whipping past your head into the contents of whatever unit's behind you.

He takes another step forward.

"Go ahead," he says about the fist your left hand is.

You look down to it too, and over to your shotgun by the office door, then shrug, hold your hand out for him and open it, blow like what you've got here is fairy dust.

Rory smiles and you sling the caliche you have in your right hand.

It catches him full in the face, swings his head around, and you're diving and scrabbling for the office door, already arcing your body away from the birdshot he must be using. Shell number four.

It never comes.

You place your hand on the fancy shotgun, lean it away from the payment slot, and look over to Rory.

He's motioning with his gun for you to get yours, and the way he's smiling you know that he's had a bead on you for the last few steps. That he *wants* you to have the gun, wants you to have a chance.

Or he wants it to look like that, anyway. For this to be self-defense on his part.

The shotgun you woke with, it wasn't from a storage unit, hadn't just fallen there for you to fall on top of. It's from Rory Gates's gun safe, his least favorite twelve-gauge, probably. A gift from Gwen's dad, something like that, to make it all poetic in his head.

You let the shotgun fall back to the ledge of the payment slot.

"That Ford you gave your son?" you say, not looking around to him.

"What about it?" he says.

"Gwen ever tell you that that's where, after the Colorado City game, y'know? Kind of funny, I mean, that of all the trucks—"

Before you can finish, he lets loose his fourth shot. Not *at* you—like you know he doesn't want to do yet, not really—but past you, into the radiator, hood, and windshield of the Ford. Like it's the truck's fault.

A crying shame is what it is.

You take your shotgun by the barrel, like you're just toying with it. "Can you see him up there?"

"Who?" Rory says, sweeping his eyes around. Following yours, up into the sky.

"The Lawler kid," you say. "Up by the 'T', in the Motel sign. He likes it there, I think."

"Dane's little—?" Rory gets out, his head automatically tracking over and up, to the boy who's been dead for thirty years, to the empty space where the sign should be, where he, like you, just forgot it *wasn't*, and in that moment of inattention you bring your shotgun around by the barrel, that six-hundred-dollar stock connecting with the side of his head.

It sends his shotgun skating away, drops him like a sack of dead cats.

You step in, roll him over to—you don't know, *something*— but he's Rory Gates. Like Toby Garrett's baby brother said, like you should have guessed, him working with his hands day in, day out: it takes more than a sucker punch to keep him down.

He takes the foot you place on his chest and he holds it, connects his work boot with your sternum in the worst possible way, and suddenly you're flying again, crashing back into the broken lamps and boxes of clothes you're being paid to protect.

You throw as much of it as you can at Rory but he keeps coming, and then he's on you, holding your shirt with one hand, pounding your face with the other until you're able to knee him away. He backs off, wipes his mouth with the back of his arm. "Should have been riding that exercise bike for years already if you wanted to take me, Nabby."

You stare at him now, no smiles.

"That's not my name," you tell him, and he shrugs, crashes into you with his shoulder, and now you're rolling together toward the front of Aardvark Custom Economy Storage, and the only reason you're able to resist him even a little is that you outweigh him by fifty pounds.

Soon enough he's on your chest, trying to work on your face, getting your forearms instead. You tell him his son hits harder than that, and manage something like a laugh.

It slows him down. Not the good kind of slow. He pulls you up with both hands, tells you to leave Dan the hell *out* of it and slams his forehead into your nose. It makes the world explode, starts your hands and feet and teeth doing their own thing until, for a hard-breathing moment, you're away from him somehow, falling into a run, crashing down over that shotgun by the office.

You roll over, the butt in your stomach, the barrel angled just generally behind you—it's not called a scattergun for nothing—and pull the trigger.

Nothing happens.

Rory lets you stand. Doesn't move out of the way even an inch.

"Think you've got to *pump* it there, Detective," he says. "You should be used to that kind of action, right?"

He scoops his dip out on his index finger, slings it away in a clump that sticks to the cinderblock of the B-units like a dirt-dobber nest, if they built out in the open.

You rack the next shell up into the chamber, settle the long gun on him, and he stares at you over it.

"Well?" he says.

"What?" you say back.

He narrows his eyes at you in reply, holds one finger up, and works his can of dip up from his pocket, packs some into his lip.

"Surgeon general my ass," he says, his mouth full of spit, sirens wailing in from north of town, all the local law enforcement still out at the Rankin place.

"There's always lead poisoning," you say, stepping in, leading with the shotgun.

"Didn't get a chance to tell you about my cute little wifey," he says, shrugging. "You know what she said the second time I brought her up from the water?"

You raise the barrel, fire over his head, right into the heart of Stanton.

He steps closer. "What she said, *Nabby*, is that that first time with you, she could hardly find it, man. That dewlap you got going?" You lick your lips, lower the gun onto him, because he's asking for it now. "Ever hear what the old men at the gin call it? 'Dicky-do.' Like, your belly, it hangs out further than your—"

This time you fire close enough to him that the pellets tug at his right shirt sleeve. It spins him around a bit but he never looks away from you, even when the blood starts seeping out from under his cuff.

"Afraid to do it, Nicholas?" he says, smiling. "It easier like this?" he adds, thumbing a shell up from his pants pocket, casting around for his shotgun. He locates it, bends to pick it up, giving you the whole wide expanse of his back for what you know is longer than he needs to.

When he stands again it's with the shotgun in the crook of his arm like it's the breakover kind, like he's a pheasant hunter on a magazine cover. He looks down to the gun the whole time he thumbs the shell in.

"Two seconds," he says, holding the gun just by the slide, chambering the stubby red shell. "Two seconds and it's high noon for you and me, Nabby. Been a long time coming."

"My beer," you say. "We can split it first, think?"

He follows your eyes around to the lawnmower, the bottle still there on the seat somehow, after everything else in the world has been trashed.

"Like gentlemen," he says, nodding.

"For old times," you say, never quite lowering your gun. "Just a couple of old Buffaloes, put out to pasture."

He keeps his eyes on you, reaches back for the beer without looking, his attention split just long enough for you to fire one more time.

This time, instead of above or beside him, you shoot below him.

The rocks and dust cut up into his face, pushing him back, off balance, his hand that was reaching for the beer going palm down onto the hood instead, for support.

The electricity there arches his back, pushes him up onto the toes of his work boots, and he sticks for a few seconds, lit up until the charger sparks out, dies.

The silence afterward crackles, hisses.

Rory Gates wavers, the steel toes of his boots smoking, and then he collapses forward onto his face, and you start the kind of breathing that always comes after, the kind that came in the shade of that fiberglass boat, once. It's like crying from the mouth, and you're not too old for it, never will be.

When Rory moves again, pulling in all the air he can, turning his head to the side, you pivot the gun around your hip, pull the trigger without even thinking about it.

The hammer falls on nothing, and you smile at yourself, lean over to the side of the A-unit of Aardvark Custom Economy Storage, finally realize that the whole place is bathed in halogen light.

You follow it back to the twin headlights of an idling Lincoln Town Car.

And the gate, it's open, the lock clipped with the bolt cutters Arnot King must have reclaimed.

He's nowhere to be seen, though. Because of all the sirens, you tell yourself, your face slack. Some lawyers run to them. Others duck.

But Jimmy Bones.

When you look back to Rory Gates, Jimmy Bones has one leg propped up on Rory's back. Descending from his hand like a long finger is something black and metal that you know is his mythical .22.

The barrel's nestled just behind the hinge of Rory's jaw.

You tell Jimmy Bones that that won't be necessary. Rory Gates has been dead for a week already. One more bullet isn't going to change anything.

27.

Sheriff Felson releases Fin at five o'clock Monday evening. You're still wearing the dark brown 1978 suit you found deep in the same storage unit you got the bench seat from. You're pretty sure it doesn't smell. It was for Gwen's funeral.

Felson escorts Fin as far as the front door. She doesn't nod to you or smile to you and you don't nod or smile back. Standard operating procedure.

The Ford shifts and complains when Fin climbs in. It's the first time you've seen him close-up, outside an interrogation room.

He nods once to you, in thanks—all you're ever going to get, you know—and sets the canister of undeveloped film on the dashboard, right under the rearview mirror.

"Don't guess you're going to be telling me what's on it," he says.

"State secrets," you say, and pull across the rest of the handicapped slots, unfocus your eyes to see the road. With the new, shattered windshield, it's the only way to drive.

"Should have kept the Mustang," Fin says, patting the outside of his door as if urging the truck on. The truck's breath smells green, like radiator fluid.

You tell him that this truck is perfect, actually, and swing up by the Town & Country. Instead of opening his door, Fin fingers up the City of Stanton check he's been issued. It's for two dollars and fourteen cents.

"I got it," you say, and nod for him to follow.

Inside, you point to four of the burritos at the back of the display, get the four at the front instead.

Fin sets a half gallon of milk down on the counter beside them.

"With burritos?" you say, paying quarter by quarter.

"Thought Sherilita kept you fed?" Fin says, pulling the milk back towards him.

You don't explain to him that the water station was closed all weekend, that you've been avoiding it all day. Instead you loosen your broad tie, unbutton your shirt, and sit on the curb under the payphones with Fin, eat one of the four burritos and wash it down with whole milk.

Somehow two or three hours slip away, locals sliding in and out the front door, tail lights time-lapsing around and around the Sonic, the Dairy Queen dead and haunted, you and Fin talking in just a general, spotty way. About the big trucks groaning past, and other trucks those trucks remind you of. About the clouds hanging out over Midland and whether they're going to amount to anything. About the way Gwen could touch the top of your forearm with the pads of her fingers, and how that could feel like the result of every wish you'd ever had.

At dusk you point through the underpass for Fin, at the Lawler kid, and Fin stands as if tasting the air, watches until a tractor trailer shudders through, all its lights burning.

"Who is he?" Fin says.

You don't look up to him, say like it's supposed to explain everything, "You're not from here."

He hisses air through his teeth, drains the milk. "And you are?"

You nod, keep nodding, guilty as charged.

Fin stuffs the milk jug into the already full trashcan. "She's really dead then?"

You study the ground between your feet, and the next time you look up, the Lawler kid's got his shadow of a hand raised to you, across whatever kind of gulf there is between the living and the dead. Whatever kind of ribbon.

You close your eyes, and inside your head, all your memories are made of the crushed lead of a thousand pencils, the grains washing back and forth against each other, polishing themselves into chrome balls too small to ever hold. But, still, you could drown in them, you know.

Or not.

You stand, follow the line of the Ford's pocked hood to the door. Fin follows, gets in his side. "What now, chief?"

You lower the truck into reverse, smile, and take him back across the tracks, to Manuel's body shop.

He opens the door, holds it there.

"Long as I'm in this town—" he says, holding his hand out for you.

Instead of taking it, you look over to him, hold his eyes. "Sure about that?"

Hesitantly, he nods, and you shrug like this is out of your control then. You give him one of Arnot King's Allegator cards. The one with Toby Garrett's baby brother's mother-in-law's address on the back.

"She needs her cars washed too," you tell him.

He breathes out through his nose. "Once a cop, always an asshole," he says, but still, he launches the card away from his forehead in salute. The last thing he does before stepping down is pull the film up from where you've let it roll on the dash, set it on the seat beside you.

"A girl?" he says about it.

"A lady," you say, then back out to 137, ease down to the liquor store, and finally have to go back to Aardvark Custom Economy Storage. On the way you see, behind the water station, Thomas's truck, the tailgate down. It means he's brought his equipment back, is maybe already jacked in, warming up, a bottle of warm beer standing on the amp beside him, his sunglasses tight to his eyes.

You have no idea what to say to him, really.

His dad's service is tomorrow, in the same place Rory's was. Because Stanton, Texas, it's a complicated place.

You step through the gate, your case of beer by your leg, and Thomas looks up from his guitar, smiles to you. The girl draped over his shoulder just stares, like you're the intruder here.

You prop the door to the office open so you can hear the music, not have to say anything, but then, either suddenly or because you've drunk more than you thought, the valley between the A- and B-units is full of headlights and voices and shuffling motion.

You make your way to the door and lean against it, your hand holding your beer high on the frame.

The band's still out there, and the band's friends, and now, moving among them but not really with them, is Dan Gates, the tails of his white funeral shirt loose.

He makes his way over, just stands there.

266 • Stephen Graham Jones

"Don't want to hire me, do you?" you say.

Dan Gates rubs his nose. "Dad says just keep the truck."

You shrug, were going to anyway, and after that you do the only thing you can: offer cold beer to a minor.

He takes it, nods once like his face is about to spill out, and then spins away right as he's about to say something, leans headfirst into the sound Thomas's band is laying down.

It's not perfect, but then nothing is.

Two hours later everybody's gone except the band and Dan Gates. Because you've been watching, you know he hasn't said anything to Thomas yet, the same way you haven't. At one point Thomas's bass player balances his bass down onto an amp, then, after lifting his chin to the drummer, smiling about something, he sets himself against the cinderblock of the B-unit, pushes off hard, running full tilt for the A-unit.

At the last possible moment, instead of slamming face-first into it, he plants one large sneaker on the wall, then a second, and runs up the wall almost far enough to grab the ledge.

The drummer laughs, likes it, and then the rest of the band is trying it too, falling back into the caliche over and over.

At a quarter after ten, Toby Garrett's baby brother eases past the gate, flashes his lights once, and you lift your hand in acknowledgement, go inside to pull the extension cord from the air conditioner socket, hold your face against the two vents until your face hurts with cold.

When you turn around again, Arnot King's standing in the door.

Opposite the couch is Jimmy Bones.

"Heard you dropped the charges against our boy," you say to Arnot King.

"Case of mistaken identity," Jimmy Bones says back, rotating the rubber foot of his cane into your carpet like being really sure a bug is dead.

Outside, Thomas is doing something acoustic, it sounds like, his fingers falling down across the strings at about the speed of fifty-weight motor oil. Beading, dripping, beading again.

In your chest pocket are the two pieces of the Brock & Associates insurance check signed by William the Kid. On the back, even, it's still signed over to you.

For two hours today, after lunch, you sat outside the bank, unsure what to do with it. If it was even good anymore, taped together, or if you can sign one over like that, or if it automatically becomes Dan Gates's.

If it is his, he owes you five dollars. That's what it cost for the clerks at the Town & Country to let you go through their weekly drawing.

In your other chest pocket are all fourteen of the Allegator cards from the beef jerky jar. Because he owes you, you told yourself while doing it, but really it's the other way around, right? You pulled his business card out of the soup so somebody local could win. Somebody from Stanton.

It's about the last thing you expected from yourself, standing up for this place. And it felt good.

"So's it in the couch again?" Arnot King asks.

You laugh a little, scratch the back of your neck. "Here for the competition, gentlemen?"

Jimmy Bones angles his head over, as if to be sure he's hearing you right. And then he smiles the way a wolf must at certain times, on certain nights.

You nod to him, see that Arnot King's still watching you, not getting you now any more than he was two nights ago after all the sirens had showed up to haul Rory off. Then, he'd sat by you on the bench seat of your living room, his hands cuffed too, and told you in his lyrical, vaguely ethnic way that you should have just shot the lover down, yeah? Because you can blame anything on a dead man.

What you'd told him back was that it was all Rory's blame anyway.

Arnot King had leaned his head back, said if you really believed that, then you *would* have shot him, yeah?

"You saying it's my fault, all this?" you'd asked.

"I'm saying maybe you think it is," he told you back, shrugging like fault mattered a whole lot less than reasonable doubt.

At the time, you shook your head no, didn't explain. Not because you didn't want to, but because you couldn't. It had something to do with how you can't help thinking that Rory was holding back Friday night, just goading you. Suicide-by-cop, something like that. By security guard, anyway.

Felson said it had probably just been a John Wayne thing, blaze of glory, all that. Blaming you for what he did to his own wife. The pretty shotgun, anyway, it wasn't from his gun safe at all, had been registered to Tom Howard. Is Thomas's now, you guess. Along with a lot else.

So, maybe Rory *was* trying to get you to off him. Shooting all around you until you looked down, had this convenient shotgun right there in your hands. Maybe after being dead for a week, he'd decided it was easier like that. For everyone.

Or maybe he just didn't know Tom's guns well enough, or lost his nerve right at the end, kept seeing Tom instead, or Gwen. Or maybe you really did just outsmart him at last, after all these years. You don't know, and you probably never will. It could be any stupid thing. Not a single one of which matters right now, with Jimmy Bones stepping over, still with that look in his eye from what you'd said: competition.

"That little table, you mean?" he says, tilting his head over to the B-unit.

You lean down to the fridge for a beer, grab three instead, then the keys on the way out. They're spray-painted the same green as the lock. You hold them in your hand and stare at them, follow Jimmy Bones out onto the caliche then look up when he does, his hand sliding into his jacket on instinct.

You touch his elbow to tell him it's okay, it's nothing. Just Thomas Howard, running from a three-point stance from the B-unit to the A-.

You track his progress, know that this is going to be another bad thing, that he wants it too much, that he's made some deal with himself about reaching the top—something to do with his dad. You reach your hand out to stop him, tell him no, that—not to let his forehead touch that cinderblock. That some things you can't undo.

But then you remember what it was like to be sixteen in this town.

Some nights you felt like Thomas must now—that if you could just run fast enough, push off hard enough, want it bad enough, that you'd rise above, maybe.

From the entry of the unit he's staked out, a long-nursed beer tilted back, Dan Gates, who could do this without the wall, he's watching too, neither of you breathing for as long as it takes for Thomas's left hand to grab the crumbling top lip of Aardvark Custom Economy Storage. For an impossible series of seconds he manages to hold on, then—more impossible, Dan Gates's fist balled tight, like urging Thomas on—Thomas hoists himself up by willpower alone, stands with his back to you for five seconds, as if he doesn't believe it either. Like he can see for miles, now.

"This is what you do for fun out here?" Arnot King says, taking the green keys from your hand, squatting down to the lock.

"Yeah," you say, watching Thomas walk deeper onto the roof, disappear, "yeah," and then all at once the garage door of E swings up and Arnot King's pulling the chain light on, touching a chip of paint up from the felt.

Jimmy Bones nods to himself about the new high-watt bulb and runs his cane through his left hand like a pool stick, probably isn't even aware that he's doing it.

"What are we playing for—" he starts, but before he can finish, Arnot King pulls you back out, directs your eyes up.

Thomas is standing at the edge of the A-unit again, only now he has a little sawed-off, double-barrelled shotgun. It's the one from Fin's trailer. The murder weapon.

He holds it out at the moon like a pistol.

"You said it was somewhere safe," you tell Arnot King where nobody can hear.

"It was," he hisses back, and then, like he knows it's the worst thing he could possibly do with this particular shotgun, Thomas takes drunk aim, starts picking his friends off one by one, making the sounds with his mouth, the recoil slow motion each time.

On cue, the rest of the band falls back into the caliche clutching their stomachs, dying like people do in the movies. But then he gets to Dan Gates, standing now, his beer spilling beside him, and all at once, from the way Dan's watching that gun, from the way he's not breathing, from the way he's holding his right hand, you know that Thomas can't shoot him, even with make-believe birdshot. Because Dan's already dying on the inside.

All night long he's been here, saying nothing. Hanging close to Thomas of all people instead of going over to Midland with his football friends.

He hasn't been hanging close to apologize, you realize.

He's been staying close to *explain*. To drink enough that he finally throws up the right words.

Ten years later, him and Thomas will be the new Rory Gates and Tom Howard of Stanton. Best friends. All these secrets between them, all this history.

But not tonight.

Tonight you step forward, hold your hand up to Thomas for the shotgun and snap once, your eyes hard, no joke.

Thomas shrugs, drops it down easy, goes looking for other treasure on the roof, and you announce in your party's over voice that it's yours, this old thing. That you've been meaning to throw it away.

"Where?" Dan Gates says, and everybody hears. It's maybe the first word he's spoken all night.

You study Dan Gates, trying to see under the hood of his question, to why it would matter to him.

"You want it?" you say, flipping the shotgun around butt-first, and he holds his hands up fast, steps back.

"Not loaded," you say, cracking it open to show, and you're wrong, sort of.

There is a spent shell in the left barrel.

In the right, though, there's a tight roll of cash.

The night crawls to a stop, slow enough for you to catch up a little.

Rory *was* trying to get you to kill him the other night.

He was trying to protect his son.

Dan Gates nods down to your hand, to the wedding band you guess you're still wearing, the one Thomas's mom gave to Thomas's dad, and he says it: "You're smarter than any of them figured, aren't you?"

No.

Because if you were you would have seen it all along, you would have seen it that day at the drug store counter. Rory's truck probably even pulled past you.

If you'd just turned around, you would have seen Dan, sitting proud in the passenger seat, trying to slit his eyes just like his dad's.

Where Rory was taking him was out to meet Tom Howard. So Dan could pay for the Ford him*self*, like a man. It's what you do, if you're trying to grow your son up right.

Goddamn Rory Gates.

Dan had already been there that morning, finally got tired of waiting in the truck and walked into the old house, careful to bring the little shotgun his dad kept under the seat for rats.

But then there was only one rat in the house, wasn't there?

One Dan already knew was stepping out with his mom. One that must have talked Rory up the creaky stairs somehow. At gunpoint, or knifepoint. Or because they were best friends.

Of course Dan followed the voices.

After that, one twitch of the finger was all it took. One twitch of the finger is all it ever takes.

Then it was just a matter of hopping Tom Howard's tractor, stepping down into the gold wrecker he'd never traded Darryl Koenig.

Only, what Rory never saw, it was his son over in the passenger seat, trying not to cry. His son confessing, slipping that roll of truck money he'd worked all summer for out of his front pocket and stuffing it into the breech of the shotgun.

Seven hundred dollars, probably. Maybe seven-fifty.

It doesn't even get close to what that particular truck is really worth, and that's still what it all comes down to, at least for you—that Ford. An instant before you saw Dan Gates washing it across the street last week, you saw the truck, and it was like looking through a tunnel to twenty years ago. For an instant you were there, still in high school, before all this, mist hanging in the air all around. Shining the truck for the drive to Colorado City. Thinking it was your lucky night, finally. Having no suspicion even that the whole rest of your life, it could come to hang on one thing, on a pool ball rolling this way instead of that way, on one person being in a motel room instead of another.

A whole life sawed-off there in your hands, the barrels still hot from the day's heat. Thick with prints.

"Rusted on the inside," you say back to Dan Gates, *for* Thomas, for all of them, for the rest of the world that's never going to know, and you hold your thumb over the roll of bills, shake the left shell out. To show how rusted it is, you stick your finger down where the shell was. Not your index, but your ring. Deep enough that wedding band wedges in, deep enough that the gun oil slicks your skin above the ring.

You jerk your hand out like you've hit a rusty snag and shake your fingers, bite the tip of your middle one so you have to hold your finger out.

Dan Gates grins in spite of himself.

"Trash?" he says, opening his hand to catch the gun because he's standing right by the barrel Thomas drags out each time to dispose of all the bottles.

"No," you say, "where it belongs," and twist the top off the pipe by the office door, drop the gun in.

It doesn't catch on anything, just keeps falling down and down, the way things do in West Texas.

Tomorrow you can pour some of the concrete from the animal cage unit into the pipe, arc a couple of recycled beers down to set the concrete.

"Staying up there or what?" you call to Thomas on your way back to the pool table, acting for all the world like nothing's happened here, and that maybe you're a little disgusted with him being up there, and Thomas smiles, steps back, then comes flying over the edge, hugging his knees to his chest.

If he lands—a thing you doubt—you never hear it, have already stepped back into the storage unit with Jimmy Bones and the short table. Arnot King stands in the wide door out of the way, his lips a deadly-thin line, the new and hardly steady bulb barely pushing enough wattage down to show the nappy green of the felt.

You run the stick he hands you along the calloused side of your index finger once, twice, and then Jimmy Bones says it: "So you bring it tonight, bad man?"

It's what he always calls you when you have a stick in your hand.

You reach into your pocket, balance the film canister on the table where a challenger's quarters are supposed to go.

"This do?" you say, guiding the cue ball over to the right bank, leaning over to line your stick up.

"It might," Jimmy Bones says, his voice already far away, and just as you cock your elbow back to break you'll look over the triangle of balls, to the back wall, the outer edge of the pool of light, and see that, while you were disposing of a murder weapon, somebody's dragged a folding chair into the corner, is sitting in it. You won't be able to see her face, just her bare knees, her hands balled up between them, nervous because her son still hasn't touched down outside, but you'll remember what she looked like in the fifth grade, washed in the brake lights of her father's tractor, hay dust spiraling up into the night sky. You'll nod to her like she's your girl, here, and maybe remember what Jimmy Bones said the first time he ever racked for you, when you asked just what the two of you were playing for here. He never even looked up, just said it like the most obvious joke—*not for nothing, baby*—and standing there, you knew it wasn't your night, that you should stay away from that table. But you didn't. You couldn't. You never can. Worse, you'd do it all over again, given half a chance.

Acknowledgments

Thanks to my Aunt Tami and Uncle Bruce, for helping me keep the Stanton details straight. And thanks to them and my Uncle Randall and my mom and my dad for telling me all the stories when I was kid. Of races and wrecks and snakes and dead kids and bumblebees and horse liniment and cats that came to bad ends, fights and dances and fires and friends, and people without names sleeping in their cars in the middle of the road, and ghosts. Those stories made Stanton a magic place, just five miles up the road. Someday I was going to make it there. And thanks to Gene Louder, for a story about driving a fence line with me when I was five, to see a flattened UFO cow. I don't remember it, but I kind of think I do. I can still feel it wriggling inside me. And thanks to my grandmother, for letting me run around White's Ford while she worked, and for teaching me colors, and thanks to my granddad, for taking me for all the best coke floats I ever had. I don't drink them anymore, now. They wouldn't compare. And thanks to Guy Intoci for stepping into West Texas with me again. It's real and forever and bigger than legend in my head, deeper than blood, but without Guy's steady hand, I don't think it'd ever get on the page the right way. And thanks to whoever it was back in 2005 or so who asked me how the detective novel works. I answered, but walked away feeling like that wasn't the whole story. That I'd only really know how the detective novel worked if I wrote one. A couple of hundred thousand words later, there was this novel. It's as close to my heart as anything I've written. Fiction for me is a lot like sneaking up to the attic to try on the old clothes your parents have forgotten they ever wore, only the attic door catches and you have to make a life up there now. I wouldn't have any other life. Thanks to my wife Nancy for coming up to that attic with me. It's dusty and there's spiders, and probably a scary clown back in the corner, but we're fast, aren't we? We'll be all right.